*WITH LOVE,*

*~W. H. Pug*

¿?

# Sesqua Valley
# & Other Haunts

¿?

*I like "AFTERWORD"* *"ilUSTRATIONS!!!*

BY     *Di-107?*

*Fir-Pine-Cedar*
*Have Pitch*
*Thats have*
*fragrance*

*P-31*
*us-We?*

## W. H. PUGMIRE

*P99*
*death*
*P106*
*not accepted*

*P-3 he sink*
*hemlock*

*spruce*
*rigid*
*no frag*

*nB2-P13*          *P 24 "happy death"*  *4-1-09*

# Sesqua Valley & Other Haunts

W. H. Pugmire, Esq.

*¿?*

MYTHOS BOOKS LLC

POPLAR BLUFF

MISSOURI

2008

Mythos Books LLC
351 Lake Ridge Road,
Poplar Bluff,
MO 63901
United States of America

www.mythosbooks.com

Published by Mythos Books LLC 2008


FIRST REVISED EDITION


Cover and interior art copyright © 2008 by Augie Wiedemann.

All stories contained within
*Sesqua Valley and Other Haunts* © 2008 by W. H. Pugmire, Esq.
except "O, Christmas Tree" copyright © 2008 by Jessica Amanda Salmonson
& W. H. Pugmire, Esq.

The author asserts the moral right to
be identified as the author of this work.

ISBN 0-9789911-4-1

Set in *Selfish* & *Adobe Jenson Pro.*

*Selfish* by Misprinted Type.
www.misprintedtype.com

Adobe Jenson Pro by Adobe Systems Incorporated.
www.adobe.com

Typesetting, layout and design by PAW.
Layout & design copyright © 2008 by Peter A Worthy.

To Edward P. Berglund,
a true Lovecraftian gentleman.

# Contents

# O, Christmas Tree

*with Jessica Amanda Salmonson*

> "There is death in the clouds,
> there is fear in the night,
> for the dead in their shrouds
> hail the sun's turning flight,
> and chant wild in the woods as they
> dance round a yule-altar
> fungous and white."

—H. P. Lovecraft

## I.

December's icy fingers wound around Richard Whitson, tendrils of a cold-blooded thing probing for any opening in his coat. Somewhere distant, carolers weakly defied the weather with a feeble warmth of song. He crossed the nearly deserted depot parking lot, hunching in his sweater and overcoat like a tortoise in its shell, and boarded the bus for Sesqua Valley. The vehicle hesitated for a moment, as if expecting other riders, then lurched forward in departure.

Although the heaters allowed a modicum of comfort, loneliness persisted, a sort of melancholy that had been increasing with the approach of Christmas. *We are all poor tortured christs reborn every day*; his mind framed the thought as profound and original, but it merely made him offer a pitiable smile to his reflection on the window. *This* year, at least, he would spend the holiday with kin. That thought alone must suffice to thaw his chilly spirit, for all attempts to converse with the driver had met with grumbling of a confirmed misanthrope.

After some twenty kilometers of monotonous beauty, a hypnotic weariness overtook the eyes that scanned dark evergreens and winter sky. That sky remained an even misty grey; yet to his dulled senses it suddenly came to harbor grave foreboding. He shuddered more firmly than he had from the cold and blinked attempted slumber from his eyes, searching for some brooding presence o'er the mountains.

Before he could apprehend any source of his irrational anxiety, a deeper feeling engulfed him, one of drifting through a vacuum of an infinite cosmos. And he imagined, or dreamt, the driver with the malignant silver eyes glaring forward into the still gray of their silent, fathomless journey.

Richard jerked upright in his seat, suddenly aware that he had dozed. His heart slowed to a normal pace as he reoriented himself in the safe, sane surroundings of wakeful reality. The bus had entered a valley. Above thick evergreens, silhouetted by a vast scarlet sunset, mountains rose in awesome magnificence. Particularly striking were two jagged peaks like wings folded on some gigantic daemon's shoulders.

The majesty of Sesqua Valley was dizzying. Richard closed his eyes, laid back his head, and would have enjoyed a more restful slumber had the bus not come to a jolting halt.

The sky had grown dark, arrayed with formless shadow. From the bus window he saw, in the distance, a huge century-old house whose architecture predated anything commonly found in the Northwest. It was certainly a place to cherish in this sad age, when houses rarely last their young owners the time it takes to pay a mortgage. Yet it was deserted and in disrepair, with lower windows boarded up. A large crooked oak, devoid of leaves in this season, had been allowed to grow so close to that antique residence that its trunk had damaged a portion of the building. The welfare of the tree apparently mattered more than the house itself.

With his father dead, there was nothing to steal him back to city life: no family, no job worth saving. As he pulled his two suitcases from the rack above his head, he was already considering the renovation of the old mansion. He had, after all, a small inheritance that would allow him a new start almost anywhere. Here, at least, he had kin, and after the lonely despair of the last two years, and after his father's wasting agony, the discovery that his grandfather lived took on an importance of inordinate proportion. Even the eerie countenance of this nighted valley seemed a welcoming aspect to the gloom crouching in his heart.

He stepped off the bus and its doors hissed closed behind him. Before, a lamppost swarmed by moths illuminated a faded sign reading SESQUA DEPOT. The 'depot' was a single building that served more often as grocery store and post office. It was closed at this hour, and unlit. A lone figure approached from its shadows, and Richard recognized his grandfather from a photograph he had found among his dead father's belongings.

Nathan Whitson looked dignified in his overcoat and cap and neatly trimmed white whiskers, clasping his cane, the ends of his scarf moving with a breeze. Richard stepped forward as the bus moved away, into night. His grandfather's handshake was firm, and warm for all the bitter cold around.

"You're your father's image," the old man said in greeting, his smile the first pleasant thing in Richard's long day. He took one of his grandson's bags and led the way to an old pickup trunk. They rode a short distance to a cottage tucked into the woods alongside a calm black lake. The old gentleman asked after news that betrayed an appalling ignorance of life outside the valley. Richard instantly adored the gentle-mannered oldster and felt that shadow drawn out of his heart. Why, he even found occasion to laugh.

## II.

Over a morning's repast of hens' eggs and home-baked bread, they spoke of many things. Eventually the conversation came around to the subject both had been avoiding. "Your father never liked this place, Sesqua Valley," the old man told the younger. There was sadness, but no bitterness, in his mild tone. Richard was still hard-pressed to understand the callousness of his father in never allowing the lad the knowledge and benefits of a grandfather.

"This is an old town," Nathan continued. "Families have lived here for numerous generations. Pioneers considered it their stroke of luck, discovering this fertile valley somehow never claimed by the Indians, who elsewhere were peaceful competitors but still competitors. None questioned this fortune; none asked why Indians shunned a place abundant with game and rich of soil. They just settled in, and it is mostly those same old families who reside on this land.

"Outsiders, for the most part, find the people clannish and unfriendly. They soon leave, as your father did when he thought himself mature enough to take care of his own life. An old Sesquan like myself finds it difficult to settle elsewhere, the roots and psychic ties run deep. I tried city life when I married your grandmother. But after she passed on (your father was a wisp of eight years at the time) I longed to return home. Here I've stayed all those years since. And so have all my clan before me."

Nathan's face took on a curious expression, one that caused his grandson's heart to beat faster. The elder man had hinted at a mysterious quality about life in Sesqua, and there was the faintest note of urgency when he reached across the table to rest a withered hand on his grandson's wrist. "I had feared the Whitson line would die out of Sesqua with my passing; but now ..."

Richard helped his grandfather clear the table of breakfast dishes and insisted on doing the washing. As he performed this domestic activity, he watched out the window over he sink, absorbing the magic of country life. Beneath the window, chickens clucked and scratched at the morning's feed. A squirrel clung to the bark of a tree, planning her maneuver past the rooster to the spilled grain. Across the small lake no other houses were visible—only a wall of hemlock spruce with their ragged tips bowed in a manner of prayer or obeisance to the snow-clad mountains beyond, all reflected perfectly on the flat, still waters.

Later, when Nathan returned from outside chores, rubbing hands together and blowing at his chaffed fingers, Richard was invited into the sanctuary of his grandfather's little study. There was a fragrance of aromatic pipe tobacco mingled with the more familiar scents of spruce and cedar burning in the fireplace. The furniture was slightly dusty, except for the wide desk, which seemed regularly in use.

Old portrait photographs hung in glassed frames on one of the walls, some of Richard's father as a child, more than one of a frail and attractive woman he supposed to be his grandmother. Two walls were built with bookshelves, on which nearly every centimeter of space was packed to capacity. These books dealt with such widely varied topics as North American Indian lore, European and Chinese mythology, archaeology, regional history, and the histories of Puget Sound and the near Pacific including, it appeared, some carefully bound original manuscripts regarding early Northwest expeditions.

Habit made it inconceivable that Nathan could relax behind his desk without a well-chosen pipe of tobacco. While he indulged in all the intricacies of this pleasant, personal tradition, Richard stood regarding the titles on the shelves. Many were in French and Spanish medieval script and looked centuries old.

"The French explorer Maurice de Reau penned these pages in his own light script in 1794—a decade before Jefferson financed the Lewis and Clark expedition to the Northwest wilderness." Nathan chuckled as he set his spectacles on his nose and turned through the brittle yellow manuscript in search of a favorite passage. "Poor Maurice! He might have been more beloved by later geographers and historians had they not found him too Poloesque in his prose; as it is, the museums with their decrepit scholars likely wouldn't do so much as catalog one more of these fanciful documents. This, his last imaginative chronicle, never made it back to King Louis (who anyway had been guillotined the year before!), who had commissioned Maurice's services, intending, perhaps, to extend the vast boundaries of the French Louisiana territory. And what became of de Reau, none discovered."

Richard took an armchair beside the oak-top desk and listened intently to his grandfather's translation.

> *I have come, my cherished and honoured King, to a land that makes all the grim occurrences in the Black Forest mere fairy tales passed on by frightened spinsters. There are trees whose sap is blood and toads with the faces of men, pixies with poisonous fangs and faceless devils that fly silently through the*

*night. There is evidence of all this and other abhorrent truths,
for much have I seen with my own eyes. There is an aborigine
legend that you would not find difficult to believe if you could
but feel the air of this unwholesome place. Two titanic daemons
(say the natives) met in battle on this unhallowed ground. The
Red daemon was of goodwill, the White would enslave all
humanity. The White daemon unleashed all manner of odious
beings upon His foe, and still the White was overcome and
turned to stone.*

Here Nathan paused to enjoy his fine tobacco and allow the effect of
his narrative to impress upon his listener. Though he reiterated the
fantasy of this tale, there was nonetheless a tinge of irony in these
avowals of falsehood, and Richard was more captivated now than by the
ghost stories told on the stormy nights of his childhood. Nathan
continued:

*The daemon-turned-stone the aborigines called Selta, and
it is a strange sight to see, a mountain which lends credence to
the legend. Yet as the story goes, the Red titan could not
entirely banish the minions of the White, for they thrive in
good proportion and await the day of their Master's return
from His stone prison. All this is to inform your most gracious
majesty that such a land is not fit for French dominion.*

The old man folded the manuscript and rested a hand upon its
binding. Though he apologized for the terse translation of a passage
much more colorful in the original tongue, Richard could not have been
more affected. He forced himself to smile and say, "What would
Christmas be without a scary tale?" But the lips of the old man were a
hard, serious line within the white, combed whiskers.

"We celebrate the Yule season differently from folks outside the
valley," Nathan explained. "Very few families exchange gifts, and we
don't succumb to the crass commercialism of wasted electricity and
injured trees."

His grandsire went on to explain the spiritual side of Christmas, but
Richard had seen as little Christmas spirit as he had decorations. He
hadn't really seen the town by day, however, so he let the subject drop as
was Nathan's apparent wont. But of one thing Richard was certain: he
would not entertain the thought of another Christmas without a tree.

That afternoon he explored the good-sized cottage. It was not big, but
spacious enough for one old man. In the cramped attic he found what he
had secretly been searching for: a box containing Christmas candles,

bulbs and tinsel—packed away and long forgotten. He hauled them down to his own small room, determined to bring Christmas back to Sesqua Valley. Or at least to Nathan Whitson.

### III.

During that pleasurable week before Christ's birthday, Richard came to know his grandfather and the countryside well. The woods were like a beautiful cathedral, the lake just beginning to freeze around the edges with lovely lacy patterns in the ice. For all the forest's comeliness, Richard was unnerved by the constant silence. Even in winter there ought to be the reassuring sounds of some wildlife, but for two days they hadn't seen so much as a squirrel.

"The drop in temperature," Nathan explained, "has sent the hardiest into hibernation." Richard smiled at this explanation, excusing his unease as the result of city rearing.

On one of their many outings, Richard became separated from his grandfather and lost sight of the lake. Completely disoriented, he was on the verge of panic as he found his way through the furiously whipping underbrush. The clearing was a relieving sight when he stumbled upon it, for in its perfect symmetry it seemed a sign of habitation. The ground appeared well trod. Above, the surrounding trees closed out the sky, so only a few of the sun's fingered rays reached the dappled sod.

A perfect circle of mushrooms encompassed the clearing's only other occupant—a brilliantly colored red spruce half again as tall as Richard. A perfect, squat, widely branched sturdy conifer, Richard was entirely unfamiliar with the type. Seeing it stand there alone in the trampled circle, the lines of a song danced into his mind:

> *… for gods in their places*
> *wore smiles on their faces*
> *for pagans who danced on Christmas.*

A wind chilled his collar. Something unseen skittered through the perimeters of the clearing (and his vision), the first sign of life that day. He did not believe in premonition, but something made him wheel around into a defensive crouch.

It was only Grandfather Whitson who stood there. His face looked stern, mores than Richard had previously seen it. "What are you doing here?" Nathan demanded.

Richard stood from his foolish crouch, all the fear gone out of him like a child found by its mother. "I … I … was lost."

The elder one eyed him as coldly as the weather gripped him, but directly his expression mellowed and he said, "Come along to the house."

The young man was only too pleased to oblige. He cast one final look back at the crimson-hued evergreen, then followed after his grandfather.

## IV.

He slammed the door of the borrowed trunk.

Now, on the street of this quaint town, Richard could only scoff at his own imagined feelings of doom when he'd been "lost" so near the cottage. The town of Sesqua consisted of a very few buildings of commerce, nearly half of these boarded up. There was an herb shop, a small bookstore. The grocery and general store was the largest of the businesses and also served as post office, and two rustic petroleum pumps stood outside the doors.

Dusk came early in that wintered valley, and Richard had to do his bit of shopping in haste as the uncommunicative proprietor was in a hurry to close shop. A pouch of the finest tobacco in stock would have to do.

It took no time to wander the length of the town. By chance (or subconscious design), Richard found himself approaching the run-down mansion that sat upon a knoll. "It oughtn't cost a lot to buy," he thought, noting the poor condition of the outer walls and roof. "But it'll cost a fortune to repair." One of the twin gables was nearly devoid of shingles.

He tested the ornamental doorknob. Locked. A back stairway led to a second-story entrance—a padlock on this. He circled and inspected the building, tramping in darkness through high grass. He found a half-rotten length of lumber and broke it while prying boards off a basement window. There was no glass behind the boards. He climbed in.

For some moments Richard stood in darkness, allowing eyesight to adjust to the shadowed gloom. An unpleasant odor came to him, reminded him of a goat den he had seen in a city zoo. Near to him he espied steps leading upward. Placing a timid hand upon the dust-coated handrail, he climbed. Silently, he inspected dusky rooms. The various pieces of antique furniture seemed in decent shape. In one room, obviously a study, he found a shelf crammed with moldy books. A volume with a violet binding caught his attention. He took it, frowning at its dampness, and turned to the water-stained title page. The lettering, however, proved too faded to read, and thus he reshelved the volume.

From the broken window of a gable he looked through the naked branches of the oak to the lightless town and surrounding woodland. A brilliance caught his eyes: a campfire far away, at what might have been a meadow or cultivated ground. It was too far away to tell, but children appeared to be playing ring-around-the-rosy and tossing twigs into the flame. This seemed a dangerous sport, unattended by adults. And—

great Jesu!—were the children naked?

He watched them dance around the fire, like wicked dark creatures, striking contorted poses that were distinctly unchildlike. For a moment, a terrible fright clutched at the watcher from the window. A thought crept through his mind: *those don't look like children at all!* But he closed some psychological lid on such an absurd idea and began to turn away.

But he didn't turn, for the dancing suddenly stopped. The faint chanting ended. Richard pressed against the wall beside the window for, though it was too dark and distant for them to know, he feared that they had ceased their play—their ritual—because they sensed mortal eyes upon them. Cautiously, he peered around the corner of the sill. The fire was gone, and without its blaze he could see nothing in the meadow.

Branches of the naked oak scraped at the walls as a cold new wind whistled eerily under the eaves. As he stood looking out, he thought he caught glimpses of two shadows melding into one at the base of the tree. He watched with knitted brow. Then a limb stretching toward his window cracked so very slightly.

Overwhelmed with sudden fear, he fled the room, ran down the stairs to the awful basement, where darkness seemed to reach for him. Where was the window? Everything was so black. He felt a wind, and followed its direction to the place where he had entered the mansion. Clumsily, he struggled up and out, as something padded down the basement steps behind him. Locking himself into the pickup truck, he rushed to the cottage in the woods, waiting for his nerves to settle before entering his grandfather's abode. He lay awake for an endless time, and shadowed images followed him in dream.

## V.

Richard wearily awoke to morning sunlight. Staggering to the kitchen he found a pot of strong coffee, left by his grandsire, who had gone for a morning stroll. With steaming cup in hand, Richard ventured into the cozy quiet of the study, where he set about scanning the shelves of books. A binding of violet cloth caught his attention, and he pulled the volume from its shelf. It was indeed a mint copy of the book he had seen the previous evening, in that haunted house. He turned to the title page. "*Visions of Khroyd'Hon*, by William Davis Manly; Sesqua Valley Press, 1955." In faded purple ink had been penned a simple inscription: "To Nathan, my fellow dreamer on the night-side, with fond best wishes, Manly."

Slowly, Richard scanned various pages, until he came upon a sonnet about "children of the valley" who danced within a ring of stones. The simple line drawing that accompanied the poem caused a chill to kiss the length of his spine. It shewed a group of curious shaggy dwarf-like creatures dancing within a circle of standing stones. Their indistinct faces were oddly bestial. Dancing with them was a woman of normal stature, yet her face, too, wore an aspect of their non-humanity.

He heard his grandfather return, and raised his eyes as the old gentleman entered the room. Nathan paused and tilted his head with curiosity at the book his grandchild was holding. He uncomfortably smiled. "You knew the author," Richard said, turning again to the title page.

"Yes, slightly." Nathan took the book from his grandson and chuckled at the image that had so troubled the younger man. "He had quite an imagination."

Richard hesitated for a moment; then softly spoke. "I saw children dancing in a meadow last night."

The book fell from Nathan's hand, to the floor. Calmly, the elder one picked it up and returned it to its place on the shelf. "Did you now? Well, children like to play."

Richard struggled for words that would not make him sound hysterical. "Yes ... but ... they were *naked.* Ice around the lake and children dancing naked in the night?"

"Perhaps," Nathan's rational voice ventured, "it was an illusion of reflected firelight. They might actually have been well-clothed."

Richard almost wanted to accept this, but then he frowned. "Did I mention a fire?"

"Was there one?" The old man was too casual.

"Yes, but I didn't mention it. What aren't you telling me, Grandfather? What's wrong with the people in this valley? You're afraid I'll return to the city, but I've a right to know."

They exchanged a heavy look, then Nathan reached for a book of Northwest lore published in the early nineteenth century, illustrated with weird steel-plate engravings. To one illustration in particular he turned. It might have depicted the solstice ceremony of an ancient European earth goddess cult, but it was not so tame as those pagan rites. And the fauna was distinctly North America.

It was a picture of a short red evergreen, around which a ring of naked imps—or children with teeth filed sharp—stood arm in arm. Above the tree, a great winged creature (perhaps an oversized bald eagle depicted by an artist who had never actually seen one) held a beaver in its talons and let the blood from where the animal's heart had been ripped out drop onto the tree.

But most striking was the background of the illustration. It was unquestionably Mount Selta, with two eyes added for eerie effect.

"A popular legend," Nathan softly replied. "So popular, in fact, that it has become a common, although I admit an unusual, children's game to act it out."

Richard felt an idiot. Until that moment, he'd thought his grandfather was revealing some legitimate and incredible horror of Sesqua Valley. But it was merely child's play. And why not? Ring-around-the-rosy was originally devised by children during the era of the Black Plague; and the line, "Ashes, ashes, all fall down" referred to people dying in the streets, and ashes from cremations. In their innocence, the grimmest situation became a source of sport.

"And that's all I saw?"

Instead of answering, Nathan patted his grandson's shoulder and said, "Let's walk to town and get some things for dinner." And the day progressed lightheartedly.

The day was a busy one, and wearying for a man of Nathan's years. Richard was only too pleased to see his grandfather apologetically retired early. It had been a pleasant day for both, and Richard intended to return the favor. Armed with a flashlight from a kitchen drawer and hatchet from the woodshed, he slipped silently from the cottage, into black night.

He had made a careful mental note of the route when Grandfather had led him from the clearing. Richard knew there could be no more beautiful specimen for a Christmas tree in these woods. So he wandered, excitedly, happily, innocently, beneath the spectral trees that swayed their heavy boughs above him. Soon he knelt before the blood-red tree, saw how it almost glistened in cold winter moonlight. That lunar sphere was high, drenching the valley with eerie illumination. The white mountain sparkled.

He severed the tree at its base. And somehow the valley *darkened*. And some thing atop the mountain wailed in woe. Richard hauled the tree back to the cottage. Once, he shone his light behind him, thinking he heard a mournful whimper. With slow deliberation, he managed the tree through the door with a minimum of rustling red needles and ruddy scraping limbs. The box of decorations had been hidden under his bed. Silently, he fetched it and decorated the tree. Balanced on a chair, he was about to place the Star of Bethlehem on the tree's top when a harsh voice interrupted his endeavor.

*"What have you done!"*

The glass star fell from his fingers and shattered on the floor.

"Grandfather. It's a surprise. For Christmas. I ..."

"You're an outsider. You couldn't have known," the old man whispered in a fatalistic manner, more to himself than to Richard. His face was ashen, nearly as white as his beard. He seemed in search of some way out, some answer. "It's too late to change it now, but perhaps I can save you." Mechanically, he shuffled in stockings to a long, low wooden box, from which he took a rifle. "This will never stop them, but ..."

Confused and strangely frightened, Richard finally jumped from the chair to the floor. "Grandfather, do you sleep-walk? I think you're having a nightmare."

The elder one stopped, seemed to awaken from dream. The emotion vanished from his face. "Yes. Yes, I was dreaming. It's late, lad, we should be in bed. The tree is very pretty, but I'll see it better in morning light. Come."

Leery of this sudden change, Richard nonetheless allowed himself to be led to his room. He bid his grandsire good night and closed the door. Lying atop the covers, he fondled the tobacco pouch that on the morrow would be his Grandfather's Christmas gift. It seemed a trivial thing now, and the surprise of the tree had been utterly spoiled. His mind fled toward the same depression, which had so incapacitated him on previous years. Outside the door, his grandfather still shuffled about fretfully, but Richard was too lost in his own despair to hear, to care.

If he slept, it wasn't for long. A loud crash startled him to awareness. A window shattering? Nathan was shouting, "Get out! Get out!" Richard was on his feet, realizing that someone, some thing, had indeed come through a window, rocking the cottage in so doing. He tried the door, but Nathan had locked it from the outside and pushed a chest against it.

"Grandfather! Grandfather!"

He rammed the door with his shoulder, and knew that it would give with a few more tries. But when the rifle fired, he froze in terror at the shrieking obscenity that answered the report. Whatever made that cry, *it was no beast he knew.* With a cowardice that would haunt him all his life, Richard sank to the floor and listened through the night. His grandsire's shouting became a scream that ended in a frothy gurgle. The flapping of some pinioned beast resounded through the cottage. The stomping of myriad tiny dancing feet prancing around the severed tree, the whining childlike voices uttering a monotonous litany, damned the night.

All through the hours of darkness it raged, the hellish nightmare festival, and Richard Whitson crouched shivering and fearful behind the door, weeping silent salty tears. Then dawn approached, and the sounds from the main room faded. Things padded or flew away from the blasphemed site. Richard cautiously pried loose the lock and forced the door open enough to squeeze through it.

The room was in shambles, the kitchen window broken inward. Blood smeared the walls and floor. He went to the sink below the broken window, glass splintering into his naked feet, and looked toward the hunched mountains. Against the violet of beautiful dawn, the silhouette of some great-winged creature was plain above the lake. It let loose the torso clutched by talons. Richard watched the corpse that fell and upset the icy stillness of lake water.

Richard turned from the impossible sight and fought the urge to retch. He stumbled like a man blinded by his terror back into the living room, there to gaze once more at the product of his crime—that once-beautiful Christmas tree. It was now a ghastly sight. The bloodstained bark had mottled and grown white with leprous disease. The dead withered branches bent to the crimson-spattered floor. But it was as he looked at the tree's topmost bough that he lost the battle to keep his stomach. For where would have been a beautiful glass star rested a blood drenched human heart.

# AFTERWORD

This was the first Sesqua Valley story that I wrote, when I invented the valley in 1974. I had recalled August Derleth telling Ramsey Campbell that rather than setting his Lovecraftian tales in HPL's New England, to invent a region of his own homeland. This seemed excellent advice. As a kid I always spent two weeks of every summer with my cousins in North Bend, and was captivated by Mount Si. When I created my own Lovecraftian set place, I knew it would be a haunted version of North Bend. Imagine my delight when the television show *Twin Peaks* chose this same locale over a decade later as the inspiration for their uncanny series.

Those early stories were very poor, and the original version of "O, Christmas Tree" was rejected by *Space & Time*. I let Jessica read the story, and she surprised me by completely rewriting it. The new version was accepted by Gordon, and later published in Jessica's paperback horror anthology from Tor, *Tales by Moonlight II*. That version was mostly the work of Jessica, and so I have extensively revised it for this edition, adding my own voice and melding the story with how the valley has changed and solidified in my imagination over the decades. It's a cool creepy tale, I think.

> *"The thing that hath been, it is that*
> *which shall be; and that which done is*
> *that which shall be done; and there is*
> *no new thing under the sun."*

*—Ecclesiastics 1:9*

## I.

The ramshackle farmhouse slanted in scarlet sunset. Its bending walls seemed at any moment likely to buckle beneath its weight of years. Here it had stood, on this plot of land north of Dunwich, withstanding elements and elementals. There was the long porch, on which in-bred childfolk had wantonly played. There was the pallor, in which had been performed many dubious entertainments. There—ah, there—the heart of the house throughout the dark decades, the cluttered library.

It was within this latter room that two men argued, one playfully, the other in profound seriousness.

"Never said it were for sale, Mr. James. Only mentioned it as a matter of interest."

"I am not a man to be played with, Mr. Bishop. I made quite clear my interest in the volume."

"Ain't for sale, that's final. Had I known you'd be like this, I'd ne'er had wasted my time. Now, look here. A bi-lingual hand-writ copy of the *Dhol Chants*, with diagrams as nice as you please, smuggled out of China. Over a century old, and in fine shape."

Oscar James ignored the proffered volume. "Sirrah, you look an educated man," he said with faint mockery.

"Went to Harvard and Miskatonic ..."

"Just so." He frowned as the other man softly laughed.

"Pay no heed, son. It's jest that you talk exactly like your pa."

"And pay 'jest' as well as he, I assure you. Now, as an educated man, you realize the allurement of rarity."

"Damn straight. But this was given me by my ma, on her deathbed. I never meant to steer you wrong, Mr. James, or make you think I would sell something that I ain't likely to part with under no circumstances. Damn me, man, you won't even look at anything else I'm offering, choice items, if I say so myself."

"No, nothing else compares to this." He bent over the book and placed a hand upon its green vellum. A surge of emotion welled within him, and for an instant he thought his knees would buckle. He had heard of this thing, this personal grimoire of someone who signed himself 'Simon Gregory Williams,' but of whom not a single fact was known. All was the stuff of legend. And yet, as he kept his hand upon the book, he knew instinctively that in this case the legendary lore had spoken truth.

"What do you find so special about that book, Mr. James?"

Oscar James was so caught up in rapture that he forgot his cunning and spoke with pure honesty. "It contains a promise of power such as I have never known. Of course, one has been aware of its legend. My father whispered of it to me, often. It has not been long in existence, and yet its legend is as profound as that of any centuried volume. Who was this warlock, this Simon Gregory Williams, as he signed himself? Where did he come by such portentous magick, such concentration of alien power? Where did he live, and how did he perish? Great heavens, how dynamic his end must have been!"

"What makes you think he reached an end?"

"He would never have surrendered voluntarily a work as vital as this book of personal spells. Either he died, or this was stolen. I am not saying this to disrespect the memory of your mother. A clever theft is a joyous occasion. I'm still chuckling over last year's theft of the *Necronomicon* from the British Library. But to steal from an institution is one thing; to rob a wizard is quite another. "

Elias Bishop reached to the book and opened it. Its pages were composed of thick yellow paper, on which a variety of entries, diagrams, even poetry had been penned in thick strokes of purple ink. "It does vibrate with power, don't it, Mr. James? Damn me, the channels he knew. But he was crafty, this one. Now," and he turned some pages, "you see this diagram here, it don't seem to make sense, the lines are kind of out of proportion. What the hell could it mean, and how could you form it so as to use it in calling? Now." He went to a shelf, from which he carried a strangely shaped brick of cloudy glass. "Ever hear tell of the Urim and Thummim? This is sort of like that. See, place it over the diagram, wait just a bit, and there you go. See how the glass slowly clears, so that you can see right through it. Suddenly, the diagram beneath it makes perfect sense—terrifyingly so. You draw that with ritual chalk, you got yourself a powerful circle."

Oscar James deeply breathed, fascinated and beguiled. "It resembles one of the esoteric signs of the Old Ones, but ..."

"But unlike most you've seen, because it's pure. This is that which calls to them that was, them who wait and will be, after the sun has burnt out and the earth is cleared."

The younger man's eyes glazed over with passionate longing, with a pining that was close to criminal madness. "How do you know all this?" he softly queried.

"From my ma. She was of the so-called 'decayed' Bishops. I like that—decayed. All it means is you're removed from common stupid folk, them as don't know shit."

"Your mother was a Bishop …?"

"She and pa were cousins. There's power and purity in breeding among ones own. As you probably know from you own studies."

There was also the threat of misbegotten progeny, James contemplated. He had heard things about Dunwich. His host closed the book and placed it on a shelf. Oscar James emotionally trembled. To be denied the book was like a refutation of breath. His mind grew cloudy, dizzy, deranged with longing. Would this bumpkin actually refuse him the marvelous volume?

He reached for the brick of cloudy glass. How thick it was, how heavy in his hand. Turning to the one whose back was to him, the one who was studying spines of books and chattering good-naturedly, James raised the piece of glass and brought it savagely down upon Bishop's skull. He heard the cracking of bone and glass. The inhabitant of Dunwich fell heavily to the floor. He lay quite still as a pool of blood began to spread beneath his shattered head. It flowed toward James, the thick dark liquid.

He heard his heavy breathing, and one other sound. Something else was breathing—nay, panting. It issued from the curious bump beneath Bishop's baggy shirt, a slight deformity that Oscar James had never paid attention to. He watched it move, and then gripped the piece of glass more tightly as tiny jagged nails ripped through the fiber of the dead man's shirt.

It pushed through the fabric, the small misshapen face that wore a semblance to the dead man's visage. It screamed with a strangled voice, and then commenced to softly whisper, chanting.

Yelling in fright, James hurled the brick of glass at the thing that gazed at him with red-rimmed eyes. The heavy object struck the creature with force. It slumped from where it extended from the dead man's flesh.

Shuddering with fright, yet tingling with excitement, Oscar James reached to the shelf and snatched the book. He rushed into dark night, into his vehicle, and quickly drove away.

## II.

Nonchalantly, she stoked the furnace fire, and then used the hooked rod to push close the metal door. Listening for a moment to the roar of flames, she pushed herself to a standing position, groaning. Yes, she had undeniably grown old. The joints in the hand that held the iron rod were stiff with pain. Leaning the rod against the cement wall, she turned to look at her son.

Oscar James was drawing with chalk upon the stone floor. She thought the diagram looked familiar, from somewhere long ago in her past, when she would watch her husband in similar performance. She remembered the excitement in Anthony's eyes, the same sort of fervor that trembled before her now, in the eyes of her only child. What else could she see? Uncertainty, worry? The young man studied the book before which he knelt, and she watched as in frustration he rubbed away a portion of the diagram and gazed with dark eyes into the air, as if to gaze into memory.

She would not ask, nor shew any interest. She had stopped caring long ago. Surely, he was as lost to her as her husband had been so many years ago. Wearily, she limped past her offspring, to the stairs that led out of the cellar and into a spacious back yard. Something, some dim maternal instinct, made her stopped and turn to look at Oscar one last time. For one strange moment she desired to go to him, to lovingly stroke his hair. Bitterly, she smiled at the absurd image, at his imagined rebuff. Reaching for the support of hard granite wall, she painfully climbed the steps, out of the cellar's musty dankness, into the clear light of late afternoon.

Within dank gloom, Oscar James entered a circle of chalk and bowed before the book. Beside it lay a ritual knife and human skull. Atop the death's-head was a squat black candle, which he lit. Shadow wavered on the skeletal face, on the yellow parchment of which the pages before him were composed.

"Within this yellow light, your violet letters seem strangely embossed, as though they were reaching out to me," he whispered, placing a trembling hand upon the pages open before him. The words demanded to be uttered, and he ached to mouth them. Taking up the sharp knife, he pushed its blade into his forearm, then pointed its crimson-dyed tip to the circle's four corners.

He had studied carefully the spell, an evocation of the dead-yet-dreaming, those who would reveal to him the key to the Gate of Sothoth. Once opened, this elemental threshold would usher in influences that would instruct him with unholy wisdom. He would learn the knowledge of the spheres, unknown to mortal man. His brain would supernaturally expand. He would resurrect his father, whose twisted bones, one decade dead, had been ceremonially buried in an unhallowed patch of sod on their spacious grounds. They would be together again, united in blasphemous wonder. Why, even his mother would snap out of her lethargy, would rejoin the fold of magick to which she once submitted.

He uttered the alien words in anxious voice, at one point vocally stumbling. Don't be rash, he mentally scolded; do not rush. With the wisdom and power he would obtain, he would survive the time of alignment, would have all of eternity in which to sing his black arts.

There came from a distant corner a pop, a hiss. It was the fire in the furnace. Why did she always want it so bloody hot? Perspiration speckled his brow.

Another hiss, and movement of light and shadow. An awful stench. Thick repugnance sailed into his nostrils, a scent of death. He looked at the candle atop the skull, at the wax that spilled over the death's-head, covering it like a ghastly sheath of flesh. Like skin, it took on features, a daemonic face that raised its countenance to him. It wore a semblance of the man he had murdered in Dunwich, a face over which there moved spilling wax, wax that oozed inexorably toward him, as once a mess of blood had pooled. It moved in flickering candlelight, from an eyeless thing with gaping mouth.

There was movement behind that mouth, from other lips, tiny and twisted. They mouthed an antient spell of vengeance. He watched the dwarfish head that pushed through a dead man's mouth.

Oscar James quaked with terror. Was this the thing he had foolishly evoked with chants to the dead-yet-dreaming? It was some cosmic jest, a deadly one. The wetness on his brow thickened and slipped into his eyes, where it congealed. His quavering hand lifted so as to brush the sweat away; but when he looked at that hand he saw not perspiration but pearls of fleshy wax. Again he rubbed at an eye, and felt the jellied orb sag within its too-soft socket.

He opened his mouth in screaming, and felt that mouth impossibly expand. The room distorted as his eyes continued to slowly slip down his face. Trying to push himself up from his kneeling position, he watched in horror as the pressure of hand on stone floor forced finger bones through the pulp that had once been human flesh. That flesh was now an insane mass that bubbled, that seeped toward that other, that darker, flow of pooling wax. They met, these pools, and indecently congealed.

Agnes James had heard the screaming, but it was the awful smell emitting from the cellar that chilled her heart. Limping, she rushed to the cellar door and once again entered the murky depths. Her trembling fingers found a light switch, and dim illumination emitted from a grime-encrusted bulb—light enough to shew her the bubbling mass of gelatinous bilge that shuddered within a chalk circle. Something that had once been a human face pushed through the mass and burbled her name.

Fear. Yes, she felt it; and nausea. But keenest of all she felt loathing, a deep and seething hatred for the web of sorcery that had so seduced her

loved ones. There it was embodied in that vile, atrocious tome that had been her son's new obsession. Such books had warped her husband's sanity and led to his tragic, his premature demise. And now such a book had destroyed her only child. Howling rage, she stepped into the circle, rupturing its magick, bringing shrieks from the shuddering thing that was her offspring. She snatched the book and hobbled to the furnace. Taking up the hooked metal rod, she clumsily opened the furnace door. Into the nest of flames she hurled the blasphemous book.

In her hurried fury, she had not noticed the other horror within the circle. A small waxen face shook with outrage and howled in agony. The occult diagram of chalk convulsed and smoldered. Agnes choked and gagged, but refused to leave the place without whatever remained of her son. She staggered through the poisonous fumes that sailed through the cellar door and into spacious night.

She knelt before the lump of waxen flesh and crumbling bone. She saw through billowing smoke the sorry remains of Oscar's face. It seemed, this misshapen thing, to beseech forgiveness. She reached out to stroke it, and at her touch it dissolved.

Her eyes closed in weeping. When again they reopened, she was kneeling before a tangle of liquefied bones. Grinning up at her were two sullied skulls.

### III.

She buried his bones beneath the elm tree, next to his father's remains. Her husband had instructed her precisely, preparing her for tragedy, as if he knew the encroaching fate that would befall his clan. She sat upon the fresh mound of earth and queerly smiled. Really, it was all too utterly boring. The young man she had married was wild in a marvelous fashion. They had been intellectual equals. But he was audacious, hungry for uncanny experience. For a time she was enchanted and intrigued at the strange hidden places he had lured her to, smiling in wonder at esoteric knowledge. She shared in the debauchery of eerie rites; but as their marriage wilted with age, he became secretive and solitary. Was it his sexism that gradually denied her entrance into his ever-darkening world of sin and sorcery? How thrilled he was to have sired a son, and at what an early age he began to share with the child the things he had once shown only to her. She tasted from a distance their intoxication, and waited in lonely isolation for fate to have its fancy.

Finding her own intoxication in the works of Shakespeare, she slipped into a world of her own imagination. There was always, in some deep pocket of her heart, an ache for her loved ones; but it was an ache that time continually dulled. She became especially fond of storms, and would venture forth into wind and rain, howling the phrases of Lear and Hamlet. She knew, at last, that she had lost her sanity, and took much solace in madness.

She fondly patted the soil near her rump. She crazily laughed and raised a handful of soil above her head, then let it gradually spill upon her face. With dirt-flecked eyes she scanned dark heaven. She pointed at the sky. "The gods look down, and this unnatural scene They laugh at," she quoted. She rose to one knee in clumsy genuflection, and moved her hand in signal to the sky, as once she had performed in haunted places with her husband. What were the gods looking down upon her now? She remembered names, and whispered them. Yok-Sotot. Nyarlathotep. Lucifer.

"No, oh no, my loved dead. The god you worshipped was thine own self. What was it you told me once, at a Sabat? 'This is what it feels like to be a god!' Oh, Iä! Iä, what pathetic farce. Your gods were dead names found in the pages of forgotten books. You might as well pray to those unhallowed tomes." She recalled the book that her son had been so obsessed with. She dimly remembered the symbol that had been embossed upon its vellum spine. "Is it magick you want, my wanton boys? Well, let a woman shew you how it's done" and smiling strangely, she spat onto the ground, then began to etch in dirt and saliva the remembered symbol. In rich lunacy, she uttered a faintly remembered chant.

In the cellar, in the furnace, among the smoldering debris, something shifted. Something moved with shaping. Metal sounded against metal as a small furnace door slowly opened. Something charred fell heavily upon the cement floor. It began to creep. Outside, Agnes James clawed at dirt and muttered. Clouds moved away from the moon, and a beacon of light fell upon the distant thing that suddenly she was aware of.

She knew what it was, knew exactly; for she had summoned it. Not all of it had been consumed by flame. Remnants of vellum and parchment, black and charred, existed still. The esoteric symbol upon the spine was clearly visible in moonlight. As it moved stealthily toward her, she took in the pungent smell of burnt matter. It drew nearer, so that she saw in amazement the formulae, spells, diagrams that were embossed in silver upon the burnt pages. And she could see the living ember that glowed with golden radiance.

She whispered, and the thing before her seemed to expand at her noise. The essence of fire brightened seductively. She reached to it, into it. There was a popping sound, and around her hand there danced a multitude of sparks. Pearls of flame sank into her flesh. She raised her moiling hand and savagely blew upon it, until it exploded into flame. How astonishing to watch it burn! She raised that paw of fire to the sky, then let it fall into her hair, upon her face. She howled an antient name until her face caved in. What once had been mortal woman scattered as sparks toward the sky, particle by particle, into dead insentient cosmos.

## IV.

The lean and sallow cynic scowled at the boy who bowed before him. "Arise, wretched fool. There is nothing so mundane than being worshipped by mediocrity. Up, coxcomb. I have no taste for your pallid veneration."

"Simon ... please ..."

Simon Gregory Williams snorted, then kicked the idiot in the nose. "Be gone, burthen me no more. I've no need of disciples. I am ripe with self-adoration." The youth looked at him with trembling puppy eyes, and the sight so sickened the older man that he kicked the boy's face once more, savagely. "Away!" he screamed. The lad, cupping nose with a hand that soon spilled blood, whimpered and fled.

"Pah," the wizard spat. "Why do they weary me, these weasels? This is what comes of being too utterly beguiling. 'Reputation is an idle and most false imposition,' as the poet so wisely penned. Something, some lingering presence, loitered among distant trees.

"Remaining still, green immaturity?" His silver eyes squinted as he scanned the shadowed place.

There was movement as something pushed through branch and nettle and hobbled toward him. It was a charred thing that spilled with shifting shape, and he knew not what it was until he saw the symbol, a symbol that he had embossed upon the spine of his personal grimiore. "Great Yuggoth, what have they done to thee," he hoarsely whispered, falling to his knees before the remnant of his wizardry. Gingerly, he placed a hand upon the symbol. "Well, I'm certain that they paid a deadly price. How long you've been away." He kept his hand upon the symbol, and hissed to feel his magick's potency still within the charred remains. And joined with his magick he could feel the enchantment of other charismatic souls.

Simon rose, with his daemonic offspring held in steady hands. He lifted it to the white mountain that towered over Sesqua Valley. "Behold, this thing of alchemy, as much a child of the valley as I myself. Assist me now, great mater. Heed paternal moan."

He deeply felt his heartbeat; and beneath his soles he sensed a deeper pulse. The trees about him grew heavy with mist that exuded from their moist bark. Shaggy things, with bestial faces, fell from limbs and danced about the warlock. They watched in marvel the miracle of Sesqua's magick. Mist enveloped the charred vestige of spell and sign and diagram that beguiled the forces beyond the rim. It changed, this wizard's work, within its father's hands. It formed a face (with esoteric symbol embossed upon the forehead), and hands of its own. Pushing out of Simon's embrace, it leapt onto the ground, a thing of wanton sorcery. Upon its nameless flesh there existed still the spectre of lines that etched diagrams, evocations, alien names.

It raised its paw unto its sire. Crazily, the gremlins danced in darkness.

¿?

# AFTERWORD

Part of the fun of writing Mythos fiction is that it returns me to
Lovecraft. I not only read HPL's immortal prose, I *study* it. I study his
life as well as his work, which is why I've read S. T. Joshi's magnificent
biography of Lovecraft five times, and will read it many more times
before my happy death. A simple phrase or imagery from Lovecraft's
fiction is often enough to inspire an idea, or a title; and often a new title
itself can suggest an entire story idea. Unlike Lovecraft, my horror
fiction is absolutely drenched in the supernatural, that is simply the way
my mind works. I find it extremely liberating, this supernaturalism,
because it frees me to be audacious in writing weird fiction. Sesqua
Valley is a place of supernatural wonder, a combination of Lovecraft's
horror stories and of his delicious dreamland. It is a place where
anything can happen.

    With this new story, I took an old vignette and imagined it anew,
creating a new tale. It appears here for the first time.

## I.

Richard Lund was not native to Sesqua Valley, yet I had always felt a close kinship to him. I liked his clumsy bulk, his big flat hands with their thick yellow nails. I enjoyed listening to his sepulchral voice as it intoned his morbid poetry. I loved the large face from which that poetry was uttered, that face with its thick lips and flat nose. Above all, I was seduced by his eyes, those dark green eyes that strangely caught candlelight or moonglow. Richard had come to the valley as a child, from Boston, with his wild, unruly mother. She had been a great beauty, had posed for a number of scandalous sketches and paintings by the men and women who were her lovers. Truly bohemian, she had experimented with hip drugs and cool booze; alas that appetite had transformed into addiction. Her relationship with her oft-neglected child was sad and peculiar, to the point where Richard had often felt an abandoned child, an image that frequently found expression in his poetry. I shall quote a typical example, from his long poem, "The Changeling":

> "For I was in strange shadow borne and bred,
> Squeezed from maternity of chilly pitch,
> And moonlight was the milk on which I fed.
> And I, the product of a nameless bitch,
> Was hurled away from my maternal place,
> Unknown, unwanted, useless, full of brine
> That seeped from out mine eyes onto my face.
> I stagger in a world not mine."

I had met his mother often, and pitied her. She was an absolute grotesque, her once-proud beauty now dissolved into a withered package of ruined flesh. It was horrifying to see her suddenly take hold of her massive son, press her emancipated face to his flesh and deeply sniff him, then move her tongue along his face. At such times Richard and I would exchange miserable glances; but he never pushed her from him.

It was clear, however, that he needed to escape her, if only temporarily, and when he turned twenty-two he decided to visit his long forsaken hometown.

"Adam, you must manage my mother while I am away."

"I will do all I can," I promised. Thus I spent much time in their two-story house, often staying the night in Richard's small room. And when his mother would call me by his name, I would answer; when she held me I would not push her away; when she climbed into my bed, I would embrace her. And when I found her dead, a needle in her arm, her face in a pool of squalid vomit, I cleansed her.

Richard refused, upon his swift and sorrowful return, to hold a funeral service. Having had the body embalmed, he kept his mother's corpse in a coffin situated in an unfinished basement room. Then he went into seclusion. Even I was kept at bay, but I would not utterly ignore him. After one week, I was bold enough to pound upon his door and call his name. For ten minutes I kept up my clamor, glancing at the blinds that perpetually covered every window of the house. Finally I heard the fall of muffled footsteps, and the door slowly opened. Richard, shirtless, a candlestick in hand, gazed at me for many silent moments. I was horrified at his alteration. He was beginning to resemble his deranged mother. He was thin and haggard, utterly depleted of the vital strength that I had found so sexually alluring. My horror must have been obvious, for finally he strangely smiled, moved away from the door and allowed my entrance into his home.

"Let me see your arms," I shouted as soon as the door was shut. "And why is it so dark in here?"

"Ah, Adam Webster, how like a mother you sound."

"It was obscene enough that she brought that city filth into these sacred confines, but that you ..."

He stopped my mouth with a kiss, then held out his naked arm. Pouting, I examined it, my Sesquan eyes seeing easily in the gloom. There were no needle marks.

"What did you expect? That I need her stimulates? Don't be absurd. And you know that since childhood I have suffered from an ailment that makes bright light a torture to mine eyes. Of late the torment has increased, and thus I keep it dark."

We entered the living room, in which another candle flickered. Richard flung himself into a large low chair, the candlestick nestled in his lap. How weirdly he studied its dancing flame. "You look tired," I said at last, not sitting, looking around the room to see if he had made any changes. He had not, nor had be bothered with house-cleaning. I ran my hand across a nearby table, then clapped thick dust from my fingers.

Richard momentarily smiled. "Yes. How weary I've become. Quite, quite so." He looked at me over the candle's glow and frowned. "You needn't look at me like that. I'm not a helpless child. I don't need you worrying over me like some surrogate matron."

"Stop calling me your mother. And I will worry, blast you. You cannot bring me intimately into your life and then push me emotionally away when things turn tragic. My feelings have been bruised. I've missed you.

And I confess to being a bit flummoxed at your bizarre refusal to have her properly buried."

"Enough."

"No I do not think so!" I shouted.

Suddenly snarling, he rose and placed a large hand at my throat. "I said *enough*. I don't need to be lectured by you, child of mauve shadow. You dare to question my behavior, while you sit in the tower and pour over those damned tomes and make outlandish signals unto darkness? No, I think not."

"Do let go, you brute."

Roughly, he pushed me from him, and I had to hold onto the mantelpiece to keep from falling. "No more about my mother. She's an outsider and no concern of yours. I'll bury her when I've a mind to do so. I am not now in the mood. I'm keeping her around. Perhaps it will give birth to poetic inspiration. God, I was having such a good time in New England. Spent a day in that weird Arkham town you told me about. That was certainly interesting. And Boston was splendid; I did some fine writing there. I felt enormously at home. To have to come back here, to *that* ... "

"The worst is over."

"The worst is not over! I'm completely blocked. And I need so desperately to write. Here I sit, pen in paw, and nothing ... nothing."

"And so you ignore the ones who love you and writhe in self-pity. How very pathetic." Turning my back to him, I ran my hand over the mantel, then looked at a painting that hung close by. Gingerly, I reached for it and wiped at an accumulation of dust. Richard's low voice filled the room.

"I found it in an old shop in Boston, a neglected place along a narrow alleyway. A homey place, so it was. Very little light, no bothersome humanoids about. The charming proprietor was a quaint gentlewoman in her twilight years. She seemed as dusty and faded as so many of the objects in her shop. I found that painting and was enchanted. She could not remember how it came into her possession. There's no signature that I can discern, although we found a title on the back—'Gallow's Hill'. I gave her a very good price for it. I gaze at it continually. It haunts me."

I leaned closer to the painted surface. Its colors were very dim, perhaps from age, but I sensed that it was due rather to the artist's style and intent. The scene was a lonely hill. A row of baying creatures encircled a corpse that hanged from a sinister gallows. I sensed Richard behind me, felt his heavy hand on my shoulder. "I love the subtle hint of color," he whispered. "See how the moonlight lingers just over the crouching beasts, as if afraid to get too close? The shadow of night blends with those powerful daemonic limbs, as if it would become one with their substance. Do you see how the nighted sky contains just a hint of purple, a subtle bruise of color so as to distinguish it from darker shadow? And most wonderful of all, observe how pale lunar luminosity is reflected in the staring eyes of the dead hag, those wide green eyes. See, too, how a darker hue of emerald is caught in the eyes of her hunkering companions. Rather superb, eh?"

I stared at the image of the woman's dead face, and Richard leaned closer. I felt his warm breath at my ear. "Do you see how her rigid visage subtly resembles those baying physiognomies beneath her? Wonderful."

But I could not listen. My mind was whirling with what I saw and numbly recognized. I turned my startled countenance to the creature at my side. "Yes, dear boy," he spoke. "Odd, isn't it? That face, that stiff dead canine face encased in a shaft of misty moonlight. I noticed it straight off, and thus I had to buy the painting. Why, that dead thing resembles me more so than my own dam."

## II.

He led me, gothic candlestick in hand, to the lower region of his house. We entered the cryptic room that had been transformed into a memorial chamber. Richard smoothed the wood of his mother's small coffin, then slowly opened the lid. A variety of unpleasant odors assailed my enhanced senses. Richard inhaled the engulfing foetor as if it were a succulent bouquet. "There she lies, finally at peace." He ghoulishly smiled. "Almost as fresh as when she lived."

"Richard ..."

"Hush. Look upon this husk of death. I've lived with her all my numbered years, and yet she looks to me like some stranger. Did we actually know each other? Betimes, when she was especially drunk, she would penetrate me with red intoxicated eyes and ask, 'Who are you; *who are you?*' I ask that very question: Who Am I? From whence did I approach? From her loins? Did she birth me, or find me in some shadowed place? Why have I always felt so utterly alien? And so lonely, so unutterably lonely."

I reached for him. "Darling ..."

His wide rough hand covered my mouth. "Hush. We all have loneliness and sorrow. Except, perhaps, you guys, you weird spawn of the valley. You seem to know exactly what you are, from whence you exuded. But one such as I—" He took his hand from my mouth and reached for the hand of the silent thing. He brought her cold and withered hand to his flat nostrils. Deeply, he inhaled. I did not like the look that slanted his somber eyes. "I don't smell like her, don't look like her." He pressed his lips to her chilly hand and kept it there for many moments. "I don't taste like her."

I tried to take the hand away. With savage fury, he shoved me from him, with such force that I knocked against a table and crashed with it to the floor. Wickedly, he smiled. I saw his dark tongue lick the dead skin, saw his crooked teeth nibble a thin slice of flesh that tore from the corpse's hand. Richard turned his face to me. I had never before seen within his eyes such a wild hungry look. "I wish to spend some private time with my mother."

I clawed at the floor in outraged anguish, until my fingers bled. Sucking at the foam that gathered on my lips, I pushed myself to a standing position and escaped the house. In a rage of fury that I did not try to understand I fled into the woodland, where I crouched beneath the swaying shadows of encircling trees. Looking up through branches, I saw the moon watching me. I shrieked at that godless sphere and laughed insanely. I gathered fallen vines and wove them into a wreath, then placed the garland on my dome and danced in the lunacy of moonlight.

Exhausted, I fell upon the ground. In my madness the headdress of strong vines had loosened and encircled my throat. I pulled at them so to free them, gagging as they tightened their stranglehold. Then I stopped, remembering his hand so forcefully around my neck. Extraordinarily, I began to weep; and as I suppurated sorrow I heard the low distant baying from the highest regions of Mount Selta. Something of consequence had occurred within the valley. Cold sweat chilled my brow as I rushed to Richard's house, the front door of which I found wide open. Timidly, I tiptoed into the living room. It was empty of inhabitant. Looking at the large old sofa, I saw the weird painting resting on it. I went to it and picked it up. The dead hag's face was moist, as if blessed by some unholy kiss.

Again, from the mountain, came the mournful dirge. Silently, I found the basement door and walked down the narrow steps. The coffin lid had been lowered, and I gazed for many moments at that ghastly box of death. From a place outside I heard the song of rushing wind. Hurriedly climbing the steps, I rushed outside, into a mayhem of tumultuous wind. Screaming Richard's name, I forced myself through the fury, to the back of the house. I took in the tall oak tree in which Richard had, as a child, built a platform that served as a place to which he could escape so as to read and write. From one of the tree's sturdy branches hanged a length of rope whose burden moved in the violence of wind. I approached that swaying figure and knelt beneath it. His dark green eyes were open wide, their dead surface reflecting yellow moonlight. I raised my silver eyes to that globe of lifeless dust and opened my mouth in desolation.

# AFTERWORD

I am particularly fond of this story, because of the character of Richard Lund, who was based on an asshole I used to date. I caught with this tale a measure of poignancy that deeply touches a place within my weary heart. I think there is something of myself in Richard's tragick loneliness. After I wrote the story and sold it, I felt an overwhelming sorrow in having killed Richard off. I wanted to write more stories about him. Thus I relished the opportunity to rewrite the story for this edition of my work. The original version of "Born in Strange Shadow" (the title is from Lovecraft) was published in *Terminal Fright* #12.

## I.

When my elder siblings and I were very young, our parents returned to Sesqua Valley, the land of their origin. As a child there had been something about the valley, and the large old house in which we lived, that affected my nerves. I often suffered queer nightmares. Things I saw—or thought I saw—in dark verdant shade beyond our yard took an unhealthy hold of my imagination. My fears were always soothingly dismissed by Mother, but the situation has had a lasting affect. Perhaps that is why I reacted as I did, last week, when my oldest sister died.

My brother, James, felt a profound distaste for Sesqua Valley and its queer inhabitants, and departed from us as soon as he came of age. Victoria, the firstborn of us children, was his complete opposite, for she adored the valley and often accompanied Mother on long walks. I was always astonished, and I think envious, of the sense of wonder that glowed in her violet eyes when she returned from such wanderings; and often I would creep silently past her slightly opened bedroom door, catching sight of her scribbling into her pad of yellow paper. Victoria was a poet, but Mother was the only family member to whom these works were ever shown. I never dared to invade the privacy of that bedchamber, until the recent and very weird event.

Oh, I was obsessed with that room, certainly. Perhaps I felt neglected. I loved Mother, yet sensed that she had been somehow disappointed in me. I felt her distance. Sometimes as a child I would get out of bed late at night so as to use the bathroom. When I passed the closed door of Victoria's room I would often hear the low chanting of her soft voice. At times Mother's accompanied her voice. At other times I imagined that I could discern other voices, strange and far off. I would stand in the darkened hallway and listen to that weird chanting, and to the valley's pulse that sounded deep inside my eardrums. Sometimes I thought that the entire house throbbed to that uncanny rhythm, as if something were pounding beneath the ground, begging entrance into the world above.

With what chill I recall that strangest of all evenings. Father was away as usual on a business trip, and Mother and Victoria had been spending every evening in my sister's room, crying to the valley in esoteric song. I remember how it chilled me to hear the beasts that lived on Mount Selta cry as if in response to the clamor. I remember the thick cloud of mauve fog that issued from the woodland and encased the ancient house. I sat at my window, watching that mist in fascination. I placed my tiny hand upon the window's glass and shivered at its chilliness. I watched the peculiar shadow-shapes that seemed to drift within that vapor just outside my window. Then suddenly the mist was gone, and the singing in the other room was replaced with joyous laughter. Cracking open my bedroom door, I watched the door to Victoria's chamber, and saw it quietly open. My mother and sister emerged, sheltering from view a third figure, tiny and dwarfish.

At breakfast the next morning I was introduced to my newest sibling, the mysterious Edith. We had "adopted" her, I was told. This newest addition to the family perplexed me. Perhaps I resented how she was obviously Mother's new darling. Once I began to tease her because of the way she smelled, like wet leaves on a stormy day, and I cruelly mimicked her ugly goat-like face, making obnoxious bleating noises. Mother reprimanded me severely, as did Victoria. Edith watched in silence, gazing at me with her odd silver eyes, eyes that were the same color and shape as Mother's.

The day came when Father never returned from one of his many trips. Nothing was ever explained to me of this event. Victoria would merely shake her head and say that Father had gone away. I was a teenager when Mother came to my room and said goodbye. This was our most tender moment together, and I loved the feel of her slender hand in my hair, her soft mouth pressed to my tear-stained face. I listened to the sound of Victoria's sad singing, watched the mauve mist that spilled from the woodland. I looked out my bedroom window at the ground below, where Edith stood holding Mother's hand. The thick mist enveloped them, and when at last it drifted back to the woodland, Edith stood alone.

It was after this that Edith began to vanish for days at a time. Victoria never seemed to mind or worry, and indeed began to take an almost maternal interest in me, encouraging my growing interest in literature and my frail early attempts at fictional composition. Yet I sensed that she and Edith had some special and unspoken connection, of which I was not a part. I envied the looks they would share when Edith would suddenly return from having been gone for days. Once I boldly asked Edith where she had been. I'll never forget the answer.

"I walk the shadows of the valley, William, those dark places that you are so eager to avoid. Of what are you afraid? If only you would close your eyes and silence your frantic fears, oh!, the things you would sense and perhaps begin to understand. Why must you remain such a dense clod? Do you never hear Mother's lullaby on the night wind? Are you doomed to stay an outsider all your pathetic life?"

An outsider. Yes, that was how I was always made to feel, by everyone I loved and lived with. Now, in these twilight years, I have a kind of understanding, incomplete as it is. I've learned to accept in silence this haunted valley's ways. I've had my career, such as it was, as romantic novelist. Still, as I mentioned, my nervous system was never hearty. When, in early adulthood, Edith became interested in sculpting, my frail imagination reacted in violence to the hideous gargoyle faces and figurines that she created. I recall one afternoon, when I had finished working on a chapter and came downstairs so to puff upon one of the scented cigarettes that I aesthetically smoked in homage to Wilde. I could hear Edith working in the sunroom at the back of the house, and I decided to be bold and spy on her. There she sat, among the potted plants, painting one of her daemonic stone faces. I did not like the way she sang to it, nor the way the thing's face seemed to come to ghastly life as more and more paint was applied. Then Edith slowly turned and gazed at me. Oh, those silver eyes beneath the thick dark brows! And when she suddenly smiled I nervously noted the resemblance between her goat face and the stony visage that glistened wetly on her worktable.

But that was aeons ago. It has, of course, been heavily on my mind since Victoria's death last week. I am trying, I suppose, to understand the events that have occurred—that still occur, and from which there is no sane escape. Even as I pen this journal entry I can hear the chanting voices and feel the swaying of this ancient house. I can feel deep within my soul the pulse of Sesqua Valley in answer to that mantra from Victoria's room. No, there is no escape. I must set this aside and go to them.

## II.

The unnerving events began two weeks ago. Victoria and I were spending a quiet evening reading in the living room. Edith quietly entered the room with something, some new work, in hand. I intuited that she was intensely interested in Victoria's reaction to the thing she set on the table before the sofa. I stared at the sculptured stone in bewilderment. What on God's good earth was it supposed to represent? It seemed to resemble a cluster of clouds, yet there was something in its form that suggested sentience. I felt oddly afraid looking at it.

"What on earth do you call that?" I stammered.

"I call it 'Shub-Niggurath'," came Edith's cool reply.

"What a cryptic name," uttered Victoria, putting down her book and approaching the low table. "It's fascinating. And how odd; for I've recently written a new poem that compliments your work. Let me see if I can recall it." I was stunned. In our many decades together, my sister had never shared with us her poetry. It was her private mode of self-expression and self-discovery, as she once explained it to me. And so I sat with mouth wide open as Victoria stood straight, leaned back her head and closed her eyes, then began to recite.

"The dark hath come with furtive stealth
To ease my mind, my soul's ill-health.
Night's pale mauve fog consumes my breath.
What revelation comes with death.
Those sifted sands of life are stopped.
Into a charming void I'm dropped
Where solace sings with lonesome tongue
From mouths numbered a thousand young."

"Oh, dear," Edith laughed. "Are you to be adopted into the Black Goat's number?" Victoria secretly smiled, and continued.

"The writhing fog transfigures me
And ushers forth eternity.
I find the realm where I belong,
Wherein is echoed Mother's song.
From shadow's realm I'll ne'er depart.
I pulse within the valley's heart."

I listened intently, and watched Victoria's eyes grow moist with emotion. The tears began to flow from my own eyes. Smiling, my elder sister took my head into her hands and kissed my brow. Then she took up the thing of stone, looked at it admiringly, and bent to kiss it before handing it to Edith. I watched as she slowly vacated the room. It was the last time I would see her as she was.

One of our elderly rituals was for Victoria and I to sit at night and read or discuss literature. I think it was her way of shewing a kind of matronly love that had been absent in my childhood. I relished the quiet companionship, something that was absolutely lacking between Edith and myself. And thus I became alarmed when three evenings went by with no sign of Victoria. She had kept up her constant roaming through the woods, an activity that she and Mother shared. I panicked, thinking that my beloved had vanished as suddenly and as mysteriously as Mother had. Yet I said nothing to Edith, who in old age had grown bossy and scolding, treating me as if I were a helpless and stupid child. And so, on that third evening, I found myself climbing the carpeted stairs that led to the second floor and our bedrooms. Bright moonlight streamed through the small hallway window, and I stopped to gaze out at the dark woods. Had I heard a strange drumming in my sleep a few days before? Had I dreamed of pale mauve mist enshrouding the house? Why was I so bizarrely terrified? Moving past the window, I went to my sister's bedroom door and opened it.

The room was cold and damp. Yellow curtains swayed at the widely opened windows. Dim shapes took on solid form, and I studied the furnishings of a room that had obsessed me for decades, but which I had never entered. I noticed the heaps of yellow foolscap that littered much of the floor. An odd shape that reclined in one dusky corner of the room caught my attention. Cautiously, I went to it, that pale thing of human form that gave my old heart a violent jolt.

I had no doubt that it was my sister, and that she was dead. But in what her body been sheathed? Candlelight filtered into the room, and Edith stood beside me. For one silent moment she gazed in puzzlement at our sister's corpse; then she handed me the candlestick, went to the body and knelt beside it. I watched as she cautiously touched it. Overwhelmed with emotion, I began to weep.

"Be quiet, William. Or if you must make that repulsive noise then leave the room."

Choking angry words, I went to join her and knelt. I gasped in bewildered horror. The candle's light revealed that with which my sister's body was covered. In what must have been a state of insanity, Victoria had pasted her nude flesh with sheets of paper on which she had penned her private verse.

Edith bent and blew out the candle's flame. I watched as she swayed to and fro, clutching her hair, moving her mouth in a grotesque churning motion. I thought she was going to be sick, but instead she suddenly pressed her mouth to my ear and hummed a haunting tune that was strangely familiar. Edith placed a hand on my chest, just above my heart; her other hand was flung upon the corpse, between the lifeless breasts. I felt the sound before actually hearing it: the heaving throbbing, deep and steady, from somewhere beneath the house. Raising her hands into the air, Edith made strange signals with her tiny fingers. Those dwarfish fingers suddenly moved to me and clutched my startled face. Her eyes were wild and moist with tears. She lunged at me and savagely kissed my mouth. Shocked and revolted, I roughly pushed her from me, spitting the taste of her kiss from my mouth.

Edith cackled as she rose upon her stunted legs. I watched her move in time to the valley's outlandish heartbeat. Her beckoning hands reached toward an opened window, and I shuddered at the sight of the approaching fog, that unearthly mauve mist that began to spill into the room. I hugged myself as chill windstorm pushed around me. The hearty breeze pushed the pages of Victoria's verse around the room. I watched those sheets sail to my sister's corpse and cling to it. I saw those sheets ripple, shining in mauve illumination. Edith's dancing became frantic and disjointed, and suddenly she collapsed and fell to her knees.

The thing that had been Victoria slowly rose to its feet as the wind roared and Edith howled fantastic alien words in her raspy voice. That which had been my elder sister opened wide its mouth. In a deep transfigured voice it uttered beautiful poetry as Edith continued to belch her alien tongue. The room was alive with language. Words seemed to whirl about us in the leaden light. I saw that light pulse with ungodly life, saw it billow and shape itself into a likeness of the sculpture that Edith had christened "Shub-Niggurath". A thousand faces flowed within the pulsation of writhing cloud.

Edith howled like a crazed creature. The sheathed figure towered above her, its rippling flesh capturing the enchanted illumination of the hazy mauve light. It raised its majestic hands to our sister, and I moaned as Edith took hold of one hand and licked its palm. Edith turned to look at me, and for the first time she regarded me with a crazy kind of love. She held to me her free hand in invitation. "Come to us, brother," she wailed. "*Iä!* Come to your destiny! Let us worship her together!"

# AFTERWORD

I relish the chance to go over these old tales and touch them up a wee bit for this edition. Of course, reading them all together shews me what I consider weaknesses, the repetition of favorite words, imagery, &c. Indeed, in this book I have two stories that contain scenes in which hands raise into the air and turn into ash. Oh well. What I also see is how my vision of Sesqua Valley has matured with age. When I first began to write of the valley, it was merely a cool place wherein I could set creepy Mythos stories. Derleth and Lumley too overly influenced me in those early days, but—happily—those days are gone. The Mythos still has a strong influence over my imagination, and although I try to keep the Mythos in the background, I don't always succeed. I am, and always will be, a Lovecraft *fan*, and that adolescent thrill and sense of wonder for the Mythos will always be a part of my writing, for better or for worse.

"Another Flesh" was first published in *The Bone Marrow Review #1.*

## I.

It has called to me from early youth, and as a child I often climbed the grassy hill to the stone edifice. The building, black with age, beguiled me. I remember how I would place my tiny hand on the rough surface and marvel at the sense of primeval potency that seeped into my fingers. Legend of the structure tells that it has stood upon the grassy hummock for centuries so to house the thing that sleeps within. Like the ancient round tower, the stone construction seems almost a growth of the valley itself, a substance of Nature.

Inside the structure is a case of golden wood. The wondrous creature that lies within this case has often called to me in dreams of the buried past. As a girl, I would stand on tiptoe so to peer into the casket, and I would gaze for hours at the thick dry skin, the elongated head. I felt an indistinct sadness that the creature had been interred facedown, as if in disgrace. The thick reptilian skin exuded a delicious aroma of decay. The round disc held in one upturned palm especially fascinated me. I could not tell if the figures etched thereon formed a peculiar alphabet or were meant to convey a representation of some unfamiliar race of creatures. I once placed my small hand upon the stone disc. At first I sensed nothing; then my vision blurred and darkened, and I heard the low hum of distant windsong. Dizziness oppressed me, and I covered my eyes as I tried to keep my balance. When at last my senses calmed, I took my hands from my eyes. Before me was an ancient city lost within a valley of sand. My astonished heart beat with wild emotion as I gazed upon the still and darkened ruins that squatted shapelessly within the deserted city. Then my pulse slowed its rushing rhythm and the prickling liquid that coursed through my veins slowed. I flowed over sand toward the ruins, moving with the rushing wind that gusted always behind me yet never brushed my flesh.

I listened to that ageless wasteland wind as the antiquity of the place kissed my soul with spectral speculation. I felt no fear; despite the queerness of everything around me, the city did not feel unfamiliar. Dusky memories filtered through my dreamy mind. I remembered clans of beings, creatures who once surrounded me as I held in hand a forbidden scroll. I did not like the way they leered at me with menace in their gaze, and so I shut my eyes. I sensed the wind that rushed behind me, never touching. I sang to its whispered song in the syllables of a forgotten tongue. I sang to the dread lord Nyarlathotep, whose chaotic image I had tried to raise with the signals etched onto the sacred scroll that I had criminally procured. I spoke His profane name, and the wind

behind me muted.

Cautiously, I reopened eyes. I stood within a dark and vaulted chamber. Along a rough stone wall was a line of golden wood caskets. Peering into the one nearest me, I saw an elegant figure draped in gorgeous robes. Its reptilian dome was crowned with a triple diadem of white gold. It was a wondrous creature, and yet I felt deep apprehension as I looked upon it. Looking up, I espied a distant corridor, and somehow I began to flow toward it. When movement ceased I found that I was inside a small dark place. Before me, naked of fabulous robes, was the mummy that I had found within a stone construction in Sesqua Valley. It lay face down. A round stone disc reposed in its upturned palm. I turned that disc and found myself within a vortex of daemonic wind, which whirled about me yet never kissed my flesh. It howled at my ears and spun before my eyes, and I covered those eyes and opened my mouth in lament. I cried until all was silent around me, and when my eyes reopened, I saw that I was standing within the familiar shadows of a stone edifice, with before me a casket of golden wood.

## II.

It is the custom in Sesqua Valley for its young to journey forth into the outside world when they come of age. Yet, no matter how far we travel, the valley always finds us and sings for our return. I had journeyed to Salt Lake City to visit my cousin, Corianton, and learn the alchemy of the Lamanite nation; but the rhythm of enchanted tom-toms became, in time, subdued by another pulsation, the living beat of the valley's soul that throbbed within my blood flow. Dreams spilled to me in time, and blended with their song I heard one other sound, the haunting hum of ancient winds. And beneath the beating of Sesqua's soul-pulse I could hear the slow and steady throb of a thing that slept within its case of golden wood. Thus I left the land of the saints and returned to my lush homeland.

The morning of my return was clear and warm, and barefoot I wandered the woodland until I came to the length of meadow that led to a grassy hill. As I caught sight of the stone construction, I was overwhelmed with ecstasy. I was home, surrounded by the verdant beauty of this immortal valley. I stretched happily in the sunlight as I scanned the trees, the gleaming white stone of Mount Selta.

I reached the vertex of the hill and stood before the thing of stone. From within the edifice came the soft high sound of a child's voice in song. Cautiously, I stepped to the narrow opening that led inside the structure, then peered inside. He stood before the sleeping beast of antiquity, a small boy with arms raised high. Upon his small head he

wore a triple crown composed of white gold. His small frame swayed in tempo to his esoteric song. One fist curled around a small black statue, a statue of a faceless god.

Entering, I knelt beside the child. His eyes were tightly shut. I listened to the song he sang, to the alien words that issued forth from his soft pink mouth. His chant was a thing that I had heard when dreaming of a lost and nameless city. The purity of his voice seemed almost too ethereal, as if he too were a product of reverie. I reached to touch him.

He opened silver eyes. Smiling, he placed a tiny hand over my trembling lips. Slowly, he closed his eyes again and began to sway. I could feel his warm breath on my face, and smell its rich valley aroma. Leaning to me, and taking his hand from my mouth, he pressed his lips against mine and began to sing his arcane song. The tip of his crown pushed against my eyeball. I tried to whisper a response to his chanting. My arms wrapped around his tiny body, and we sat upon the cold hard ground, our backs supported by the ancient wooden casket. We surrendered to strange slumber. In dream I heard our twin breathing accompanied by the low hum of distant desert wind. In hazy vision I beheld a small and shadowy chamber, and saw also a golden case within which reposed an ancient mummy. Reaching out, I touched its flesh, the undead skin that weirdly warmed my hand. Poignantly, I climbed into its bed of death and spread myself beside its musky flesh. Lowering my face before its reptilian mouth, I hungrily drank its hot delicious breath.

I awoke in darkness, with moonlight streaming in through the cavity of doorway. The child had vacated my embrace; standing next to me, he leaned over the coffin's perimeter. The crown sat upon his dome at a lopsided tilt, and the black statuette was hugged to his little chest. He gazed steadfastly at the motionless beast.

"They're hungry," he whispered.

I knelt beside him. "They?"

"They are legion," he sighed. "Can't you feel how they want you?" Reaching into the casket, he took up the round flat disk. His silver eyes shone like starlight as he pressed the object into my hand. Nodding slowly, he held the statuette before my face, closed his eyes and began to sing. Rising, I removed my clothing. Naked, I climbed into the casket. In darkness, I pressed the stone disk to my flesh, smoothed it along my neck, my breasts, my thighs. I ran my free hand against the dry skin that I had straddled, the dry flesh that somehow beckoned me. Bending low, I stroked the dead thing with tongue, with burning lips. Heavily breathing, I placed the stone disk upon the back of the dead thing's head, stretched myself along the body. My breasts pressed against its back, and my loins smoothed the dry buttocks.

The child swayed and sang, and the words of his chant became familiar. Softly, I whispered his song, then reached for the stone disk. I held the disk tightly, then opened my hand and let the object rests upon my palm. The reptilian skin beneath me began to ripple, to soften. I felt it slowly melt into a mound of moving sand, sand that flowed about me. I moved my face into the substance and let it fill my mouth. I moaned as it flowed between my legs and entered there. It covered me, this stuff, like some strange new skin. My face began to shift as my flesh began to ripple and reshape. The stone disk felt hot on my palm. I smiled as a triple crown of white gold was placed upon my elongating dome.

Years have passed. As I lay here, dreaming of antediluvian wonders, I behold a nameless city that slumbers beneath a valley of drifting sand. I dream of a faceless god that stalks among starlight. Joined to my dreaming self are the other selves that form my multitude of souls. We sigh and dream within a stone edifice that stands upon the grassy hill of an enchanted valley. We dream of Nyarlathotep, sire of the million favored ones, who will bless us in the age of crawling chaos. It is a sweet dream. And equally as sweet is the one youth who sings beside our bed of golden wood; the youth who, in time, will join our eternal throng.

*6?*

# AFTERWORD

Unlike Lovecraft's cosmic fiction, my own yarns are decidedly subterranean. And yet there is one spectre that haunts his fiction, the quintessentially cosmic creature known as Nyarlathotep, with whom I am profoundly obsessed. Indeed, afore I crawl into my grave I shall probably have penned enough tales of Nyarlathotep to fill a small volume. His fictive influence has been immense, from the Lovecraftian tales of Robert Bloch to Stanley C. Sargent's brilliant tale, "Nyarlatophis, a Fable of Ancient Egypt," found in Stanley's newest collection, *The Taint of Lovecraft*. Lovecraft's fiction is filled to overflowing with such delicious daemons, and the spell he weaves is so overwhelming that no one can ever take his place as the finest weird fantasist of all time.

"Immortal Remains" was first published in *The Cthulhu Codex* Vol. VI.

# I.

It was early in September, on a chilly afternoon, that she came to us. The valley had been oddly silent, as though holding its breath. It seemed to me an oppressive silence, and to dispel the clouds of gloom that had gathered in my head I took my flute to the woods and played soft low music to the windless air. Strangely, I did not play any tune from memory; rather, I let my feelings intuit music. My heavy melancholy sailed as measured sound into the aether. Then came the subtle change. Gradually, I became aware of my body's pulse, could feel it in my blood and hear it in my ears. And beneath the ground on which I stood I felt the paranormal pulse of Sesqua Valley as it matched my body's rhythm.

A hand was placed upon my shoulder. Turning, I looked into the eyes of Edith's goatish face, at her high wide nostrils, at her ancient smile. She ran her withered fingers through my hair, then pointed them toward the woodland. My anxious eyes followed the direction of her pointing, as around and beneath us the valley shuddered into life. I knew this consciousness. A new child of the valley was about to arrive. I sensed behind us a growing crowd of townsfolk.

The day darkened, and from high on Mount Selta's arched peaks snouted things bayed to shadow. I gazed into the woodland, and watched the thick mauve fog that began to billow from it. I watched the figure that daintily stepped from out that swirling haze, and felt my flesh grow prickly cold as I looked at her. Her face was incomplete, like some forsaken portrait. Her features came and subtly went, with merely the mouth and one silver eye staying permanent. Her black flesh was as dark as midnight, a solid pitch that seemed of another realm. She was of astonishing beauty.

Edith went to her, took her hands and kissed them. Other women of the valley joined her, their hands welcoming the new one with soothing touch and adoring eyes. "You are as beautiful as a goddess," Edith cooed. "Shall we call you Selene?"

"Selene. Yes, it is beautiful. I heard music, and followed it from the place of shadow and ghostly trees. Such beautiful music ..."

I approached and shewed to her my flute, letting her touch it. Then, placing the instrument to my lips, I played. The new one closed her eye, and as I watched her facial image subtly melted and reformed. She raised a lovely hand and with it touched my face, then lifted both her arms and exotically began to dance. Usually I shut my eyes when lost in the wonder of song, but I did not want to stop gazing at this phenomenal beauty, and so kept my eyes wide open. Moving closer, she danced against me, and I was astonished at the smell of her, the potent valley scent that emanated from the taut breasts that pushed against my body. Selene smelled of the valley as none of us ever had, a rich redolence of wood and flora, of earth and stone. Intoxicated, I joined in the dance, and others moved to accompany us.

Selene reached for my flute and took it from my mouth. "What are you called?"

"I am Nelson."

"I like your face, Nelson. There were beasts in the place of shadow that had faces such as yours. I'm beginning to forget the things I knew in that place of misty shadow, but when I look at you, I shall always remember vaguely my former home. Do you know the song of the shadow's wind?"

"I don't recall such a song," I admitted.

"Let me teach it you, before it slips from me entirely." And she placed the flute to her mouth and, with weird instinct, began to play. Oh, the low tones, how they touched us. We shuddered, as chilly breath seemed to swell from the earth beneath us. It was my turn to dance close to the woman who played the flute, to move behind her and bury my face in the flowing redwood hair, to slid before her and nestle my visage between her fragrant breasts. She took the flute from her mouth and playfully tossed it to Edith. Yet still the low music sounded all around us, from the woodland, on the wind. I felt that wind play with my hair and kiss my face. Then I watched as Selene blew her magick breath onto my eyes and into my ears. Her potency was too overwhelming, and I fell to my knees, gasping. She fell beside me and touched her full lips to mine. I closed my eyes in ecstasy.

## II.

Edith and I sat before her library hearth, watching the flickering images of a log fire. Above us, in a small room, Selene heavily slept. A book of verse by William Davis Manly lay open on my lap, utterly ignored. "Strange," I said at last, "that she came to us too early."

"Too early?"

"Her unfinished face, and her scent. That must be how we smell in the place of shadow, before we are borne into this woodland realm."

"Perhaps," Edith said, smiling oddly.

"You know something, don't you?"

"My dear child, I know everything. Oh, ho, that hungry look in your eyes. Read to me poem thirty two from the book you continue to neglect."

I turned to the indicated page, but my attention was caught by the illustration on the page next to it. William Davis Manly was a crude artist, and yet he caught things in his illustrations that hinted, in line and delicate design, of extraordinary things. The illustration shewed a night-gaunt bending before a pool of water. The fabulous creature had no face, as is the way of the gaunts, those strange creatures that have filtered to this dimension from beyond the realm of dream. Yet as I investigated more closely the thing's reflection in the pool, I saw that its mirror image did seem to have a kind of countenance, and I was astonished to see in the vague uncertain features a distinct resemblance of Selene's unfinished face.

I gazed at that illustration for many moments, then moved my eyes to the poem and read aloud.

> "I hear your song in breath of wind and see
> The core of your immortal entity,
> The nucleus of what you are and will
> Become when legend's presage you fulfill.
> I genuflect to you on Sesqua's sod.
> You are one aspect of the faceless god."

I shut the book and furrowed my brow.

"Oh, dear," Edith laughed. "I fear I've increased your curiosity rather than diminished it. But, hark, I think she awakens above us."

Pushing out of my chair, I found my way to the steps that led upstairs. Entering Selene's room, I sat on her bed and smiled as she looked at me with her single eye. "Nelson," she whispered. "Did you see my friend?"

"No," I answered, confused.

"It was here, just now. Perhaps it will come again. May I taste your mouth?"

Smiling, I bent to her and shared a kiss. "Mmm, you taste of things I but vaguely remember. I don't like forgetting."

"We all forget, but our link to the place of origin remains with us. We are borne of the valley's shadow, and that place is ever near us, awaiting our return once we have experienced this mortal realm."

"How strange it all is. But I like this mortal realm, with its solid form and firm sensations. I like the touch of you."

I touched a finger to her brow, and watched in wonder as her features faintly displaced and reformed. I kissed that goddess face, then kissed her breasts and thighs. I could taste the valley in her loins. Overwhelmed, we made love, and afterward we dozed. In dream I could hear the rhythm of the valley pulsing in my brain. Visions, dark and indistinct, whirled within my mind. When at last I awakened, I was alone in bed. Selene knelt at a window, stroking the head of a faceless thing. I called her name, and the creature before her spread membranous

wings and vanished. Its black flesh had been exactly the pitch of Selene's.

Standing in the bedroom doorway, Edith smiled and nodded her ancient head.

## III.

I found the two women, the next morning, in the plant room. Edith had dressed Selene in a gown of beige cotton and was brushing the young creature's long red hair. Edith smiled at me, and her eyes twinkled excitedly. "Ah, the young flutist, risen at last. Excellent, for we three have a wee journey to which we must attend. You've sought answers, and now you will discover them."

She laid down the brush and stroked Selene underneath the chin. Selene slowly rose, and with her movement came a drifting scent of rich Nature. They each took hold of one of my hands and led me out into early morning sunlight. There was a vigorous north wind, the kind of current that I adore, alive as it is with scent and sound. We walked in woodland toward the bulk of Mount Selta, into a grotto near the mountain's base. It was a place where Edith did much of her private sculpting, and we of the valley never bothered her at this site. Our silver eyes adjusted to the darkness of the place, and I glanced at the chiseled faces that sat on various ledges carved into the rocky walls we passed. At last we came to a life-size figure composed of obsidian marble, and I could not help but gasp in exclamation. The figure was the identical twin of Selene, and yet something in its nature seemed very old. I let go of hands and touched the thing of mineral, then bent to smell and kiss it. Yes, my Sesquan senses could detect that this was a centuried creation.

"You did not compose this, Edith."

"I wish I could claim it, but you are correct. I found it here when first I encountered this potent place. It was this thing of dark beauty that inspired within me an interest in artistic creation. How could it not inspire one? I believe it is the work of the gaunts, who frequent this place, this place that serves as portal between the waking world and the realm of dreamland. You've sensed that the black substance of which the figure is composed is very old, and—how shall one put it?— unearthly."

I smoothed the statue's countenance with my hand. "How can the face be complete in form, if our friend here is the model?"

"Not model, dear boy. The statue, I believe, served as icon of a thing beheld in vision, a goddess in the bud, so to speak. I have knelt with gaunts in supplication before this frozen image, waiting for the time when starlight is aligned and gods and goddesses awaken. The time hath come." She put her arms around Selene's waist and led her to the statue.

The young woman touched the mineral visage.

"This is me, and I am it," Selene whispered.

"Borne of the stuff of dreams, the splendor of cosmic darkness, the shadow of this supernal and everlasting Eden. Borne to be worshipped." And Edith slowly knelt before the figures. I felt the ground beneath me slowly pulse with Sesqua's haunted heartbeat. I saw a swirling void above me spread, from which there filtered a race of gaunts, who supplicated before Selene, raising their awful talons which moved in esoteric signal. I raised a hand and made the elder signs. My mind was impregnated with a language that was as compelling as it was arcane. I spoke the ancient syllables. The gaunts spoke too, with their silent talons, echoing with claws the *outré* language that I mouthed.

And then another voice spoke the words I uttered, a voice that was the music of the heavens. Selene sang to her obsidian twin, then leaned unto it and kissed the hard cold surface. When at last she took herself away, I saw the statue's face had been utterly erased. I watched, and saw the living creature move her hand as I moved mine. The statue seemed to shudder, then convulsed with cracking. I watched as it shattered and crumbled as a cloud of dust. I watched as Edith, kneeling still, reached into the debris and took from it the one piece of marble that had remained whole, a strange shape that resembled a triple tiered crown. Rising majestically, Edith placed the tiara upon the woman whose back was still toward me.

Slowly she turned, this deity of darkness. Unhurriedly, she held to me her hand. I looked at where a semblance of a face had been, but where nigh there was naught but smooth blackness, like unto the encircling gaunts. Trembling with awe, I took her proffered hand and licked its palm.

*6?*

# AFTERWORD

I was thinking about Robert Bloch when I originally wrote this story, in the fall of 1995. Bob had recently died of cancer. He was the first horror author with whom I came into contact, and his letters became a beloved treasure, especially when I was a lonely missionary in Ireland, knocking on doors and preaching the gospel of the Latter-day Saints. It was at that time that I first began to collect horror anthologies, buying books that contained stories by Bob. Thus I became a fan of the fiction and eventually an author, all thanks to my mentor, Robert Bloch. So I wrote this story in his memory, touching upon the myth of Nyarlathotep, but fusing it with my own myth of Sesqua Valley. This story was first published (under an alternative title) in *Tales of Sesqua Valley*, published by another good buddy, Jeffrey Thomas, Esq.

*To ye memory of Joseph Payne Brennan*

## I.

Thoby Whateley took up the pen with long lean fingers and began to write.

"My dear Adrian:—

"You have certainly missed out by not coming with me. This valley is as wondrous as our sisters have suggested; and, we have more kin here than either of us have realised, from the distant Dunwich branch of the family. We had some of them over for coffee two evenings gone; strange, furtive folk, so they are. They had a manner of gazing at one, with subtle inquisition, while asking questions relating to family background. My absolute ignorance of such matters seemed to distinctly dishearten them—oddly so.

"The town is rural, with few paved roads or sidewalks. People seem to enjoy walking along the sides of dirt streets; and there are so few vehicles that this is not at all hazardous. The simplicity of life here is like nothing I've elsewhere encountered. Townsfolk are amiable but distant. Children are few, and thus the quiet is absolute. I've seen a minimum of canines, but everyone seems to own at least one feline.

"I arrived by train, and it was a quaint experience. The 'depot' is an absurd little shack. There is a much larger bus depot, with frequent activity. I believe many of the residents work out-of-town, using the bus line to reach their place of employment.

"One large and sturdy old building serves as post office, general store, motel, and lord knows what else. This is located on the main street, which is paved with a kind of black pitch. I noticed a hardware store, one small café, an extremely popular bicycle shop (which also sells hiking gear, Virginia informed me), a bookshop, and our younger sister's hair salon. On our walk (yes, *walk*) from the depot to our sisters' spacious Georgian residence, we passed a church; well, it looked like a church, although I could espy no cross. It had a steeple, ergo … Probably Mormons, those critters are everywhere these days. I stopped to investigate it yesternoon on my way to town for groceries. The massive brass doors were locked. Upon each door there was embossed a curious toad-like design. Peculiar.

"Vanessa's salon brings in, so it appears, enough income for them to subsist in easy comfort. Thus Virginia—who is looking older, but still quite lovely—can concentrate on her writing. Ginnie says that the valley is filled with writers, with artists of all kinds. Indeed, while strolling the woods one early evening I came upon a number of rather odd statues, in the most unlikely of spots. Sesqua Valley seems to be an aesthetic hot spot, so I think I shall feel at home for the few weeks I am to stay. This afternoon Nessa is to shew me more of the local sights. I've asked about hiking up Mount Selta, but neither are thus inclined. It is a magnificent sight, this mountain of sparkling white stone. Situated northeast of town, it rises some 4,190 feet. The white rock of which it is composed must contain some kind of crystal residue; to see it sparkle in the valley's misty light is quite bewitching. Most unique are its two peaks, narrow and curved, resembling folded wings.

"An enchanting place all told, dear boy. And now I'm off to lunch—Virginia has blossomed into an accomplished cordon bleu—and then off with Ness to investigate the flora and fauna of this enchanting valley. I miss our debates, and most especially my library; but there are books and disputations here aplenty, we lack only your good company."

Thoby read over what he had written, signed the epistle and set it aside. When he entered the capacious dining room, he found his elder sister spooning hot soup into bowls.

"Ah, Thoby, I was just about to call you. Please, sit. Vanessa is tending to the casserole, which I think you'll find quite excellent." In a lower voice she confided, "I'm glad to have another literary soul here, I must admit. One cannot really talk books with Nessa." She smiled a comrade's smile, and he took in her appearance. Her tall, angular body moved with easy grace. Violet eyes twinkled above the aquiline nose. The dark hair, beginning to grey, was wound in a conservative bun.

What a contrast to his younger sister, who now sailed through the kitchen door carrying a casserole dish. Thoby took in her astonishing, almost youthful, beauty. She wore a pretty dress, white with a design of yellow flowers; low cut, so that one could easily admire the milky smooth complexion of her dainty bosom. Her dark luxurious hair fell onto her shoulders, and it had been scented with some kind of lavender ointment. She wore a modicum of makeup, expertly applied.

"*Do* sit down, Thoby," she happily scolded. "You don't have to play the gentleman here. Lord, I've never seen such manners in a man!"

They ate slowly, speaking rarely between bites, as had always been their family way. He liked being here, with them; he liked this easy, familiar feeling of intimacy. They ate in a realm of shared memory, and the years of having been absent from each other melted away. When the repast was completed, the two younger siblings prepared for their walk.

"Wear your warmest coat, Thoby," said Virginia. "Though not as cold as mid-autumn in northern New England, it can grow rather chilly here. The woods are dark and the air quite cool in places."

"Not to worry. I have quite an excellent coat, which I wear when walking the winter nights in Granbury. I'll go fetch it," he said, turning to Vanessa, "and then I can walk off those two full plates of dinner that I so shockingly devoured."

He rushed upstairs while the sisters smiled at each other, and then quickly returned wearing coat and scarf. As they went to the front door, Vanessa took a hooded coat from a coat rack. October wind greeted them with the rich scent of the valley, and Thoby also took in the faint fragrance of his sister's scented hair. She took his hand as they stepped along the wooded path. The cool green shade felt soothing on his eyes, and he enjoyed the simple cracking sound made as he stepped on small twigs. Now and then he heard beating wings and saw shadows sail among the distant trees. Thoby smiled at the patches of moss that spotted the thick trunks of towering trees. Now and then a slate-colored sky was seen above the outstretched branches.

They suddenly came upon a sight that startled him, a bust of what looked like Pan, sitting on a pedestal of black stone. "My dear great god, what pagan practices are here revealed?" Thoby lightly laughed, running thin fingers through thick dark hair.

"It's a custom of the valley, brother, to place creative pieces here and there. I can shew you some rather amazing creations. This is the work of a woman who went away. She did some wonderful work. There's a far more curious piece in the clearing up ahead; rather grotesque, actually, if you care to see it."

"My curiosity is at fever pitch, Nessa darling. I'm only thankful that I'm not tramping trough these mystic woods alone."

"Come on," she laughed, linking her arm in his. Before long they came to a clearing that was encircled by pale willows. Thoby unlocked his arm from Vanessa's and slowly approached the unsettling object that knelt in the center of the glade. Of what it was composed he could not say; pigskin, perhaps, or bleached leather. Its worn and tattered feminine clothing moved in moaning wind. As the young man knelt before the enigmatic figure he could not suppress a shiver. The thing was utterly queer. The arms stretched skyward, as if reaching for the stratosphere.

Upon the left palm was etched, in yellow thread, a curious symbol, one that was repeated, inlaid in gold, on a clasp of black onyx that was fastened to the figure's blouse. He did not think the symbol Arabic or Greek or Hebrew—it was like no alphabet he had seen before.

Most strange of all was the mask of yellow silk that veiled the figure's face, beneath which, with suggestive folds and hollows, appeared the semblance of a death's-head, with mouth open wide. He reached to touch the onyx clasp. How cold it was, with what an unearthly chilliness. Thoby kept his hand upon it, not wanting to take his fingers away. Oddly, there seemed to emanate from the kneeling figure a slow and subtle vibration, a pulsation that sounded in echo in the darkening firmament.

Thoby Whateley lifted his face to empyreal dusk. How did it grow dark so quickly? Why did starlight move, encircling the smouldering sphere that drifted downward? He reached with shaky fingers to the sky.

"What?" Vanessa fell to her knees beside him, perplexed by the expression in his cloudy eyes. "What is it, Thoby?"

"That sphere. That star of obsidian inferno. It hums my name. Its eyes, those myriad eyes, they summon the sign. Oh, god, it calls my name!" He reached for the onyx clasp and tore it from the figure's blouse, then raised its golden symbol to dark heaven. Shaken and wild-eyed, Vanessa tilted toward him and clutched his arm.

"You *see* it?"

"It speaks my name with voice of storm." Thoby tried to rise but could not. Heavily, he fell to the ground. His breath issued as a torrent of gasping. When again he looked skyward, there were no stars or daemonic globe to be seen. The heavens were just beginning to shade with the blue-violet of early evening. Thoby's heaving breathing eased as he shook his startled head. He spread his hand on the sod upon which he kneeled. "What's this?"

"This?"

"Look. They seem to be prints, circling this work of diabolic art. Are they children's bare footprints? They appear almost human, don't they? And yet—not quite human. Something's wrong with their shape, it's not quite right ..."

"Actually, they aren't the prints of anything. My dear, it's a part of the aesthetic creation."

He turned suspicious eyes to his sister. "This certainly is a queer creation."

Vanessa smoothed his hair. "Are you feeling better? You were acting strangely."

Thoby tried to shrug. "I haven't had a spell like that in ages. Must be this heady valley air." He deeply inhaled. "I can feel it so heavily in my lungs. It seems to linger there, floating around my heart." He smiled at the serious expression on his sister's face. "What strange enchantment lingers in this darksome valley?"

Vanessa smiled and lightly laughed. "I think you've had too much supper. Come, let's continue our walk." They slowly rose to their feet.

Thoby hesitated. "Funny, I feel reluctant to leave, as though I were somehow rooted here." He tried to laugh, but the feeble effort failed. Looking into his sister's eyes, he noticed at last their very strange expression. Slowly, Vanessa reached to the iron clasp held in her brother's hand. Leaning close, she pinned it to his coat lapel. Keeping her hands upon it, she deeply gazed into Thoby's troubled eyes. Gently, he covered her hands with his. "You're trembling," he whispered.

"Yes," she uttered, moving from him. "It grows chilly. Come, let us go from this place. Ginnie will worry." She began to walk toward the spreading willow branches, the green-yellow vines that streamed toward the ground, that moved sinuously in evening wind. Pausing, she turned to her brother, who stood staring at the grotesque figure.

"What happened here?" he asked in a subdued voice.

Strolling to him, the woman smoothed the back of her soft hand against his face. "Nothing, Thoby. Nothing happened here." Strangely, she smiled. "*Do* let's go." He sighed and shook his head, then took her hand. Together, they walked toward the trees, into Sesqua's sequestered shadow.

## II.

For the following two evenings, Thoby Whateley experienced unfathomable dreams. He walked beneath the awning of Sesqua's spectral forest, followed by diminutive silhouettes that hid behind the trees. Those twilight trees bent low so as to observe his phantom progress. The evening air was pierced by the cry of something that lingered in its mountain lair. Thoby came upon the long pale branches of ancient willows that rustled damp leaves against his face and hair. He saw the figure that danced within the clearing. Entranced, he drifted to it and took it into his aching arms. They danced in darkness, accompanied by small shaggy forms that pranced about them. Around, around they whirled, until falling in laughter onto the ground. They wound their limbs together. He kissed her pallid mask, then gazed beyond her into the obscurity of a haunted heaven. She bent her straddling body to him and breathed into his ear.

"Do you see it, cousin, the dark star of Hastur? Oh, call it, dear one; summon it with the yellow sign." She pressed her face into him, and its dreamy essence melted into his being. His fingers tightened around the object in his hand. Roaring at the sky, he hurled the clasp into the pulsating void of seething firmament. The clasp sailed above him and transformed with mutation; it heaved and expanded into an opaque star that blistered with black fire. This flame transformed, turned into melted gold, a blinding radiance that formed into a living emblem. He saw the symbol that burned into his eyes and found his soul, that found his tongue and shaped his lips. He spoke the unknowable name.

Ah, the force that thundered his name in nightmare. Oh, the power that soaked his body with secretion. It was a phantasm that echoed in memory as he trembled toward wakefulness.

Below, thoughtfully sipping hot almond milk, his sisters spoke in hushed voices. "Fate is so curious, and utterly inescapable," Virginia sighed. "We felt influenced—nay, compelled—to invite Thoby to the valley. We are puppets in the paws of ancient beings."

"I longed to see it," breathed Vanessa, more to herself than to her companion. "Oh, I burned! I could sense its power, its longing ..."

"It dreams beyond the rim, awaiting the alignment. We mean nothing to it. It will liberate itself in time, to rule the universe in chaos. But we can hurry the night of glorious pandemonium, and thus it sends us dreams."

"I could *feel* it influencing me to give him the clasp."

"Aye, thus is our heritage. We be of Whateley blood, no matter where we dwell. An element of *otherness* flows through our veins. Monsters have been our kinfolk. Our fate is assured, and our birthright calls eternally, like the Old Ones who slumber, never dying."

They silenced as the sounds of movement came from the room above. As a dishevelled Thoby stumbled into the room, they greeted him with magical smiles. "I've the damndest headache," he complained, dropping onto the sofa.

"Poor darling," cooed Virginia. "Nessa, heat your brother a glass of almond milk." The sisters exchanged a heavy look, then the youngest rose and vacated the room.

"I can't believe it's so late," Thoby mumbled as he looked at the mantelshelf clock.

"You've been oversleeping, which explains your headache. We need to go for an early evening stroll. The air will calm your throbbing head."

"Yes, this valley's air does have an affect. I'm happy that you invited me. I was surprised to learn of father's being born here. When was that?"

"1929. I do so love delving into our genealogy. We are a fascinating family. Why father chose to settle in Westborough I cannot imagine."

"Better than Dunwich. I could not believe the way people treated me when I asked for information on family gravesites. One old woman gave me some kind of sign with her hand, as though I were a devil child. I found a small clan of the so-called 'bad' line of the family, but they were dirty hillbillies and so revolted me that I didn't extend my cordiality."

Vanessa quietly entered the room and handed Thoby a glass of steaming milk. "Here we are, our favorite childhood drink. The glass is hot, use this napkin as a holder." She stood next to Virginia and together they anxiously watched him bring the glass to his lips.

"Mmm, very nice. But what's that other taste? You've altered the sacred family formula." The women nervously laughed as they watched him drink the remainder of the liquid. Thoby set the glass on a table next to the sofa. "I'm suddenly quite warm. I think, Virginia, I'll take you up on that walk you mentioned."

"Excellent." Thus they found their coats and journeyed out of doors. The sky was ablaze with starlight, and Thoby apprehensively scanned the sky. One sister held each of his hands, and sleepily he allowed them to guide him through the woodland. He smiled as they neared the pale willow trees. Yes, this was where he wanted to be, the place where he belonged. He was sad to see no kneeling figure; perhaps she would join them later. Virginia walked with him to the center of the clearing, to the circle of peculiar footprints. She bent with him as they lowered to their knees. He wanted to call Vanessa, but could not find the energy with which to open his mouth. Dreamily, he smiled at her as she anxiously scanned the sky.

Virginia petted his hair, and he leaned his head against her shoulder. He watched the small shaggy figures that crept toward them from behind the willows. He liked how these beings gazed at him with shining black eyes. He moaned as they touched his face and hair with rough leathery hands, as they unfastened Ginnie's hair and let it fall to her shoulders. How beautiful she looked. Shutting his eyes, he listened to the ancient song that issued as humming from his sister's mouth.

Other voices joined in, chanting the songs with words he did not understand, in a language he could not fathom. His half-open eyes watched the others of his distant kinfolk who gathered around them, who swayed and sang as they hungrily watched the sky. How he longed to join in the singing. He seemed to know one of the alien words, an antediluvian name that he had heard in dreamy vision, from the mouth of a veiled face.

The shaggy beasts danced around them. With blurring vision he watched as Virginia took his hand and kissed it. He saw the silver needle that glistened in the cosmic light, and smiled as his sister pierced it into his palm. Another presence knelt next to him, and Thoby sniffed her perfumed hair. This other woman covered his face with a piece of soft yellow silk. He slowly opened him numbing mouth, aching so to sing, as the pallid mask of silk was sewn into his tingling flesh.

Yet even then, with face covered and eyes closed, Thoby could somehow see into the sky that called his name, could see the distant star of darkness that yearned to kiss the yellow sign. He reached to heaven with a bloodstained hand. Oh, how he longed to touch that star, to watch the black fire that swirled within its thousand eyes, to listen to its beating wings. How he hankered to float to it in that sky that pulsed and hissed, that firmament that has waited strange aeons for the shifting of dead starlight.

Thoby Whateley could not close his mouth. Its lips stretched as he heaved at last the unholy name, the name that echoed in the haunted valley, an echo that was answered by the snouts of things that howled atop a twin-peaked mountain. It was a wail that was imitated by the dancing folk who moved around him in that place of nameless providence. He somehow knew that they would dance forever around him, in patient ecstasy, until the end of time.

*¿?*

# AFTERWORD

This tale was inspired by my reading a rather poor story by Joe Brennan, a rather sad guy with whom I briefly corresponded, and whose weird fiction I have long enjoyed. An image in Joe's story, of a figure that resembled a ramshackle scarecrow, inspired the image of a strange figure found in woodland, something decidedly not a scarecrow. Does anyone know the family from whom I borrowed the names of my characters? (Clue word: Bloomsbury.)

"The Darkest Star" was originally published in *Tales of Lovecraftian Horror*, in an issue edited by Joe Pulver, the author of a Mythos novel published by *Chaosium*.

*Dedicated to Jeffrey Thomas, Esq.*

*Visions of Khroyd'Hon.*

> It stands titanic in the gloom of twilight;
> Majestic, like some god beneath the skies.
> You cannot turn away your spellbound eyes.
> You long to kiss the stone of sparkling white.
> Among the dancing trees old wingsong sighs,
> Rushing 'neath the shadows of the night,
> Seeping toward the antient, ageless site
> Where ant'diluvian power never dies.
>
> In dreams you sense the passion of the daemon
> That lures you from the slumber of the sane.
> Your soul is lost and never can regain
> The happy joy of sweet unfettered reason.
> But never fear, you'll find your fate anon
> Beneath the arch'd peaks of antique Khroyd'Hon.

*The Outsider's Song.*

> Why have you brought me to this godless place,
> This place of haunted shadow, haunted sound,
> Where dream and dark reality compound
> To breed a wild, a weird, a godless race?
> Why do the shadows follow me around
> And sink into the texture of my skin,
> So that I feel a monstrous mannequin
> Composed of poison bred of Sesqua's ground?
>
> I sink to trembling knees upon the sod.
> I claw the dirt that dares to call my name.
> I feel the potency that aches to claim
> My wretched soul for some chaotic god.
> And you, you smile at me with silver eye
> And whisper secrets to the hungry sky.

## Immortal Moon

Weary with the toil of trivial life
I gaze upon your lush lunatic glow
And curse this mortal season, oh so rife
With deep despair and lingering sorrow.
With misty eye I dread the coming morrow,
Smeared with golden light of hateful day.
In shadow'd realm of candlelight I borrow
A semblance of your cunning wolfish ray.

I smile to sense your cool and crazy kiss.
I reel to feel your shadows in my heart.
With your unholy light I can subsist
On madness which to mortals I impart.
But then some hateful cloud forms to eclipse
The poison of your pale daemonic kiss.

## Elusive Sunset

I lean against a mountain wall and watch
The slanting sunrays beam in golden light
Upon the dreaming town that holds my heart
Within a spell of wonderment serene.
The cosmic fire fills my soul with such
A keen expectancy of sense and sight
That fantasies of vision subtly start
To clothe in hues of red and curious green

The vista that before me is outspread
Of roofs and river, wooden bridge and tower,
Of dancing trees and tombstones of my dead,
This ageless vale of preternatural power.
But shadowed twilight soon engulfs the sight
And sunset melts into eternal night.

*Alchemy*

When maggot ostentation sets me on
To weave a web of wizardry and fear,
To summon from some outré exosphere
Chaotic madness as some cunning daemon;
When overwhelm'd with rich iniquity
I conjure forth atrocity and death,
When passion utters with hot anxious breath
A spell once spawn'd in chill antiquity:

Then do I pulse with pantheistic rage,
Impatient with pungent inquietude;
Then lawless Nature cannot be subdued,
But thunders with my wizard lineage;
Then windsong echoes in unholy hymn
To those who dream on Yuggoth on the rim.

*Returning*

Come hither, shadow, usher my return,
Swim among my bones and wash my woe.
This mortal cesspool nevermore will churn—
I'll sink into a blackness absolute.
Come hither, darkness, drown my mortal moan,
Seep between these teeth that clatter so;
Help to temper my tempestuous groan
And lead me to that realm where pain is mute.

Come hither, all you voices in the air;
Come hither, all you tremblings 'neath the mud.
I hearken to the cries of Selta's lair
That call to me and others of my blood.
Mauve shadow I wholeheartedly embrace
For 'tis the heritage of Sesqua's race.

## Minion of the Moon

Shall I compare you to the beauteous moon—
You, far more lovely, twice as lunatic?
Rough etchings carved into an antient rune
Are not more covert, more esoteric
As your pale eyes in which I nigh behold
The lazy luster of your hungry beam,
That self-substantial fire, twice more cold
Than those refracted rays of lunar stream.

I'll chance to sink the smooth length of my tongue
Into the crater of your crazy breath;
And sighs of midnight pleasure, ever young,
Will ne'er succumb unto a sunrise death.
I'll howl for an eternity this rhyme,
For my forever Mistress masters time.

## Nightmare from Crete

Stand within a ring of standing stones,
Tremble as you touch the hungry air,
Answer that which haunts a Cretan lair,
Night-usurper of King Minos' throne!
Language from a dim forgotten age
Eagerly develops on your tongue;
Yowl an antient name forever sung,
Stimulate a nameless heritage.

Appetites that ravage ev'ry nerve,
Rabid as a lust you cannot quench,
Greedily devour your soul, and hence,
Esoteric blasphemy you serve.
Netherworld of Darkness spiraling,
Titan Qom-maq is your Ever King!

## *Ides of March*

Cry the crystal river of your woe,
Heave unto the hills your heavy moan.
Valley windsong weaves into your groan
And reflects your song of dark sorrow.
Hear that daemon wind in dancing leaves;
Watch it stir within his shock of hair.
Gentle cheater, there is nothing there.
'Tis not his voice that echoes in the trees.

Hold his corpse, embrace it to your breast,
Hold him tight and never let him go.
Clutch his chilly limbs until you know
The echo of your heartbeat in his chest.
Bend to him and kiss his clammy frame.
This was the love that dared not speak its name.

## *The Scythe of Time*

Within the spacious time of golden youth
I played on sunlit hill, in velvet wood,
And laughed at what could not be understood,
Cared not if I were clumsy or uncouth.
Then in the auburn autumn of my time
I wearied of this mortal mockery,
And sought to find in dreamy phantasy
An atmosphere of peace, a quiet clime.

When silver winter frosted sight and sound
I stumbled, deaf and blind, in Time's twilight,
Bereft of hope and sanity, contrite,
Toward a darkness absolute, profound.
Nigh I play in Sirki's silent womb,
In timeless liberation of the tomb.

## The Outré Violinist

I saw him standing on a dusky street,
His face a thing demented, lacking eyes.
An empty plate had been placed at his feet.
His empty sockets seemed to scan the skies.
I listened to the strains of violin
And watched his visage twitch in time to song.
My pulse began to match discordant din.
My eyes began to watch the sky e're long,

To watch the cloud whose form seemed slightly strange,
The cloud whose roiling substance seemed so odd;
And as I watched that cloud began to change,
To shift so as to form a nameless god.
In abject fear I flew from that dark place
As laughter echoed from an eyeless face.

## Blood Drench'd Shadow

The blood drench'd shadow flows beneath my feet
And leads me down a path I've yet to trod,
Beyond the solid ground of valley sod,
Unto a realm where wondrous horrors accrete.
The crimson shadow takes me to a depth
Of ling'ring darkness where the lost ones roam,
And silently I stagger through the gloam,
Among that crowd whom shadow banisheth.

The wet red shadow softly starts to glide
Across the mud to where the dull knife gleams.
I add my voice unto the choir of screams,
Pay homage to the dread god Suicide.
I kneel unto the scarlet shade, conjointed
Unto that god, with dripping gore anointed.

*Romance*

The tolling chimes announce the midnight hour,
She enters in my dank and dim demesne
To creep among the ruins and obtain
The solace found within my windswept bower.
The heavy fragrance of my midnight arbor
Protects her from the neoteric age
From which she feels a deep alienage,
And thus she dwells within this shadow-harbor.

She dances to the song of midnight wind,
The wind that moves my torn, tattered sinews.
She weaves her fingers through my useless thews
And deeply drinks passion undisciplined.
Thus loving what most mortals deem disgrace
She crawls into my carrion embrace.

*Starlife*

How wan and lonely seems your misty gleam,
Like bones that nestle in an Arkham pit.
To your dead glow I thrust my arcane dream,
My mouth whispers a blasphemous obit.
My syllables awaken your demise,
With scarlet wash your lifeless light is dyed,
With cosmic crimson tint you volcanize,
Like sunset bleeding on an Innsmouth tide.

An opaque darkness shadows your visage.
I watch you drift in answer to my prayer.
You nestle in some Sesqua foliage,
Like horror dreaming in a Dunwich lair.
Now Sesqua hums daemonic harmony,
Like some *Rue d'Auseil* cacophony.

## Logos

In the raw light of dawn I spoke the word,
The sleepy vowel that dreamt within my brain,
A monstrous syllable that did not deign
To smile upon mortality's swineherd.
In noontide heat I would not be deterred,
The scorching solar teeth could not restrain
My mouth from uttering again, again,
The name I echoed in the haunted verd.

And nigh the darkness that eternal slept,
The shadow that had called to me in dream,
Has fumbled and awakened to my prayer.
And from this sphere humanity is swept,
Its humid breath is stifled in a scream,
And Darkness is Time's universal heir.


## Reawaken

Come, bend your shadowed visage to our own,
With your lips nurture our unnourished mouths,
Press your living flesh to our dry bone,
Breathe into our millennial drowse.
Let the living luster of your eyes
Glisten our centuried sepulcher.
Let your essence richly moisturize
Nightmare's dead-yet-dreaming ancestor.

Once we boiled beyond terrestrial slime,
Serving darkness, daemon-avatars,
Shrieking like a madness out of Time
In between the spaces of the stars.
Now, unaligned, we crave your alchemy,
Till once again we riot in ebony.

## Legions of the Lost

I stumbled like some clumsy Caliban,
Sought maternal nectar in the dust;
But when creeping despondency outran
All hope, I fell in sorrow's underthrust.
I tumbled to a pitch of mental shade
Where gleamed no ghost of lucid sanity.
Oh, there I howled insanity's tirade.
Ah, there I cried the dirge of misery.

I fumbled on my knees in dark despair.
I feared that I was fearfully alone.
And then I heard queer whispers in the air,
A sound that sank into my narrowbone.
And now I shriek and screech in frenzied glee,
With legions of the lost who shout with me.


## The Eyrie of Imps

I move beneath their homes of branch and leaf,
Stepping in a ring of antient stone,
And although neither innocent nor naïf
I nonchalantly sing to Sesqua's drone.
I hear them humming in the restless breeze.
I sense their swaying to the wind's mayhem.
Their silver eyes shimmer in leafy lees,
Like Nyarlathotep's white diadem.

With shaggy mouths they join in my chant,
In necromantic accompaniment,
Then jump to join in my wild *courante*,
As Selta trembles, subtly sentient.
And thus we move beneath the dancing wood
And summon chaos with our black priesthood.

## Ye Old One

Ah, if this antient hoary beast could speak
What secrets would it spill into my ear?
I'd hear of havoc that some storm did wreak,
I'd hear of madness, suicide, of fear.
I'd know of passion, desolate and grim,
Of fever'd love that could not be contain'd
And ended with a rope tied 'round this limb
Of bark, departed, nevermore regain'd.

I'd hear of creatures curious and queer
That leap among the thickness of dark leaves,
That cause the lonesome traveler to fear
The forms of blackness one almost perceives.
Ah, if this hoary tree could utter sound.
My *gawd,* the tales that, told, would quite astound!

## Oscar

I entertain'd the evil things of life,
Those panther boys whose beauty I ador'd;
And for this crime I lost my sons, my wife,
And I became a thing grotesque, abhor'd.
And so what can I do but live in dream,
Where my fine name is not a thing of mud,
Where kissing handsome lads does not blaspheme,
Where, seven-veil'd, I dance in pool of blood?

Ah, Dorian, the mirrors of your eyes
Shew unto me youth's golden little time.
Ah, Sphinx, how beauteous you are, how wise.
Oh, Bosie, teach me passion's poison'd crime.
I deign to dance in Dante's holy flames.
Judiciousness I leave to Henry James.

## Vision

My eye has pierced into the rolling cloud
As congeries of globes shine on my face,
And in this eldritch vision thus allowed
I watch the wonder of an elder race.
I watch the wonder of an elder race
And see the seepage of its liquid flesh,
A flesh that flows with such an alien grace
Into my skin, a supernatural mesh.

Into my skin a supernatural mesh
Of tissue links me to the behemoth.
I gaze into the future, eyes afresh,
Into a time of universal wrath.
I eye a time of universal wrath
Which elder tomes have titled "Yog-Sothoth".


## Celestial

What are these globes that shine into my eyes,
These iridescent suns of primal fire
That pull my brain toward celestial gyre,
Toward a vortex churning in the skies?
What are these mouths that weirdly rhapsodize,
Like some daemonic and discordant choir,
The consonants that taunt with dark desire,
That with unholy wisdom catechize?

I answer to the void of midnight heaven.
I pray unto the dark pulsating sun.
I abdicate all pleasure of the earth.
My fingers move in elder genuflection.
My voice is raised in riot unison.
Within my god my being finds new birth.

*Storm*

While making love within this ring of stone
We feel the wonder of this sudden storm,
This pouring water, slick and strangely warm,
That seeps into our skin, into our bone.
The frantic wind arises to intone
In shrieking that assails us, like a swarm
Of devils, syllables that nigh inform
Us of those secrets mortals have not known.

This tempest, uncontrollable and wild,
This Nature, heaving in the midnight skies,
Drowns us in delicious anarchy.
It sings to each and ev'ry Sesquan child,
Its chaos burning in our silver eyes,
And thus we weld unto its revelry.


*My Experience of Love*

What is this canker on your rose-red lip,
This spoil spreading like some fungal stain?
The beauty of your mouth begins to drain,
And foam begins to form, begins to drip.
What is this soil in your liquid eye,
This dirt that muddies your pale jelly's hue?
With fearful glance I watch the rank mildew
That webs upon your orbs as thick fungi.

Why does the moon becloud as you draw close?
Why do the shadows blend into your form?
Your ghastly moaning echoes in the storm
As in my sight you split and decompose.
And thus love's promise wrinkles, withers, warps;
Nigh all that I embrace is passion's corpse.

*Diseased*

I hear your midnight call in deepest dream
As your bright shadow dances in my dome.
My eyes awaken to the lunar stream
That takes me to the place of tainted loam.
I watch the sallow sand begin to sift
Like seconds spilling through some broken Time,
Then gasp to see you sinuously lift
Your limbs from out the stuff of Sesqua's slime.

The starlight seems to dim in supplication
As windsong rises so to taste your sigh;
And your black eyes shine in felicitation,
Approving all the madness they espy.
I flow to you in dream of lunacy
And happily discard dull sanity.

*Grotesque*

I watch the wildfire witchcraft of your eye
And know the guilt of those who are grotesque.
The phrases mumbled cannot justify
The boldness of my one—my small—request.
I simply know that on your devil's lip
I sense a danger to which I gavotte;
And when I trace it with my fingertip
That I am a grotesque is quite forgot.

But now I touch your cold, your mirthless smile,
And phantasy of love is shattered quite.
Reality reminds me I am vile,
A wretched freak of ridicule, of spite.
And when you leer at me ferociously
My abject ugliness is shown to me.

*Delusion*

But then your daemon arms surround my waist,
And eerie fragrance floats upon the air.
With anxious mouth I suck the breeze and taste
The wonder of some promised otherwhere
Where I will hear the music of the spheres
And sense the scents that leak beyond the rim,
Where I will taste the liberating tears
Of one beloved by a seraphim:

For though from Sesqua's mud you rose in birth
Your throne is in the depth of deepest sky.
Together we will flee this sullied earth
Toward that place where pain will purify,
Where love will beautify grotesquerie,
Where pain is dead and I am not ugly.


*Destruction*

And thus you lift your arms among the trees,
Those trees that sigh with sibilant windsong,
And I hear hissing laughter on the breeze;
I sense the ebbing of a brief élan.
I hear the breaking of a Sesquan bough,
A sound that echoes deeply in the dark.
I feel the beads of fear form on my brow
As laughter mutates into hateful bark.

I know myself to be a hopeless fool
As you stand smiling like some mirthless Pan.
I feel the savage tip of your sharp tool
And watch in awe the width of your wingspan.
You smile and thrust the branch into my breast.
Heartbroken fantasy finds final rest.

## Celebration

We hear the valley call in song of storm.
In darkness we approach the ring of stone.
We chant in time to Nature's antient drone.
We watch the clouds assume a deiform.
Our bodies throb to Sesqua's heavy pulse
As Old Ones call to us beyond the rim.
We answer to their call with elder poem.
We watch the clouds continue to convulse.

We watch the liquid clouds that toss and teem,
As chaos crawls among humanity,
As kindred daemons join our ecstasy
And teach us how to enter mortal dream.
And humankind will taste chaotic kiss
As nightmare hurls them into deep abyss.


## Shadow's Flesh

A nucleus of shadow waits outside
The window, breathing secrets to the dusk.
I listen to the darkness subdivide
In particles that float around this husk
Of flesh that freezes as the shadow sinks
Into me, breathing secrets to my heart.
My body burns with vision as it drinks
The wisdom only shadow can impart.

I feel my frail mortality implode.
I feel my faint humanity collapse.
My senses settle into new abode
As impulses mutate in new synapse.
I breathe outside the window, darkly bright.
I spin my secrets in eternal night.

*Jerk*

My god, you are a decadent young child,
You, moaning in your solitary sphere;
And, lord, your longings cannot be called mild;
Your cravings, lad, are rather cavalier.
And what are these rare inkings, white and black,
These creatures elegant and sinister?
When did you, child, acquire creative knack,
Become art's diabolic minister?

And what is that you do with your free hand,
That hand that delves so deep in your desire?
How strange to taste your lust, to understand
This growing passion, this perverted fire.
Satanic Priest, I kiss your dripping pen
And pant your praises evermore.  Amen.


*Twilight*

My eyes take in the velvet time of twilight
As shadows fold away the light of day.
My specter sighs into the silent dead night,
My semblance shimmers in the lunar spray.
I melt into the mists that rise from tombstone,
The mists that smell of long-dead memory,
The vapor reeking of dead flesh, of dry bone—
A substance that was once a part of me.

Outsiders die within this haunted region.
We sink into a wretched restless void.
We twitch in time to Selta's howling legion,
Our faces famished and our hands fungoid.
Cursed to roam in haunted ever-after,
We weep in time to Sesqua's mirthless laughter.

*Muse*

In dark of Providence you dreamed and dreamed
And shew'd to us a most fantastic place
Where sanity unsettled and unseamed,
Where shadow knelt unto an elder race.
With pen and ink you formed your fabled Dreamland,
And there you conquered Space, you conquered Time.
You penned of wonder in your famous longhand,
In graceful prose, in quaint and genteel rhyme.

Within our haunted hearts you live forever.
With story, essay, poem we keep alive
The genius of your rich, your rare endeavor.
Your work will all of mortal time survive:
"That is not dead which can eternal lie,
And with strange aeons even death may die."

*¿?*

# AFTERWORD

Entranced by the sonnet cycles of Shakespeare and Lovecraft, I have long wanted to compose a sonnet cycle of my own. I knew that I would be overly influenced by my two great predecessors, to an absurd degree, but I didn't care. I wear my influences openly. Indeed, the foremost reason I write is to be *identified* with my literary heroes, Shakespeare and Wilde and Lovecraft. So, to have penned this series of poems, flimsy though they be, is a profound creative accomplishment. The original series was published by Imelod Publications, but as with everything in this book, I have revised many sonnets, and replaced certain boring old ones with hopefully less boring newer poems. I can—at last—consider myself a poet, and that feels so very sweet.

## I.

He stretched onto the dilapidated seventeenth-century slab and squinted through the willow branches at late afternoon sunshine. Shadow and light played upon the surrounding graveyard ground, the numerous trees, the tall iron fence beyond which he could see the venerable town of Arkham. Everything around him whispered of a time long past. Even the living tree, whose trunk had nearly engulfed the unmarked slab on which he lay, was a creature that had long existed. When Adam pressed his hand against its bark he seemed almost to touch the hoary past.

As a child of Sesqua Valley, Adam was well-versed with the legends of this New England town. Many of the valley's children had been to visit, and he would listen on their return to their whispered lore of this place and its haunted past. It was a past that never died, that seemed to taint the very air. It was evident in the twisting lanes of cobbled streets, in brooding centuried houses. And here, in this fabulously timeworn necropolis, it was most apparent.

How many solitary souls had stretched upon this aged slab of stone? He could imagine them, in the various costumes of distant eras. And there was one whom he did not have to imagine at all, one whom he had known and could clearly see in memory. Adam reached into his jacket's inner breast pocket and produced the small book, with its thin hardback covers wrapped in scarlet cloth that had been embroidered with squiggles of woven gold. It was Richard Lund's private diary, written in his strange poetic idiom.

"The mists of light that play upon the tombstones;
a light of peculiar cadence not unlike the radiance one
sees in clouds above Mount Selta. Oh dim light of
Arkham, play on stone and dance upon dates of death
and birth. Swim through tall grass and trembling leaf.
Illume the oh familiar faces. Ah! They look down.
They would whisper what I fear to know. In dreams
of madness they sought me, and found me in this
Arkham light. Ah, dreams of Witch Town! Shake
loose the clogs of mortal coil and see the leering face.
There mocks my dark destiny. Borne in strange
shadow, unto that shade return. Brethren, stone
Brethren—brothers of silent stone."

Adam Webster returned the poet's diary to its pocket and pushed off the slab that lacked inscription. He walked the cool hard ground, glancing at tilted tombstone, at silent tree, at the town beyond the fence. He stared at the nearby house, a structure that looked as if it had withstood the elements of two centuries. How had it survived? Although incredibly old, it looked structurally sound. The place was obviously inhabited, judging from the clean curtains and various objects seen at windows. He saw a faint twinkling from the high attic window, a window slightly open. Swaying gently from invisible wires were prisms of slender glass, glass that reflected dying sunlight in rainbow hues. And there, just behind one glimmering prism, he thought he saw a small pale face watching him.

But other faces were more intriguing, and to one of these he now turned. Yes, he could see how such a thing would have so affected Richard Lund. It was gigantic, this thing of weathered stone, an awesome figure that seemed to have shuffled forth from decadent dreaming. Its face had been worn away by time and elements, yet Adam could just make out the faded canine countenance. He looked at another corner of the graveyard, and saw another sentinel of stone. Approaching it, he noticed that it had been chiseled from newer stone. Adam gasped as he beheld the face, for it so resembled his departed friend. Here was the same width of nose and eyes, the large and slightly tapered ears. Although the substantial lips were shut, he knew that behind them were thick strong teeth like those he had so often seen when Richard had loudly laughed.

Late afternoon deepened toward dusk. Adam closed his eyes and raised his face to twilight. Mentally, he called to those who slept and dreamed. He sought to taste the dreams of this old town. He slowly breathed, sensing something dark and strange, a thing that fumbled in the blackness of his brain. Something near. He opened silver eyes. He had touched a sense of lurking shadow, and of stench. It was here, close at hand, something nasty that had answered the call of dreaming, something deep-buried. Scanning the burying ground, he espied a grassy hill that was almost hidden in a thick growth of trees.

The moon began to rise, and in its light he ambled to the shadowed knoll. Near it stood a daemonic statue that spread its wings to early evening wind. The graven image was the figure of an odd crouching hound or sphinx with canine countenance. There was in the way its limbs had been positioned a kind of Oriental grace. Adam had seen its like before, in a tome of arcane lore; but no diagram could have prepared him for the electric thrill of seeing this tremendous thing cast so massively in ancient stone. He observed the hound-like face and saw that the sculpture had been damaged by vandals. One of its wicked eyes had been strangely disfigured.

Adam looked beyond the statue, to the grassy knoll. He approached it and saw at its base a circle of darkness where tiny things bent so as to peck at dirt and debris. In an instant they frantically darted as a horde, winging beyond the swaying trees. He bent before the cavity of earth and took up one of the scraps of dry and dirtied flesh upon which the scavenging birds had been feeding.

An unclean smell exuded from the hole in the hill. Despite better wisdom, he moved toward the opening. Adam sensed the thing before he dimly saw it. There was a bulky blackness, a sinister shadow that crouched and watched. The moonlight vaguely gleamed onto large green eyes, and the form of a face became slowly discernable. Chilliness kissed Adam's spine.

"Richard?" he whispered.

The eyes slanted for one confused moment, then grew large with violence as the thing sprang for him. Its padded hands dug nails into his neck. The hungry face grimaced, then grinned at his panic and fear. That face bent to his, and he nearly gagged at the reek of rotted breath.

A gunshot pierced the night. The thing lightened its murderous hold and looked up, annoyed. Another shot. The fiend snarled and spat at someone who was fast approaching. It sneered at Adam as it clenched a massive fist that savagely batted its captive's head.

Adam's sight grew static, then went out.

## II.

She bent to his face and deeply sniffed. Never had she smelled flesh so strangely scented. Daintily, she smoothed a petite tongue against the dusky skin. He moved and moaned. He slowly opened silver eyes. She gasped at their beauty. He saw a small round face that smiled amusedly. He took in the flawless skin, the short dark hair, the pretty mouth and blemished eye.

"It is the beating of his hideous heart," he groggily mumbled, before cleared head and better sense could stop him.

"Pardon?"

"What?" he stupidly asked, then moaned and touched a hand to the bandaged bump on his head.

"Your noggin has taken quite a thumping," she lightly laughed, bringing a cool damp cloth to his sweaty face.

"Thanks," he said, taking the cloth and smoothing over his skin.

"Do you do coffee?"

"God yes," Adam assented. She reached to a low table and poured from a silver pot into a tall mug.

"Cream or sugar?"

"Heaps of both." She stirred the substance into his liquid and handed Adam the mug. He sipped the sweet hot drink and noticed the curious way in which she regarded him. "Who are you?" Then he remembered the leering face that had violently emerged from a hole of darkness. "Great god, did you shoot it?"

"I shot into the air. Doesn't take much to shoo them off."

"*Them?*"

"The band of vagrants who sleep in the cemetery. You're lucky you weren't robbed."

He shifted in the sofa on which he slumped. "It wasn't money that was sought."

"To answer your first question, I'm Hannah Wilcox. And you ...?"

"Adam Webster."

"Not from around here, else you'd know better than to roam that place at dark."

"No. I'm from the Northwest."

"From Sesqua Valley," she stated, then huskily laughed at the look of astonishment on his startled face. "This fell out of your pocket as I was helping you into the house. I recognized it as Richard's." She held to him the small red diary.

"Ah, yes. Thanks."

"Is he with you? You two are obviously close."

"We were when he lived. He took his life, I'm sorry to say."

It was her turn to look startled. "Oh, my. That shocks me. He was so young and rugged."

"Physically, yes, quite vigorous. But emotionally another tale. He grew morose over his mother's sudden death."

"Oh, my. How sad," she said, fingering the amulet that hung from a chain around her throat. Without thinking, he reached out to touch the small green object that swung at her bosom.

"Not as ferocious as its ancestor in the cemetery, but impressive nonetheless."

"My mother made it," Miss Wilcox informed him. "She copied it, of course, from the 'ancestor' you saw tonight."

"It represents the face-eating cult of Ancient Leng."

She quizzically smiled. "How the hell do you know that?"

"From an old book."

"A book of legend?"

"That it was. There are numerous legends concerning face-consuming cults scattered here and there around the globe. But why eat the face, I've always wondered?"

"It houses the brain, which is the root of the soul." She took hold of his hand and pressed it against her cheek. "Plus it's so deliciously tender, don't you find?"

Adam took his hand away, wondering at the peculiar ease with which they had so revealed one to the other. He leaned back and pretended to rest his eyes, but kept them slightly open just enough to subtly study the blemished eye. He could not tell if the pale milky orb had been damaged in violence or was a product of birth defect. The sight of it was weirdly disconcerting.

"How did you meet Richard?" he asked, eyes still closed.

"Oh, I saw him when he was sitting on that slab in the boneyard, writing in his little book. He looked magnificent, and I wanted to do him." Adam opened his eyes in confusion. "I sculpt," Hannah informed him, smiling at his expression. "Drink your coffee, Adam, before it chills."

He brought the mug to his mouth as she rose and went to a bookshelf, from which she took a large folder that was crammed with glossy eight-by-ten photographs. He took the proffered portrait shot of Richard's massive head; then another of Richard's full figure, fully nude. Adam raised an inquisitive brow.

"He was impressive, wasn't he? Such a body, one that oozed physical force. I wanted him to stay and pose in the flesh, he so intoxicated me; but he was anxious to leave for Boston, so I took these shots and worked from them and memory."

He studied the firm nude body and remembered how it tasted to his kiss. He then studied the facial shot, and puzzled at how these photographs so resembled the various statues in the cemetery. "Did you create any of those statues in the graveyard?"

"No, those are all before my time. My grandfather made most of them after moving to Arkham in 1929. I was a mere kid when he died. He was cool. I used to sit with him up in his attic studio and listen to his recollections. He had some stories to tell. And such talent, but slanted toward the macabre. Just a tad too weird for the unimaginative milksops in Providence, but right at home in this old town."

She took the photos from him and returned the folder to its shelf. Adam looked to a curtained window, letting his mind wander to the place outside. "And these gargoyles in the graveyard ...?"

She grinned appreciatively. "That's actually an apt description, Adam. The graveyard is older than time, hasn't been a burial there for at least a century. Has a history of legend, that place. Decades ago some dreamy young dudes got it into their heads that there might be some valuable antique booty buried in those graves. There's an old rumor of a merchant being interred there with bags of gold. So there was vandalism. My grandfather was very fond of that old boneyard, so he built those stony sentinels in his work shed and hired some laborers to help him place them among the tombstones. Of course even Arkham found this a bit odd, but it seemed to work. People stayed away. Why, there was even talk from folk who swore that they had seen some of those statues loping through the graveyard grounds at night, ha, ha!"

"And that other statue?"

"Now that's interesting, because supposedly it's always been there. If that is so, who built it? Because it's not like anything found in local aboriginal totem art. Some say it is the work of weird cults that have been in Arkham since the beginning of time, the originals of the Arkham witch of history and legend. Obviously, it was built by someone who knew of ancient Leng and its infamous cult. Queer thing is, there are tales told of faceless corpses being found around it. Oh, the whispers of this old town. Arkham loves to murmur and scare itself."

She joined him on the sofa. "How's your head?"

"Better. So, your mother made this amulet for you," he persisted, curious and excited at this talk of diabolic lore.

"Yeah. She had heard grandpa talk of the legend. He was full of stories about stuff like that. Had a great library of queer old books, but gave most of them to Miskatonic near the end of his days. They even have one of his statuettes in their University library, some water daemon or some such thing. He was a great influence, was grandpa. I'm glad I inherited his artistic genes."

"Your sculpture of Richard ..."

"It's just a bust, but life-size. It's up in grandpa's old study. Come on."

She led the way down a dimly lit hallway, past a doorway that led into a kitchen that was charming in an old-fashioned way, to a narrow back stairway that took them up and up. Adam delighted in the feel of ancient wood, in the vague faces that gazed from oval portraits. One faded photograph touched him with slight unease. It was of an older woman whose facial structure was similar to Hannah's. The dark hair was worn much longer, and the mouth was not as pretty; the blemished eye was identical.

His head slightly throbbed with pain as he attempted to keep up with his hostess. Hannah took the steps two at a time. He examined the strong legs that spilled beneath the woolen skirt. He took in her muscular arms. It occurred to him that she must have literally carried his prostrate bulk from the burying ground to her house. A woman of strength, indeed. Perhaps that was why she had found Richard so alluring.

They reached the attic and she switched on an overhead light. The ceiling was low, almost touching his head. There were rows of books and large sketchbooks. Here and there he saw macabre statuettes, some representing monsters of classic myth, others suggesting beings of diseased fancy. But it was the bust upon an old and sturdy desk that took his breath away. She had caught to perfection his nigh-departed friend. There were the sad, dreamy eyes, large eyes that had in life worn a liquid hue of dark green. There was the long unruly hair worn in imitation of Oscar Wilde at the time of the Irishman's tour of America. And there—the wide sardonic mouth.

Adam Webster slowly approached the desk, pulled out the chair before it and heavily sat. He smoothed a finger against the lips of stone. The silent woman moved behind him and pushed her long tapered fingers through his hair.

"You seem very sad, young man."

"I miss him more than I can say."

Something in his voice alerted her intuition. "You loved him," she sighed.

"Body and soul," he confirmed.

There was a silence between them, then she moved away. "Listen, have you eaten? I usually have a light meal around now, soup and cheese sandwiches."

"That would be wonderful, Miss Wilcox."

She lightly laughed at his civility. "Cool. Stay here with your memories for a while, then join me in the kitchen. We passed it below, did you notice?"

"Yes, it looked quite quaint."

"That it is. Most of the appliances are decades old, and the table and chairs are antique."

Adam turned to face her and reached out a hand. She took it in her own. He brought her long slim fingers to his mouth and kissed them. "You're very kind."

She raised his hand to her lips. Her gentle kiss was a prolonged thing. She seemed hesitant to release him. He oddly smiled. Was she smelling him, tasting him? Was that a weird kind of hunger that danced excitement in her eyes? She looked a thing of pure appetite. Gently, he pulled his hand away. Hannah gazed at him with wide wild eyes and licked her trembling lips. Then she was gone.

He raised his hand to feeble artificial light, saw upon his flesh the moisture of her kiss. He brought the hand to his mouth and licked. Then he reached for the stiff stone hair of the bust that he tenderly stroked. He tucked that hand into the inner pocket of his jacket and took out Richard's diary. He turned its pages until he came upon a sonnet that had been hastily composed in nearly-illegible handwriting.

"The midnight constellation calls my face

As I stargaze into eternity
And midnight daydream promises to place
My weary visage far from misery.
Far from misery I ache to soar,
Far from flesh, this coil of mortal mud
That forms my face, this visage I abhor,
This countenance of flesh and bone and blood.
This countenance of brittle bone, of blood
That filters through the hunger of my face
And aches to freeze in cosmic nothinghood,
To freeze in chill of lightless cosmic space.
To freeze in chill of nothinghood, oh boon
Of nothinghood, as silent as a womb."

Adam closed the book, leaned back into his chair and emotionally exhaled. He listened to the sound of rising wind, to the gentle tinkling of chimes. There, at a window to his left, he saw the slender prisms of glass that swung from slim pale wire. He suddenly knew what house it was he occupied. Pushing out of his chair, Adam went to the window.

The moonlit graveyard spread below. He could see the stony sentinels, could almost make out the bulk of a gigantic winged hound. He noticed the small white figure that struggled toward the knoll where he had met with violence. The child-like being was dragging a large shapeless bundle toward the opening in the knoll. The creature stopped and gazed upward, to him. Adam stared at the small pale face. Clouds obscured the moonlight, and the cemetery was cast in momentary blackness. When again the moon's light gleamed, the figure was absent from view.

### III.

The kitchen was spacious, and very quaint. They sat in silence, eating. He looked at her and wondered what secrets she was keeping from him. That she had some weird dark secret he had no doubt. How easily they had confided in each other, as though fate had brought them together. Unobtrusively, he studied the blemished eye. The more he saw of it, the more it seemed an object of genetic defect. Adam remembered the oval portrait, the woman who must have been Hannah's mother.

He closed cool silver eyes. Her voice came softly to him. "Richard told me a bit about this curious valley of yours."

Adam secretly smiled. Ah, here it was. Within his inner ear he could hear the trembling urges of his far-off homeland. He knew what he was meant to do. "Why curious?"

"It was something he said, the way he phrased it. About how I'd feel at home there, because I was as wild and wanton as the valley itself."

Lightly laughing, Adam opened his eyes. "That's so like him, poor dramatic lad. But, yes, he was correct. The valley is a thing of impiety. A thing of special properties."

Hannah felt the steady gaze of silver eyes. "Special?" she lamely echoed.

"Not only to those of us borne of its sod and shadow, but to those who are called, those chosen few."

Something chilly kissed her soul. Hannah shivered. "Called?"

"Called by dreaming," said his soft low voice. "Called by whispering wind. Called to Sesqua's hunger." His eyes darkened. Beneath the music of his voice she seemed almost to hear the murmur of other voices. "There are sensitive folk, Hannah, who are outsiders no matter where they dwell. They are the creatures, Hannah, who dream the dark dreams, who sing the decadent song. They are the poets of madness, and oh how Sesqua Valley hungers for their insanity. The valley feels them, it knows their name. Hannah."

She tried to smile. "It sounds crazy, certainly." Her voice was laced with odd emotion. She saw his eyes grow darker still, those metallic orbs that held her in their spell. She could not move as he began to reach for her.

A sudden movement at a small-paned window broke the spell as it took his attention from her. Hannah slowly shook herself free from enchantment and followed Adam's gaze. Pressed against the window was a small round face that angrily watched. Adam took in the thin colorless lips, the shock of filthy hair. He saw the blemished eye. Snarling, he pushed out of his chair and rushed to a nearby door.

"Adam, stop!" Groggily, Hannah rose and struggled to follow. She saw the childlike creature that swiftly scampered across the road and into the graveyard. The strange man chased after it, across the dirt road, into the place of silent death. Hannah shrieked his name again, but was ignored. She watched as he entered the necropolis and sought but not find the wild wee one. There were others who watched, whom he sensed but could not see. They were bulky shapes that hunched in darkness, creatures pent in shadow. They were creatures of vicious hunger.

Hannah stepped onto the familiar boneyard sod. She saw the young outsider stop beneath a large tree, saw the pale thing that fell from that tree and push the outsider to the ground. She hissed with hungry pleasure as the small one bent low and tore with rotted teeth into the stranger's throat. Reaching for a heavy chunk of broken tombstone, Hannah sauntered toward the couple. Kneeling next to the prostrate man, she savagely brought the piece of stone down upon his still-bandaged head. The sisters groaned in pleasure at the fragrance of his strange dark blood. This scent of wounded mortality wafted toward those who lurked in shadow. Hannah smiled at their hungry snuffling.

"Are they satisfied?"

"They ne'er are. I brought 'em some dead feed early on, but they twitch to taste this 'un." She pushed her tongue into his flowing blood. "Ooo, his taste, his taste!"

"Aye, this one is different from all others. Comes from some strange place far away, a place that requires investigation. I'll be leaving you for a time."

"What was he doin' in there? Ye looked all whacked out?"

"Not sure." Clouds moved above them and began to obscure the moon. "Don't matter." They bent in thickening darkness and began to eat his face.

## IV.

The beast of Arkham breathed in the scented valley air. She bent and clawed slender fingers into dirt, then smeared the mud of Sesqua on her mouth. Its taste was vaguely familiar, like unto flesh recently devoured. This was the taste that had beckoned and beguiled, irresistibly. She had left her wild sister to tend the homestead so that she could wander and savor new experience. Wild as the young creature was, she could, in her wanton way, be absolutely responsible, and Hannah knew not to worry. The pack that hunted the ancient graveyards and dank Arkham tunnels would be fed. And Hannah would feed as well. She had waited a spell before making her first kill, on a lonely roadway outside the valley confines; but it was disappointing, being merely human. She hungered for true Sesquan flesh.

She looked into deep memory and conjured Adam's singular face. There were others of singular countenance, with silver eyes as equally bewitching. But these especial folk tended to shun her. Well, she would bide her time. Raising her face to scented air, she seemed to hear beneath the wind a voice that spoke her name. Nearby stood the amazing mountain of white stone. How her grandfather would have reveled at the daemonic sight of it, this titan that stood against the moving sky like a thing of subtle sentience.

Hannah smiled at the memory of her grandfather. She had especially loved the time of his senility, for then he spoke his secret thoughts and arcane knowledge. Her mother and she had known that he had been an ardent student of the occult. They could see it in his sculpturing, especially the work of his youth. When the old man had begun to lose his senses, it loosed his tongue. His talk flowed with the secrets that fumbled in his rotting brain. His words had fed the flame of lust for occult adventure that had burned inside his daughter and granddaughter. Then he had expired, and they had secretly buried him in his beloved age-old boneyard, erecting one of his gruesome statues over his unmarked grave. With wisdom gleaned from queer tomes in her grandsire's library, they began to journey to secret corners of the world. They had entered blasphemous temples, diseased grottoes, haunted hills. Hannah's monstrous matron had taught her new sensation, filled her with unnatural appetite. They had participated in a ritual that had given birth to Hannah's younger sibling.

And then they had found the Asian plateau of spectral legend, and there had paid homage to a devil beast. It had blessed them with its brush of leathery wing. It had kissed them upon one eye so that they wore for all time its special insignia. It had taught them unholy hunger.

Yet even it was not as beguiling as this wondrous valley. Richard Lund had been correct: she did feel strangely at home here. She had come in answer to psychic call, and it mattered not that the townsfolk kept their distance. She would linger here, and feed.

The thought of flesh filled her with a pang of unwholesome hunger. She sniffed the motion of wind. She pressed her face against a tree and licked. She listened as once more a voice beneath the wind called to her. It was a voice that was familiar. She kept her face against the tree, that tree whose taste upon her tongue was like some dim memory of ecstasy. She dreamed that the trunk was shifting, softening, subtly moving beneath her face. She dreamed of strong arms around her waist. Lifting her face, she looked into the eyes of Adam Webster. She stretched her tongue to his, and trembled as they tasted of each other.

"You seem not at all surprised, Hannah Wilcox."

"I'm no stranger to strangeness," she answered, shivering at his scent, his taste. "So it was you calling me …"

"Not always. We sing in single voice."

"We?"

"We of the valley. I confess I hated leaving that cozy hole in the hill in which you hurled my body. That pack of midnight creatures was upset not to find me dead and ready to be fed upon. But I gave them a special offering."

"My sister …"

"Alas, she is no more. Ah, how you shiver. But not with rage, is it? I think it must be appetite." A hand pressed against the back of her head. He pushed her face once more to his. She tasted him with trembling kiss. "Partake," he whispered. Consumed with unyielding hunger, she chewed into his face. His flesh easily pulled free. She could feel coldness at her ankles, and looked down at the pooling mauve mist that seeped from the ground on which they stood. She watched that mist rise and embrace Adam's face, his face that stretched and smoothed into perfect wholeness. He gazed at her with smoldering eyes. "You have fed upon the valley. Now it will feed on thee."

She knew what she had never known before—pure terror. Her arms shot up in fear, into low-hanging branches. Those sultry limbs coiled around her wrists and pushed into her hair. Hannah felt the soil beneath her give way. She slowly sank into the hungry earth that pulsed in time to the tremors of her heart's wild beating.

The valley pulled her down, deeply into it. She could feel its particles of sod spill into her pores. She gagged in trying to call the one who stood before her, that child of the valley who watched the soil that seeped into her mouth. The fleshy organ of his tongue came toward her, impossibly expanded. It tickled her blemished eye. The beast of Sesqua Valley moaned with inhuman hunger, then wildly laughed and howled as the one beneath him sank from view.

*¿?*

## AFTERWORD

It's a game played by those of us who are deluded into thinking that we pen Lovecraftian prose, to take a plot or aspect of plot from Lovecraft and rework it into a story of our own. Most young Lovecraftian writers seem to have written their own version of "The Outsider" (mine was called "The Kiss of Corruption"). With this tale I took a character from "The Call of Cthulhu", although I never actually shew him. Then I took elements from "The Hound" and "The Unnamable" (two of my favorite HPL stories, minor though they be). I blended in different aspects of hunger, and tried to write as poetically as possible a story about ghouls and face eating. This tale was a lot of fun to write, but I know it is little more than amusing entertainment. We'd all like to be Ligotti, but some of us are doomed to be Derleth, alas.

"The Heritage of Hunger" is original (sic) to this collection.

# The Imp of Aether

*To ye memory of August William Derleth*

## I.

When Wilus Shakston returned to Sesqua Valley I barely recognized him. He seemed much altered, older than when he had left six months ago. He had lost weight. His lean epicene face, more feminine than I remembered it to be, gazed at me with brilliant flame-like eyes. Those eyes alone were familiar, yet even they contained an alien alchemy, and seemed the eyes of one who had beheld and remembered weird wisdom. Wilus stepped off the bus, his tall frame elegantly draped in a flowing coat. His face smiled beneath a wide-brimmed hat, a hat that hid his long dark hair. He tightened a light cloth scarf, then held to me his welcoming hands.

"My dear Adam."

"Welcome home, my dear." We embraced.

"Yes, here at last. And how much I've missed, according to your melodramatic letters. I was very sorry to hear about your friend. I cannot say that I was an admirer of Richard Lund's poetry, the little of it that you've shewn to me. Such a morbid boy, not at all surprising that he took his life. But what was this you mentioned in your last letter, of your leaving so as to journey to New England?"

"Yes, I plan to visit some of the places to which he wandered and compose therein a cycle of sonnets to his memory. But that won't be for some time yet. Come, let me help you with your luggage. I've brought my large wheelbarrow, it should hold most of your items."

"Delightful." And so we packed my wheelbarrow with his bags and walked the dirt road that led to his residence. The day was hot, and I observed how queerly he would look up and gaze at sunlight. "How it burns in cosmic aether," he said at last. "Like some bubbling throne of Azathoth." I looked up and beheld the disc of golden fire; but after a few seconds its light hurt my eyes, and so I looked away. "No, your silver eyes cannot gaze for long upon its supernal splendor. Much too used to shadowed gloom, eh, my child of the valley? That sphere of living flame has blazed for a billion years. We live by its light. Beyond it there are other orbs of cosmic fire, strange alien globes dominated by alien beings beyond mortal comprehension. But not to we, my chuck, not to we who have spent our evenings reading the lore stored in the room of an ancient round tower."

"How curiously you speak, dear fellow. What aren't you telling me?"

In answer he kissed my cheek, laughed like a wee child, and mischievously ran before me, expecting me to chase him with a wheelbarrow stuffed with bags. I did not do so, keeping at a moderate pace until I came to his large old house. I found him in his spacious library, turning the pages of an ancient tome. I set the few bags that I could carry onto the floor, sat in a wooden chair and patiently waited. He had thrown open all the shades of the many windows, and brilliant sunlight filled the book-lined room. I gazed again at his face, the countenance whose strangeness I could not place. It was the visage I had known for thirteen years, but with some added element that I could not place. He had not yet removed his hat, which was peculiar.

"I've told you that my maternal ancestors were highly assimilated Dutch Jews. I've long been fascinated with Dutch culture. A queer people, with queer elder secrets." He went to one bag and unzipped it, took from it a book, opened the book and took from it a piece of yellow parchment. Then he returned to the tome on his desk and seemed to be comparing its text with whatever was on his piece of parchment. I could contain my Sesquan curiosity no longer, and pushed out of the chair so as to join him in his study. Wilus raised the parchment to his face and pressed it lovingly to his nose. Then he handed it to me.

"You know I cannot read this," I told him.

"Yes, poor child; language has never been your *forte*, has it? That's the province of Simon Gregory Williams." He took the parchment from me and examined it. "I found this in a forgotten hillside tomb, a tomb that has slept undisturbed for centuries beneath a Holland hill. It's most curious, the sacred things that are buried in hillsides. One thinks of Qumran or Cumorah. Within this neglected—or should one say shunned?—sepulcher I found buried a woman of delicious legend. From certain papers entombed with her, I discovered her succulent history. She was known as 'the fire hag', and her legend is whispered still. It is written that those who crossed her met with a blistering termination. Stupidly, one religious fanatic condemned her to the stake. Yah! The amber flames devoured her bonds and then danced into the frothing crowd, turning many, including the minister, into crispy critters. They left her alone after that."

I smoothed the parchment before me as he spoke and gazed in bewilderment at its foreign language. My informant continued. "The language is in a forgotten dialect. Took me forever to find someone who would help decipher it. We thought at first that it was some kind of poem or unholy psalm, but upon further study discovered that it is a prayer to something called Cthugha. Supposedly a fire element. You know the idiotic notion that Great Old Ones represent terrestrial elements, as if these cosmic creatures could be molded by corporeal law or understanding. Utterly absurd; but in this case, there seems some sustainment. I journeyed to Miskatonic and found in their library an explanatory volume. But that was not required; I had only to wait for the dreams."

"Ah," I suspired as he took the parchment from me.

"Ah indeed," he mocked, and I did not like the look that slanted his yellow eyes. "Her marble coffin, dear boy, had no lid. She was remarkably preserved. Seemed to be waiting, so she did. Seemed almost to beckon and beguile. Her perfumed hair, yah, how intoxicating! It seemed, this hair, to shine with ethereal life. I caressed it with my hand, watched as it shimmered with shades of firelight beneath the glow of burning candles. I bent to kiss it, and as I did so a thick strand came loose—a gift from the grinning ghoul."

"What has this to do with dreams?"

"Don't be such an impatient sod. I took that strand of hair to my wee digs, and spent the evening twining it into my own. I fancied that I could feel her soft warm hair weave around my head and seductively enter my dome. That night I beheld what I can only describe as memories. I had somehow conjoined with this yummy sorceress, entwined soul to soul. Ah, such visions I beheld. The next morning ..."

Dramatically, he removed at last his hat. His hair fell to his shoulders. Soft fragrance wafted from his thick dark hair. I leaned close to him and took hold of the length of pale hair that seemed to oddly catch the shimmering sunlight that filled the room. That hair felt warm to the touch, an unnatural warmth. Soft, sentient. I lowered my face so as to sniff, and the strands move of their own volition to meet my face. I gasped, and Wilus chuckled.

"Rather wonderful, my dear boy, isn't it, what a witch's hair will do?" He turned from me and walked to a window, where he stood and gazed directly at the blinding sun.

## II.

I spent most of the next day in the round tower wherein is collected the massive occult library of Sesqua Valley. I searched thoroughly, but found no reference of an Old One who was aligned to fire. And so at last I leaned against the wall of ancient brick and searched my dreams. Hazily, an image came to me, but of what I could not fathom. It was a dark and formless entity, like some ash-hued offspring of Shub-Niggurath. And as I saw this thing in dream, my senses were tainted with a smell of burning. I opened my eyes, thinking a candle must have extinguished itself. I saw something drift quickly from me and ooze out one of the slender carved openings in the wall that served as window. I

sat where I was for quite a while, until footfalls climbed the winding
steps that led to the tower room.

"Ah, dear boy, I thought I might find you here. What a strange
expression sits upon your charming face. Come, link your arm to mine.
I've been away too long, I need your company as I wander this
enchanting, enchanted woodland."

I rose and took his arm. Playfully, we skipped down the winding
stairway, into night. "We've missed you, Wilus."

"We? Oh, you mean the valley. Yes. I've missed it as well. No matter
how far I journey, the valley has much influence over my mind and body.
I can feel its rhythm coursing through my human blood. It's interesting,
how we outsiders become adopted into the nameless pack. We discover
Sesqua Valley—by chance? Who can say? We experience its wonders,
we are seduced by its shadow, by the spawn of that shadow. Marvel
consumes our startled souls. We begin to feel that we belong. We dwell
among its people, those natives borne of magick, and slowly we learn the
secrets, the rituals, the rules." Here he stopped and leaned against the
trunk of a narrow tree. "But just as we are bewitched, so are we
disturbed. In time someone we know goes away forever. We are told
that they have 'returned unto shadow'. More disturbing still, my dear
boy, is the high percentage of mortality among those of us who are
outsiders."

"Meaning what, Wilus?"

"Do any of us die a natural death? I cannot think of one. We are
somehow consumed by the valley, doomed to drown in its waters or
become buried by its sod. Most peculiar, and how peculiar is that smile
of yours, that monstrous knowing smile. But, behold, my smile is just as
eccentric; because I shall *not* be consumed of the valley, delicious an
experience as that may be. This valley is your temple and your god; but
there are other gods, who also call in dream."

The night grew cold, and I saw him shiver. Wrapping my arms about
him, I led him home. We made love by moonlight, and as I lay beside
him his hair embraced my face. Wakefulness was ushered by the
whispering of a husky voice. I smiled, for I had never heard Wilus talk in
his sleep. I listened carefully to the words of a Dutch language, then
pushed away his hair so as to put my ear nearer to his lisping lips. His
mouth was still, unmoving. Deep and steady breathing alone issued from
it. Yet still I heard the whispered words, in a voice from the other end of
the bedstead. A potent fragrance wafted from where the darkness
whispered. A patch of crouching darkness rose above us and whispered
my friend's name. I felt upon my face its hot scented breath as I gazed
into its yellow eyes. Pale streams, like strands of ghostly hair, floated
from the eyes that hungrily gleamed. I could not turn my eyes from

those bright amber orbs. My eyesight blurred, until I could see naught but red writhing shapes.

Beside me, Wilus moaned. I weakly turned my face to his. My lips found his salty human flesh. He moved away from me, with deep suspiration, and moaned in ecstasy an alien name. Oh, how seductively that name sounded in the quiet room. I tried to name it on my lips, over and over again, until slumber conquered me.

## III.

I awakened, with flesh consumed by fever. Wilus bathed my face with a cool wet cloth. "You'll be fine," he reassured. "Do be still, dear boy. It came for me, to teach me the way home."

"It was *she*!" I insisted, then reached to touch the dark gray bruise upon his throat. I did not like its soft ashy substance.

"No, no. It was the fire vampire. You looked too long and deeply into its burning eyes. Your cool silver eyes took in too much of its property, and thus you burn with strange agitation. One borne of the valley's shadow cannot withstand such cosmic brilliance. Don't look so wild, Adam. I've left a note explaining all."

"A note? Why, are you leaving again?" How queer was his smile. I gazed at his face, the face that seemed more altered than before. The womanly lips smiled.

"It came to seal the covenant, and will guide me home to Fomalhaut, where I shall sit beside the bubbling throne. *Ia!!* The rapture that will flame in me forever!" And then he chanted words in a Dutch tongue, all the while stroking my brow. I think he enchanted me toward slumber once again.

In darkness I awakened. My eyes could barely open, encrusted as they were with sleep and rash. How painfully they stung. A heady redolence issued from somewhere in the house. It was the smell of that enchanted hair, tenfold. I kicked the damp bedclothes from me and staggered to my feet. Like someone lost in nightmare, I moved out of the bedroom, down a flight of stairs, entering at last the library that glowed in golden candlelight. Wilus lay within a circle that was composed of chalk and melted wax. A piece of yellow parchment lay upon his naked chest.

A thing dark and formless crouched above him. It raised its smoky head and hissed to candlelight. I could not help but gaze into its voracious eyes, those eyes that hungrily burned into my own. Then it lowered those eyes to my friend's throat, as its airy substance spread like liquid smoke along Wilus's bony frame. He writhed and whimpered. His hand took hold of the parchment and held it high as his mouth voiced a curious chant in an antique Dutch tongue. His dark hair moved as if he floated in water, and I watched that slim strand of pale hair that moved over his face and slipped between his lips.

I watched, as the parchment in his hand darkened and turned black. In horror I watched as the hand that held it darkened also and turned into a thing of ash. Oh, how his flesh crumbled and separated. Ah, the hot burning wind that came from nowhere, that encircled Wilus and the thing to which he was conjoined. A cyclone of ash rose toward the ceiling, and from within the mania of storm I could see the lustrous eyes of an ageless daemon. It raised an amorphous face and opened wide an expanse of mouth, an orifice that puckered and exhaled. A flake of ash sailed from out the tempest, drifted to me and floated into my heaving mouth.

The storm grew wild, then vanished. Simply that. I fell upon the floor of a pitch dark room where burned out candles weirdly smoked. I wanted to call his name, but my tongue would not move. For on that fleshy organ I could taste the thing that had floated into my mouth, that tiny flake of ash that tasted of a remembrance of my friend's beloved flesh.

*¿?*

# AFTERWORD

In 1995, after my lover's heroin overdose and death, I began to write a series of Sesqua Valley stories dedicated to deceased members of the Lovecraft Circle. I suppose I was trying to take my mind off personal tragedy by sinking into creativity. It worked quite well, and many of those tales became the core of my first American collection of fiction, *Tales of Sesqua Valley,* published by my good buddy and fellow author Jeffrey Thomas. With these stories I mentioned briefly the addition to the Mythos created by the gent to whom the story was dedicated. It was a fun wee game, although the results were not stories of importance. The original version of this story had its first appearance in the chapbook that Jeff published in 1997 under his Necropolitan Press imprint; it has been substantially rewritten for this edition.

# The Million-Shadowed One

*For Colin*

*"What is your substance, whereof are you made,
that millions of strange shadows on you tend?"*

—Shakespeare

## I.

I knelt in a shadowed place, smiling at my young companion. Reaching into the burlap bag that I held open for him, he took from it a skull. A moonbeam shaft filtered through the spreading trees and fell upon this ghastly treasure. Oh, how we sighed to darkness at this display of gothic beauty.

"It's as oddly shaped as my own," Nelson replied.

"Yes, I chose it because it reminded me of you. It seemed to call to me the instant I beheld it. All of these selected fossils struck my singular fancy, and so I seized upon them. Before I left Dunwich I slept with this bag of bones as my pillow. Yah, the dreams I dreamt that night!"

Nelson softly laughed. "Yes, I can easily imagine. The Whateley clan who settled here has often spoken of the deposit of human bones that littered the domed hills of Dunwich. It seemed to make them homesick to speak of them, and of those hills. And yet they so seldom return, ever since the original members settled here in 1928. A strange bunch, aye."

"Aye. Look at this elbow bone. See how the one end is almost melted? Whatever fed on these remains, it was not of this earth. The Whateley's are so secretive about their past. You know they have gobs of arcane books in their personal libraries that they refuse to take to the tower?"

"So I've heard. Did all of these skeletonic remains come from Sentinel Hill?"

"They did indeed. I followed your directives to the letter. I still don't understand why you didn't come with me."

"I never leave the valley. I'm not like Simon Gregory Williams, who never stops his madcap journeys. I don't trust the outside world, Geoffrey. Neither do I need it. I need only Sesqua Valley and its intoxicating wonder. There is magick here, and with such enchantment I shall bring into being a creature that will shew me the secrets of Dunwich and help me apply them to this realm. You will assist me, of course."

I smiled. "Of course."

He plopped the skull into the bag and rose to his feet. I followed him beneath a blanket of starlight to the ancient necropolis wherein outsiders to the valley are interred. Silently, we strolled past tilting tombstones and the reedy branches of willows, stopping at last before the rose bush that grew within that place of death. I gazed at the mauve petals of its perfumed flowers, then knelt with my companion upon the graveyard ground.

"I want you to concentrate on these vestiges of mortality, Geoffrey. I want you to taste their marrow on your mouth, to feel their elder essence in the innermost compartment of your soul. Your soul is dark with the shadowed alchemy of this haunted valley, outsider though ye be. These bones have sat for decades beneath the spectral sky of old Dunwich. We'll combine their elements with the magick of our valley, and hopefully give birth to something wonderful." He took bone after bone from the bag and tossed them onto the ground. I listened to the bewitching music of his voice as he sang to the rose bush, and marveled at how the pale petals trembled and broke free, drifting softly onto the scattered bones.

"What is this song you sing, Nelson?"

"It's a song of potency that Simon taught me. He'll be back in a few days, from his journey to Illinois."

"A strange place for him to visit."

"Yes, he was very mysterious. Something about a town called Nauvoo, and some supernatural circumstance that was about to unfold there. You know how impossible it is for him to disclose his little secrets. But he taught me this chant, the vibrations of which trigger the alchemical properties of this rose bush and its silky petals."

Nelson continued singing, and I concentrated on the bones. I *could* taste their olden quintessence, and something more. Strangeness entered into my soul, found my brain, began to fill my mind with outlandish shapes and shadows. Some of these ivory relics were not, I knew, of this terrestrial realm. They had been brought from somewhere else, by things called forth atop the domed hills of Dunwich. Nelson's shoulder touched my own as he swayed on his knees beside me. My human heart pounded in my breast, and from beneath my bended knee I could feel the pulsing heartbeat of the haunted valley. Opening my eyes, I watched the rose petals continue to fall upon the bones, and saw those petals liquefy and melt over the bones from Sentinel Hill. A potent fragrance overcame my wits, and I began to weep. Nelson placed his cool hand over my mouth, bent to kiss my tears. Then he sang more clearly the alien syllables, and I watched as the rose bush madly twitched, showering petals onto the heap of ivory debris, all of which writhed and coalesced. I grew dizzy at the potent perfume that wafted into my nostrils, and shutting heavy eyelids I tilted and fell onto the ground. Wakefulness departed, and I entered a realm of eerie dream, where I floated among the shadows of other dimensions.

I awakened to the sound of laughter. Rubbing slumber from mine eyes, I blinked at morning sunlight. Some distance from me, prancing naked in the warming air, were two figures. Nelson, tall and lean, with his shaggy black hair falling in his face, looked immensely happy. Next to him, twisting its misshapen form in imitation of Nelson's play, was an impish thing. Seeing that I had awakened, Nelson pranced toward me, followed by his scampering companion. The wee imp watched as I lifted myself to a kneeling position. The rose petals that had fallen onto me fell away, and others I brushed at with my hand. And then I froze as I carefully looked at that hand and saw how some of the petals has liquefied and melded with the flesh of the hand that hand been closest to the pile of bones. Mutely, I raised that hand to Nelson, who merely grinned.

The small creature hobbled close, and I took in the weird shape of its head, the cloudy and colorless eyes, and mutation of its ungodly form. It took my hand and brought it to its wide nostrils. Smiling, it shut its awful eyes, began to shudder, and I felt my blood grow cold as its fleshy form began to blur, to grow momentarily indistinct. And my hand, the hand it held, faded as well, and with that invisible hand I seemed to touch another realm, a place beyond the rim of time and space.

Nelson knelt next to us and touched the undulating face of the strange new being. Its form solidified. I took from it my numbing hand and placed it on the ground, where it touched the creature's shadow. Yah, how I shivered at the unearthly chilliness of that malformed silhouette! I watched that black outline slightly spread and eerily reshape itself of its own volition, in an undulating delineation that did not conform to its fleshy source.

Nelson placed his hand upon my own. "Ah, what an unfamiliar chilliness that is, as if from another cosmic place. Our supernal offspring isn't entirely of our sphere. Its bones have slept too long among the shadows of Sentinel Hill. And in other places, of which we cannot begin to imagine. And now we have wedded all of that with Sesqua Valley's occult nature." The child of Sesqua Valley picked up a handful of rose petals and, holding them over my head, let them drift onto me. He took my altered hand and bent to kiss it, to deeply inhale its redolence. Reaching for my hand, the wee imp took it in its own and lifted it to its nostrils. Then it opened its mouth and sang in a high wailing voice. I recognized the song as Nelson's magick chant, but here it issued in purely alien syllables that even Nelson's weird mouth could not imitate. It sang, the nameless issue of our sorcery, and held to me its hand. I watched in spectral wonder as that hand began to mist and spread with shaping. I watched as from the creature's palm there blossomed a diminutive growth of pale mauve petals that opened so as to form a perfect rose. Shining its translucent eyes at me, the creature plucked the rose from its palm and placed it into my altered hand, then pushed that hand to my face. The flower and my flesh smelled as one.

## II.

"It's quite singular," said Simon Gregory Williams as he took from Virginia Whateley the proffered glass of almond milk. "Really, Geoffrey, you are to be congratulated. I never would have thought to try such experimentation myself."

"And yet you are the source of Nelson's outlandish education," I countered. He daintily closed his eyes and bowed his head in modest acknowledgement of this. "And yet I fear that Nelson's original plot is absolutely foiled, for the thing does not speak."

"No, it's all whimpers and pleading eyes, like some friendly hound. And yet it does communicate something of its nature to the lad. Most fascinating."

We watched as Nelson and the imp played on the lawn with the youngest Whateley woman, Vanessa. Virginia handed me a glass of sweet warm milk, and as she placed it in my hand she wound her free hand around my altered flesh. "This is most peculiar, Geoffrey. Do you say you actually *touched* a cosmic otherwhere?"

I sighed. "So I believe. You've been to Sentinel Hill, Simon; you've seen those littered bones. Some of them are of outlandish shape and structure."

"Yes, extremely *outré*, so they are. What does your family legend say of those bones, Ginnie?"

"I've never visited the domed hills myself. They are the dwelling place of the diseased branch of the family. You must remember that I never lived in Dunwich. My father fled the place after the Horror tainted forever the family name, moving to a different part of New England. I was raised with the family secrets, warned about our infernal heritage, and urged to resist its temptations. It wasn't until Nessa and I followed our cousins to this region that my interest in supernatural wonder coagulated and took hold. But in answer to your question, some of those fossils, so family legend whispers, have been there for centuries, having fallen from the skies when certain early Whateley wizards opened holes in cosmic aether. But we cannot be certain of these old legends. Some of the bones, most perhaps, are human, probably sacrificial victims. Dunwich magick is entirely too messy, I fear. I much prefer the quiet magick of this valley."

"Quiet, yes—but just as diabolic," said Simon with a chuckle. "The valley hungers just as deeply as do those cosmic beasts we call the Old Ones. We've had our human sacrifices, however less untidy than those performed in Dunwich and Arkham."

Nelson came to join us. "What secrets are you pack of devils speaking?"

I smiled. "We're merely speculating on the origin of our new friend."

"Oh, but I've seen it, in dream, when those malformed limbs are twined around my own in slumber. Something, some influence, beyond the rim of reality is our new one's sire. And it's calling to him in the cosmic void. It breaks my heart to say it, but it's inevitable that sooner or later the wee one will return unto its pa."

"And what, pray tell, has come of your original plan, of leaking from this being the secrets bred on Dunwich's domed hills?"

"That's the strangest thing, Simon. I no longer care about such secrets. It's enough to bask in the unearthly nature of this new-borne being. My gut tells me that we've magick enough in Sesqua Valley. Unlike you, I don't need to seek it elsewhere."

Simon snorted. "That, my child, is blasphemous talk coming from a child borne of Sesqua's shadow. The dark universe of magick rules our existence."

"So be it," Nelson countered. "But I'm pregnant with our provincial power, I don't need it from any other place. Nor will I ever leave the valley. I am of the valley thoroughly."

The sound of laughter came to us. Rising, I vacated the porch and went to join Vanessa and our little imp in their play. "Doesn't he smell wondrous?" Vanessa enthused. "Like some lovely combination of the valley and the cosmos. He is potent with the fragrance of the blossoms of which his flesh was formed. Here, little one, can you form an unfolding rose in shadow? Watch."

And she joined her hands in sunlight, in such a way that the shadow of those hands, silhouetted on the grass, formed a folded rose. Tenderly, she unfolded her fingers, and the rose-like shadow began to open its petals. Wailing in amazement, the wee imp clasped its hands together. I watched its shadow on the grass, then shouted as that shadow began to heave and surge in monstrous growth, expanding impossibly in size. The others on the porch rushed to us.

"What on earth—?" gasped Virginia.

"No," Simon excitedly proclaimed. "'Tis nothing from this sphere."

"Is it the shadow of the thing that calls to it from cosmic aether?" Nelson asked.

"I think not," said the wise first-borne offspring of Sesqua Valley. "We all looked at Simon and waited for his explanation. He smiled as we waited, then shrugged. "It is merely the shadow of that which our little imp will some day become, in true Dunwich tradition."

### III.

For three months our little friend was with us. But we knew that the end was nigh, for more and more its outline would dim and fade, as if reaching for that nameless otherwhere from which its essence had ultimately issued. Nelson had been especially gloomy all that day, aware of something. I realized more fully how absolutely a child of the valley he was, more in tune with Sesqua's secrets than anyone other than Simon Gregory Williams himself. Perhaps this came from Nelson's never having left the valley, even when he came of age, as is the tradition here. Finally, he looked up at me with his sad face. "Our little friend is leaving us today."

"How on earth can you know that?"

"I know. He's at the cemetery, and he's fading away absolutely."

I stood and began to walk to the place of death, followed by my friend. The wee imp stood before the rose bush, wailing in its high ethereal voice a chant of familiar alchemy. Its outline was very dim. Portions of its shadow seeped about it, climbing its limbs, clouding its darkening eyes. Weeping, Nelson knelt before the creature. He opened his mouth in chanting, and together they called forth the name of that which pulsed on the other side of sky, that thing that claimed with titan authority our little friend.

I stooped before these two and tried to utter the weird words they chanted. The wee one took my altered hand and kissed it with its malformed mouth. Staring steadfastly into my eyes, it slowly chanted. My aching lips began to form the wondrous words. And then the flesh of my palm began to ripple, to surge and spread. Something pushed out of my palm and opened crimson petals. The imp reached for the rose, tugged at it and pulled if from my flesh. It tore apart the petals with both hands, then raised one hand over Nelson's head, the other hand over my dome. We closed our eyes as the petals drifted onto us. The heady fragrance was all we sensed. I cannot say for how long my eyes were shut. But when again I opened them, Nelson and I were utterly alone.

*6?*

## AFTERWORD

I wrote this story for the autistic son of Rose and Jeffrey Thomas, and the original version of the tale appeared in my first American collection, *Tales of Sesqua Valley,* published by Jeffrey's *Necropolitan Press.* I've rewritten portions of it for this collection, bringing in some of my new Sesqua Valley characters and tying it more firmly to the Whateley's of Dunwich. As with many of my Sesqua Valley stories, this one is preoccupied with the theme of Love. As a child I was such a freak that I never felt love from family or society. I was always being critiqued and made fun of for being so stupid, lame and weird. Perhaps part of the reason I created Sesqua Valley was so that I could have a place where all the weirdness that is within could find a home of acceptance and love. I often visit Sesqua Valley in my dreams, and I am always accepted absolutely for who I am.

# The Child of Dark Mania

*To ye memory of F. B. Long*

My weird and amusing cousin, with whom, in childhood, I was very close, wrote to me one late September day, asking if I would set some time aside and visit her. The letter's tone was warm and easy, yet something between the lines worried me. I had not seen Diane since her return, eighteen years ago, from Greece, to which she had journeyed with a gang of lesbian witches. A creature of wild abandon, she was always on some exotic journey to some strange land. I have a collection of postcards that come from every corner of the world.

She shocked us all by becoming pregnant and settling in a place called Sesqua Valley. I had, when her letter arrived, been recovering from a serious epistolary row with my editor and publisher. My last two novels had sold amazingly well and it was time, they informed me, to drop the reclusive author 'pose' and go on an extended book tour. I absolutely refused. My solitary ways, I informed them, were not a pose but a way of life. I saw no one; I went no place. I would not own a telephone. If my books were selling briskly, I saw no need to journey hither and yon to pitch an already popular product. These battles with my publisher leave me extremely distraught, and I felt a huge need for escape. Thus, one splendid morning, I boarded a bus and journeyed to Sesqua Valley. I felt an almost criminal thrill in making my escape from everything. No one had been informed of my sudden departure. No one would be able to find me.

The motion of movement soothed me, and I napped. On awakening I found that we were entering a valley. Hugh hills, thick with evergreens, rose all around. I gasped with joy at the magnificent beauty of a titanic twin-peaked mountain composed of sparkling white stone. After the bus had pulled into town and stopped, I stepped off, smiling at the quaint lamppost from which a sign reading "Sesqua Depot" hanged. Beneath the sign, grinning widely, with a huge clean wheelbarrow at her side, was Diane. Her blond hair, faded and streaked with grey, moved lightly in the wind.

"Frank," she said, hugging me, "you look great, exactly as a distinguished author should. And how kind of you to have more grey hair than I." We got my luggage, which she placed inside the barrow (a valley tradition, she explained), and which she insisted on pushing as we strolled the dirt road that led to her residence. I found myself immediately relaxing, charmed by the quiet place, by the lack of cars, by the large old houses. My senses seemed somehow to fully awaken, to come alive. I could actually hear the soughing of the wind as it brushed against treetops. I could smell Nature, a captivating aroma. The verdant beauty felt cool and soothing upon my eyes.

We came to her large yellow house. I was delighted to see its long wide porch, the porch swing and rocking chair. I longed for sweet and easy comfort, to sit and smile and do absolutely nothing. We carried my luggage to a spacious room on the second floor, then went to the kitchen. A tray of fruit and cheese was placed on the table before me. I ate slowly, drank hot fresh coffee. I felt indecently at home.

"I'm glad, if a bit amazed, that you've come."

"Amazed?" I queried.

"Of course. In every review of your work that I've read you are always described as the 'reclusive author'. Makes you sound extremely distant."

I smiled. "I insist on being so described. It's my little theory of hope that it will keep people away. I need peace and quiet in order to write, need it profoundly. It feels at times almost an obsession, my insatiable need for solitude."

"Then you've come to the proper place."

"I would probably have come before now, but you've been rather distant yourself, these past many years."

"It comes from being the oddball of the family. Whenever I was with kin I felt a constant need to defend or excuse myself. Especially after Melissa's birth. So I found this secluded place in which to settle—this wonderful valley."

"You never get lonely?"

She hesitated and thought. "I do feel a bit lonely, I confess. That's why I suddenly wrote. It was impetuous of me, but I'm a creature of mood and impulse. The fact is, I think that Melissa is soon to leave me. We've become distant, but the idea of losing her has me a bit freaked."

I loved her modern way of talk. I took her hand in mine. "It's natural for her to want to someday go her own way."

"Natural? That word has no meaning for me. Do you remember, when we were kids, how I fancied myself a voodoo queen, how we danced in darkness to ethnic strains of exotic music? I've traveled to shadowed lands and knelt before strange gods. I've witnessed things that even you, with your wild imagination, could not conceive of. Phantasms, ancient tomes, weird moods and wild mania." Diane's eyes focused inward, like one lost in memory. I watched her in silent fascination, until at last she blinked and grinned. "Supper is at seven. Vegetable stew, your favorite as I recall. Go relax. No publishers or fanatics will find you here."

I kissed her hand and rose to my feet. I looked at the lines that crinkled the corners of her eyes, and felt a tinge of sadness at our lost youth. Her eyes seemed to subtly betray a sadness of their own. Silently, I turned away. The autumn day was mild, and I opened my bedroom window, so to enjoy refreshing wind. Stretching atop my soft bed, I shut my eyes and placed hands on chest. I could feel the hypnotic pulsation of my heart. I slept for a few hours, until awakened by a faint and distant howling.

I knelt before my bedroom window and looked out at the black valley, with its pointed silhouettes of surrounding trees. Clouds obscured the moon, and as I looked at Mount Selta, as it was called, its colossal bulk seemed absolutely sinister, especially the wickedly arched peaks. It looked like some daemonic god that was biding time. Then there came once more the chilling sound, from the darkly shadowed hills, a low unnatural baying.

And from somewhere beneath me, from some place in the silent house, there came an answering howl.

I shivered as my flesh prickled with fear, a sensation I had never known in my placid existence. Weakly, I stood and walked out of my room, down the carpeted hallway and steps that led to the floor at ground level. All was dark, but I could see a sliver of light beneath the kitchen doorway. Diane sat at the kitchen table, her face drawn and pale. Looking at me, she tried to smile.

"What was that unearthly howling?"

My cousin bit her lip and furrowed her brow. "It's taking place more quickly than I expected," she said at last. "I was wrong to bring you here, forgive me. I just did not want to be alone. I'm not like you, can't abide the solitary life. And you've such a wild imagination, as displayed in your thrilling novels, so I somehow thought perhaps you'd be a comfort and not condemn my past."

"I have never done so, nor shall I."

"The worst is that I feel almost apathetic. I knew that he would come for her eventually."

"My dear, your enigmatic talk is less than elucidating."

"Yes, of course. I'm babbling. She's asked to see you. Go through that doorway and follow the stone steps that lead to her dungeon. I'll be in the living room if you need me." With this she rose and left the room. I hesitated, for the creepiness of the situation was too confusing and uncomfortable. Quietly, cautiously, I opened the door and stepped down the narrow step way, pressing moist palms to the rough concrete wall for support. Down I went, to the creature that awaited me.

She wore a simple dress of amber cotton. Her hair was long and dark. Grey eyes gazed at me from behind the cloth mask that completely covered her face. Those eyes seemed to smile. "Cousin Frank. How good of you to visit. I've been rereading your earlier work," and with a gesture she indicated a small pile of paperback books. "I prefer your short stories to your novels."

"As do I; but novels are ever so more popular with the public herd. They are the necessary bread and butter." She had not risen from her chair, but indicated that I was to sit in the vacant chair by which I stood. I tried but found it impossible not to study the grotesque cloth mask, and the strange unsettling shape that, nigh and again, moved beneath it. I had known that Melissa had been born misshapen; we had assumed that this was the result of Diane's consumption of foreign opiates. I had always supposed that this was the authentic reason for Diane's not having anything to do with her family. Perhaps she felt that we would look at her with blame in our eyes for the defacement of her beloved offspring.

Melissa gazed at me in silence, and I blushed, thinking perhaps it was obvious from my expression on what I was pondering. "My mother was mistaken to bring you into this matter," she finally uttered. "Diane's always been an impulsive woman. I like that, usually; it's made for a remarkable existence. She's been an excellent companion. Perhaps she has told you that I am leaving? It is so. My sire comes to claim his own. Mother's just a tad bit nervous, I fear."

"You and your mother have the most extraordinary way of talking! You speak of outlandish mysteries as if they were things of common knowledge."

"No, not ordinary at all, these things. But they shouldn't seem alien to the author of your books. Surely you have done much research into the dark arts so as to display the *outré* knowledge that one finds in your imaginative fiction."

"Fiction, my dear."

She rose and wearily sighed. Then she picked up one of my books, opened to a page and read. "What was this thing before me, this sick pulsation from diseased dreaming? It seethed in midair, an incongruous mass. A multitude of mouths opened wide and sang my name, and I shuddered at this chorus of damnation that seemed to know me."

"Not one of my best, I fear."

"Where did those images come from, Franklyn?"

"From dreams, I suppose."

"And dreams are such curious things, containing knowledge we did not know we possess. And deep within our subconscious dreaming are other layers of night vision, unremembered and unsuspected. Sometimes we need assistance so as to unlock those compartments of dream." She went to a stand and unwrapped a piece of plastic, from which she took a small cone of incense. This she placed in my lap, along with an incense burner shaped as an Eastern deity, an elephant god whose nomenclature

I could not recall. "These will help you to understand. Burn this incense before you go to sleep. Perhaps someday my mother will overcome her sense of guilt and tell you all. Please watch over her, she can be so childish at times. Oh, what a creature of wild dark moods she is, with what an intricate mind she is possessed. She's mentally feral, at times savagely so—and I was borne of such madness. I thank her for it."

It came again from some distant place outside, the low and bestial baying. That now familiar chill pricked my old flesh, and I shivered. I watched Melissa's eyes, and shuddered as they flashed with queer sentiment. Then she dreamily closed her eyelids, tilted back her head. The bizarre shape that bulged beneath her mask expanded, and from beneath the moving mask there came a spine-chilling howl. Clutching the tokens she had placed into my lap, I quickly leapt from my chair and fled the basement chamber.

## II.

My room was cool and welcoming, and kneeling before the window I welcomed fresh air with gulps of greedy inhalation. Without undressing, I sat on the bed and placed the figurine onto the bedside stand. I studied for a moment the cone of incense, studying the weird minuscule symbols that had been somehow etched into its surface. Then I placed the cone in its place on the ornament and lit it. Musky smoke found my nostrils, and deeply I breathed it in. My heavy eyes closed. Blurred lines and muted moving spots writhed before my tightly shut eyelids. They moved with shaping, until they formed an image of ancient ruins that stood upon the apex of a black hill. I floated closer to the ruins, saw within them a spot of unhallowed ground where a woman danced. She was Diane, and she danced with provocative movement before an enormous statue of an elephant god that squatted upon a jeweled throne. Dream had altered—horribly so—the features of the silent god. Its ears had lengthened, as had its blasphemous trunk. The trunk and tusks and ghastly mouth were coated with dripping gore.

Diane danced, completely nude. I marveled at her grace, her exotic beauty. But then my blood froze as she lowly bent and kissed the shadow of the frozen god. I saw that nameless silhouette blur and bend. I saw the taloned hands that reached for my kinswoman. I watched in terror as they lifted her to the creature's hungry trunk, that shaft that ended in a moving maw. I watched the trunk move over her body like some ravenous lover. Then the creature raised its eyes to me. Atrociously, it offered me the writhing body of my blood relation. I gazed at her blood-soaked nudity, at the heaving, swollen stomach. I opened my mouth and yowled in protest.

I awoke to the sound of howling, and at first was uncertain if I listened to an actual sound or to the memory of my own pathetic cry. A gathering wind whimpered at the bedroom window. I went to that window and looked toward the dark hill that rose behind the house. I saw Melissa moving toward it, as wind pushed clouds from before the moon. Lunar illumination fell upon the girl's unmasked face. She turned to suddenly gaze at me, and my blood froze with fear. And yet the image lured. Thus I staggered out of the house, into gale and yellow moonshine, stalking toward the dark beckoning hill. Melissa danced before it, with movement that was monstrously familiar. I watched her swaying form, the elegant and intoxicating movement of her arms. Strangely, my loins surged with longing. I moaned. Melissa turned to face me, and I watched the weird appendage on her face unwind. She held to me her beckoning arms, and passionately I rushed toward them. Melissa pulled me into her embrace, kissed my throat, my face. Her writhing trunk nestled against my ear. From somewhere on the dark hill there came an unearthly baying.

"He calls to me. 'Tis time, Franklyn. Can you feel it, the shifting of the stars? Can you taste the cosmic wonder on the wind? Oh, delicious, delicious!"

I pushed her from me so as to gaze once more into her wondrous eyes. She clutched her breasts and shook with crazy zeal. She bent to me her writhing stem of unwholesome flesh. Its fanged godbox fastened to my mouth. I drank my blood. Above us came the sound of insistent baying. Melissa unlocked from my embrace and hurriedly climbed the grassy hill. I fell, exhausted, to my knees. Up on the grassy crest I beheld the faint forms of shadowy things that raised their trunks to dead moonlight. I watched them blend together and ossify into a bulk of solid blackness that towered unspeakably before me. This titan outline reached for the girl who ran toward it. I shrieked with rage and grief as she vanished forever into the unhallowed paternal essence that engulfed her and then was gone.

*¿?*

# AFTERWORD

This story appeals to me more than most of the things I've written this past decade. I am fond of the image of the woman with her weird masked face, and was delighted when *two* pictorial renditions of that image were included in my first American collection, one by my editor and publisher, Jeffrey Thomas, and the other gracing the superb cover illustration by Earl Geier. There is a lot of peculiar passion in this story, and it gets to me, deliciously. I was delighted to be able to write it in memory to HPL's great buddy and fellow weird author, Frank Long. "The Child of Dark Mania" originally appeared in *The Pnakotic Series.*

*"Behold, I have graven thee upon
the palms of my hands ..."*

—1 Nephi, 21: 16

## I.

Lisa came to me on that fateful evening of revelation and beguilement. Her purple hair was almost as wild as were her eyes, those wide intoxicated orbs. Her pixy face had lost its usual mirth. She was dead serious.

"You must see Nyarlathotep," she panted, refusing the chair that I had offered her, preferring to frantically pace the wooden floor. One hand clutched a large canvas that was covered with a thin sheet of cloth.

"It amazes me," I said, smiling patiently, "that hair as short as yours can look so disarrayed."

"Screw the hair," she shot back, at the same time running a gloved hand through the thick unruly mess. "You've been moaning for over a year about your inability to write, to dream fresh vision. I tell you, go see Nyarlathotep, and he will drench your brain with phantasm."

"I doubt that the tricks of a cult figure will inspire new work from my dead pen. I recently had two squeaky clean young boys leave me a copy of some new sacred book, an absurd thing about a Great Old One filtering through the clouds and dwelling among the mongrel hordes of ancient America."

"Ah, Joe Smith's gold bible."

"And now this new lord of disillusion. Stephen was over recently and told me all about this new bloke, some darkie who arrived three months ago to our city of chaos."

Lisa sighed. "You know, its really stupid, the way you use your tired, boring cynicism as a way to stay cooped up in this pathetic little apartment and hide from the outside world. Things are happening in this city of chaos. Can't you feel it?"

I wearily shrugged. "All I feel, dear child, is this intolerable heat wave. I've never known such appalling weather in October. Autumn is my favorite season because it heralds absolutely the death of tortuous summer, that redoubtable period when human apes strip off their gaudy attire and shriek to the cancerous sun. How you can wear such thick gloves when it is so grotesquely hot is *quite* beyond me."

Oh, how oddly she smiled as she quickly placed one gloved hand before her face and gazed at it in rapture. As she did so I noticed two curious things. First, the gloves that encased her slender hands were not composed of cloth but rather of some fine mesh of mauve metal, the likes of which were utterly foreign to me. Second, with the swift movement of her hand there came to me a wave of fragrance, a scent not unlike the festering of dead lilies. Something in her expression slightly unnerved me, and I felt the need to jabber on. "I've not been able to sleep because of this diabolic temperature. When I am able to fetch a few winks, I have the most monstrous dreams, horrid visions that soak my flesh and shake me awake."

"He will make you dream," she sang. "You would find your muse again if you knelt before him."

"Oh, please. You speak of this freak as if he were a god."

"By god, he could be! He looks supernal, with his golden eyes and scarlet robes. I worship him. My knees grow weak with reverence whenever I think of him."

"Great Jesu, you're worse than that timid little Stephen was when he came to tell me of his encounter with this strange black beast."

"Screw that little gay boy. His teeny brain couldn't endure stunning revelation. The prophecy of Nyarlathotep augurs ill for pea-brains. His vision may be brutal, but it *rocks*!"

"Ah, what a modern girl you are, with your punk rock parlance and thrift store clothes. Such stunning vocabulary makes one feel ones age. I fear I'm far too faded for such radical visions and wonder as you hint of."

"You see, you do that all the time, using your age as an excuse to be a vacillating little shut-in who can't make up his mind about life. Will you write today, or merely whine? Will you dare to really dream, or merely sit in bed and fantasize about cowboys?"

"Don't be crude. It's been ages since I've wanked about Clint Walker. And you have gone on long enough about bold new vision and great creative guts. Stop your muscled mouth and *show* me this new thing you've done that it supposed to induce me to dress in fevered pitch and rush to kiss the palm of this moron with the theatrical name."

Deeply inhaling, Lisa placed her hands together, in a semblance of prayer. With the movement of her hands I became aware once more of some peculiar odor, one that did not inspire my lips to smile. Expecting her to remove her gloves, I frowned in perplexity when she did not. Pulling from my desk my straight back chair of solid oak, she placed it in front of me and rested the covered canvas upon it. She seemed so excited, and yet a wee bit apprehensive as well, and to try and lighten her mood I thought to playfully annoy her by yawning in feigned *ennui*. She took no notice of me, however, choosing rather to place her face into her sheathed hands and rock nervously to and fro, humming a weird little melody beneath her breath. I knew that she could be a creature of raw unregulated nerves; yet I had never witnessed in her such queer behavior.

"First," she whispered, in a voice that was almost musical with veneration, "tell me what you know of Nyarlathotep."

I was growing quite weary of that obscene name; however, I complied. "Very well, as you wish. Now what did young Stephen tell me? Let me rack my brain." Delicately, I touched hand to brow. "This person with the preposterous cognomen came to our city in middle or late June. He rented that old lecture hall where the J. Dubs used to hold meetings so as to lure souls to dreary salvation. Rumor whispers that this darkie crawled through the blackness of several centuries to our modern age; thus we see proven that the more outlandish a cult leader's claim, the more anxious are fools to follow. Stephen tells me that they *do* follow—in droves."

I watched as Lisa stopped her swaying motion and dreamily listened to my utterance. She continued to clasp her face with gloved hands. I disliked her alteration of character because it utterly befuddled me. Disturbed and irritated, I continued. "I'm told that he won't allow his image to be photographed or his voice to be recorded. Early on some poor chap smuggled a wee recording device into a lecture, but when the tape was played, all that could be heard was a weird variety of buzzing which drove the wretched bloke insane. He is, this Nyarlathotep, a splendid showman, and works a multiplicity of mechanical gewgaws with which he spellbinds the rabble. Funny, how little Stephen *shuddered* when he mentioned these devices. Like you, he urged me to go and witness for myself this fantastic creature. I declined then, as I do now. The only beast I chose to worship is myself."

Lisa's hands slowly fell from her face. "What a lonely religion yours must be. You're so full of clever empty talk. But I recall a dim and distant time when you spoke beautifully, when you wrote exquisite verse."

I sadly sighed. "Dim and distant indeed."

"Look, Hyrum, I know what it's like to lose energy and vision. But you can regain it. You can return to creation instead of sitting in this dingy apartment and uttering tired boring witticisms. Look at how Nyarlathotep has inspired me!"

Summarily, with almost fevered movement, she pulled the sheet from the canvas. I shouted in shock and outrage. Lisa's wonderful work had always been delightfully inventive and filled with brilliant color, rather in the style of Gorky. I was thus expecting a work of multi-hued genius. Instead, my eyes were insulted by a vile composition of filthy soot and blurry ink and wash, with here and there an insignificant tint of blue or purple. The scene was a titanic ruins set deep within a riotous growth of jungle. Standing among the debris of antiquity was a shrouded figure that wore no face, yet by its stance seemed haughty and implacable. The entire thing unnerved me. I knew not the origin of the ruins, for they were like nothing I had experienced in art or history. Oh yes, it was an original vision, but not one that I could embrace or applaud. I hated it absolutely, yet could not turn my eyes away. The image beguiled as much as it appalled. My senses were stunned by the aspect of antediluvian age that the artist had been able to evoke. But what a horrid medium for she who had once been so clever and outlandish with color! Quavering with emotion, I turned to the witch.

"*This* is your new achievement?" Oh, how I wailed. "This *sorry* and soulless depiction of a dead and haunted past?"

Great heavens, how oddly she smiled! "My dear Hyrum, this is a vision of the dead and haunted *future.*"

I gasped with choked fury, seethed with emotions I did not understand. "Really, this is too utterly nauseating. Please, *do* cover the wretched thing. I'm sorry to be so blunt, but it has shocked me." Lisa made no movement, and although I turned my face away, my eyes slid inexorably to the painted surface. Savagely, I suddenly pointed to the shrouded figure. "And what in the blessed name of all the gods is *that* supposed to be? You've not given the silly creature a face!"

"The faceless god wears no visage."

I could not refrain from shuddering. Muttering profanely, I reached for the sheet of cloth and tossed it over the canvas. Yet even as I did so my eyes ached to look again upon the painted surface. My companion smiled in eerie triumph.

It was my turn to rise and pace the hard wooden floor. "I simply do not understand why you would surrender your wonderful sense of vibrant color and sensuous lines and replace it with ink and ash and whatever the hell this insidious current medium is. The thing lacks life. It is naught but a concoction of blur and blotch. What did you use, an old bath sponge?"

Ye gods, her peculiar smile! "I used my fingers." She moved a few steps nearer and raised before me her hidden hands. Great Saturn, what was that monstrous stench? It was the stink of decay, yet tainted with a fragrance as I had never inhaled. It revolted and enthralled, like unto her painting. "I used these fingers that he has kissed." We stood facing each other, and I watched as she slowly removed the gloves of metal webbing. Horrified at the nefarious sight before me, I cried in fright and fell into my chair, in which I cowered from the sight.

Yet even as I wanted to turn my eyes away from the festering horror, I wanted to gaze upon it. The pale mists of smoke that spilled from the tiny wounds and bruises were the origin of the unholy stench, that disgusting odor that was extraneous to any earthly redolence. She stretched nearer, and I pretended to cover my eyes. What could have caused such mutation in hands that were once so lovely? How could fingers become so mutilated and disfigured? What could have caused them to become so *flattened*, their tips so erased?

"These hands that he has blessed."

"No ... no ..." Yet even as I whimpered I reached for one of her smoky hands and brought it to my lips. It tasted of nightmare. The nauseating smoke plunged into my nostrils and found my brain, which it ruthlessly teased with esoteric shape and shadow. I curled my nails into her transformed flesh. Lisa hissed with pain and drew her hands away.

With cloudy sight I saw her indistinctly. I beheld the fuming appendages that bled from where I had clutched them. I watched them slide into their *outré* gloves. I watched as they reached for the sheeted painting. "New vision requires radical treatment. This is the sacrosanct gift with which I have been blessed. Perhaps you lack backbone and prefer to sit here and quiver in your impotent existence. But there was a time when your world was filled with magnificent language and stunning vision. You could find that world anew, if you would visit Nyarlathotep."

Her words were like needles in my brain. Weakly, I tried to rise from my cozy chair, only to slip weakly from it to the floor. Trying to blink streaming liquid from burning eyes, I crawled to where she stood. Oh, how I ached to kiss again the palsied hands, to taste their baleful substance. My fingers found her shoes. Weakly, I clung to her clothing and pulled myself to a kneeling position.

"You must see Nyarlathotep." Her strong clear voice echoed from above. "He is wonderful, and dreadful. He will show you prophecies of the cold bleak abysses between the stars, those places where dead gods fumble in dream-infested slumber. The great ones were. They are. They shall be."

Lisa knelt beside me and put her mouth to my ear. I listened as she sucked in breath, then jolted as she unearthly howled.

Instantly afterward, I was alone.

## II.

Thus it was in that hot October that I ventured forth one night in pursuit of Nyarlathotep. As I crept along the silent sidewalks, I passed certain individuals who looked at me queerly and askance. I sensed that they had been to see this foreigner from a land unknown. How anxious they seemed to speak to me, and yet how timidly hesitant they were, watching in silence as I slipped past them. I came at last upon the lecture hall and stopped to gaze in amazement at the throngs of lingering rabble. They leaned against the building and sat upon the curbing, congregated near the open door that led to a narrow stairway. One man was especially fidgety. I watched as he snatched at his hair and muttered loudly to himself. Then he vanished into an alley, and I shivered when from that alley there came a high and mournful howling. The baying sent a quiver of emotion through the lingering crowd.

Pushing through the horde at the doorway I slowly climbed the silent stairway. From somewhere above I heard the soft low sound of fluted music. I walked down a dimly lit hallway that led to the double doors of a lecture room wherein I would confront an unfamiliar alien. The piping of discordant music came from behind the closed doors. My flesh prickled at the sound of it. Closing my eyes, I leaned my throbbing forehead against one of the doors, and it pushed open against the force of my leaning frame. With eyes still shut, I staggered into the room. I could smell scented candlelight. I opened heavy eyelids.

He stood upon a slightly raised platform, the shrouded one. Swarthy, slender, sinister, he was robed in scarlet silk. On a table beside him was a device similar to a child's magic lantern. Its diseased illumination cast obscene and spinning shapes upon the black walls. My attention was caught by the nebulous form that squatted at the feet of Nyarlathotep, the thing that held in clumsy paws an apparatus of tinted ivory or pale gold. It was from this instrument that the fluted music emerged. Yet the more I tried to scrutinize the gadget, the more it seemed to subtly fluctuate in form, reshaping with a sensual and seething movement that ached my skull. I listened to what sounded like whipping wings, as the music melted into silence. My eyes demanded closure, and on their lids I beheld swirling shapes that madly moved before me. These spinning shapes inspired dizziness, and suddenly my knees weakened and my legs crumbled. I fell to the floor.

Weakly, I raised my agonizing head. He stood before me—grim, austere, merciless. My hungry mouth kissed his chilly feet. The room was still, silent. Slightly raising my head I looked about, but the creature that had performed music had vanished. Boldly, I clung to Nyarlathotep's scarlet garment and climbed to a standing position. Swirling light and shadow played upon his regal face. Fantastically, he smiled; and as he did so his visage slightly slipped, as though he wore some tight-fitting mask that had momentarily lost hold. He lifted a hand, and I saw upon his palm an emblem that pulsed with sentience. Tilting my head to it, I licked the captivating insignia. It was sharp and ripped the tongue that touched it. I drank my blood as the creature moved his hand away, then jolted as he swiftly pressed that palm against my forehead. It felt as though splinters of bubbling ice had pierced my brain.

I was inside Lisa's painting. The awful heat that had so plagued our autumn season hung heavily in the dead air. To breathe was to burn. He stood before me still, the ancient one, composed of shifting shapes that composed and decomposed his semblance. I looked beyond him at the mammoth buildings, the ruins of a far distant time. It was a time over which Nyarlathotep was Master Absolute. But how could he still exist in future epoch? How had he escaped the nip of Death?

"That cannot die which stands outside time and space," he lowly uttered.

Behind him I detected a throng of writhing black gargoyles that mindlessly pranced beneath a dying sun. Why did I ache to join in their danse? Oh, how his liquid mark burned upon my brow. Scorching wind arose and pushed into my eyes, burning wind that forced my eyes to close. A large rough hand poked at my face. Opening eyes, I beheld a lean young man who gazed at me in desperation. I watched the mouth that twitched in an effort to talk but was unable to function. I watched the blackness that crept into his trembling eyes, and watched as he raised his head and howled in lunacy.

I escaped him and rushed along the nighted pavement, to the seedy house that Lisa shared with her epileptic mother. My brain blazed with vision, with a prophecy of disaster that I ached to share with one who knew and understood. I was filled with a kind of lust so as to gaze once more upon the image of her painting, to bow before the likeness of a faceless god. Not pausing to knock, I boldly entered the dark and dusty living room. A lamp glowed with pallid light beside a worn and battered sofa, upon which was sprawled an elderly woman. Her twisted body oddly contorted, and puzzled eyes watched the crooked fingers that locked and unlocked.

She did not look at me as she spoke. "You don't need to stay. She's quiet now. I'll leave it up to you. I didn't like the way she howled in that funny way. But she's quiet now. You don't need to stay, it's up to you."

I left her to her confusion, and walked the cluttered hallway that led to Lisa's studio. I could smell incense, and also that other fragrance borne of my friend's altered state. Pausing before the studio door, I leaned my brow upon it. Slowly, it pushed open.

Her lifeless form lay on the floor, its arms sprawled over a large white canvas. An overwhelming stench emanated from the stubs that had once been hands, those nubs that stank and smoked. I knelt beside her. The terrible eyes, wide open, still wore their wild expression. I looked to the image on canvas, the image composed of the filament of transfigured flesh. I saw the hooded figure composed of soot and shadow. From deep within the folds of its hood I could discern the shifting features of a regal and inhuman façade. Yet even as I gazed the features faded into blackness.

I raised my shivering face. I closed my liquid eyes. I stretched my mouth with baying.

*¿?*

**AFTERWORD**

This is one of my favorites of the new stories penned exclusively for this collection. Nyarlathotep is the one creation of Lovecraft's that continually haunts me. I remember how thrilled I was when the brilliant Robert M. Price edited an entire anthology of Nyarlathotep tales for one of *Chaosium*'s Cycle books. This dark god reappears in my fiction time and again. He is an awesome creation. With this story I feel that I've finally written my definitive tale of the Crawling Chaos. It appears here for the first time.

> *"Empty your heart of its mortal dream.*
> *the winds awaken ... "*

—William Butler Yeats

## I.

I sat at my shop counter, inhaling the heady scent of olden books, my thoughts drifting and transforming into nebulous dream, when the bell sounded at the door. Chill evening wind moved the brittle pages of the book that lay before me. A figure entered and silently shut the door. I took in the male attire, clothes that hung askew on so lithe and feminine a frame. I took in the buttonhole, a large green carnation, and the tall black hat that was shiny with age. Beneath the hat's rim dark eyes peered from a wan and worried face.

"Have you seen Jonathan since his return from Thailand?"

"No," I answered, closing the book before me. "I've been rather preoccupied with a new shipment. But I expect to see him before the grand affair of your Black and Red party, which is ..."

"Three weeks away." She sighed and leaned against a tall and sturdy shelf, looked at her black silk gloves as if she couldn't decide whether to remove them or leave them on. Again, the deep sigh. "Perhaps I'm being foolish ..." The pause was pregnant with implication.

"Do tell me everything," I coaxed.

"That's just it. I don't know what it is. He's been distant, mentally preoccupied. Usually, when he returns from some far off place he's excited to tell me about it. Now all he does is sit in is pagoda and whistle to himself."

"Hmm. You don't think he's heading for another breakdown or any such thing?"

"I don't know. I don't think that's it. There's something secretive about his actions. I guess that's what really bugs me. I hate being left out. Jonathan's been my intimate companion ever since father died. We have a bond. In the past, when something had troubled him, he would confide in me. I've tried bullying him, you know how he enjoys a bit of brutality. But when I castigate and question he dismisses me as though I were a clueless child. I know he likes his little secrets, his strange and naughty little pleasures, whatever. But this ..."

"Perhaps he's caught the clap. There is, so I read somewhere, an internationally famous bordello in Bangkok. Or is it Saigon?"

"A case of the clap wouldn't induce him to spend the night in his stupid so-called pagoda." Inquisitively, I arched an eyebrow. "Yeah, I got up at three to go pee and saw him from my window. He was sitting in the cold wind and swaying back and forth. When I called to him, he completely ignored me. It was weird."

"Indeed, most curious. And what is it you want of me?"

"Talk to him."

"Well, yes, of course …"

"Tonight."

"But, my dear!" Helplessly, I lifted my hands in a gesture to indicate how questionable I found her course of action.

"Please, Henry. There's no one else."

"But, my dear, *listen* to that brutal wind. Surely it can wait …" But I saw from her expression that it could not. With melodramatic sigh I heaved off my stool, wrapped myself in heavy coat, and escorted her to their car. The house in which they lived, in a well-to-do lakeside residence, was almost a mansion. This had always been their home. After the death of their father, the two siblings had made few changes inside the house, comfortable with the furnishings their had known since childhood. Their personal lives, however, altered absolutely. Alisha often held gala gatherings for her collection of dubious comrades. Jonathan began his series of journeys across the globe, often sending me fabulous old books that he had discovered in far off lands.

I watched the nighted lake as we drove along the boulevard, until at last we came to the graveled driveway that led to a high metal fence. Alisha pushed a button and the gate began to silently slide open. Their property was so densely populated with towering firs and evergreens that it had a solid air of seclusion. The trees grew so close together that even on the brightest of days the house stood in lush shadow.

The gate closed behind us as she stopped the car. "He's in his pagoda," she said, as if dismissing both her brother and myself. I watched her disappear into the house. A line of swaying Japanese lanterns dimly lit the stone path that led across the lawn to the structure that Jonathan called his pagoda, although it but faintly resembled anything found in the Far East. It was like an open garden pavilion with roofing in Oriental fashion. Inside could be found a gigantic Buddhist bell, a miniature waterfall, and an amazing assortment of wind chimes.

The young man sat on a mat, his legs crossed in what I took to be one of his yoga positions. It made my knees ache just to look at him. His long brown hair was tied into a ponytail. He wore sandals, khaki cut-offs, and a Wonder Woman t-shirt. With eyes closed, he could not see me. I examined his handsome profile, the lean face with prominent cheekbones and goatee. Even in the dim lighting from the single lantern that swayed inside the structure, I could tell that he was darkly tanned, probably from his time spent in Thailand, where he had journeyed with a yoga instructor. He looked remarkably composed, and I began to question his sister's histrionics.

The chill evening wind died a little. The music of wood upon wood and metal upon metal subdued. "Henry." I crinkled my brow in perplexity. He had not moved, nor opened his eyes. How, then ...? "I can smell you on the wind. You reek of dust and old books." Chagrined, I grinned. How to take this comment on my personal aroma? Then: "I suppose that Ally has asked you to see me."

I spoke as I strolled to him. "Yes, but also to ask my aesthetic advice regarding décor for the upcoming festivities. But she does seem just a tad bit worried. Are you behaving beastly? In one of your tiresome moods?"

"No. I've merely been preoccupied. She simply wants something to fret about, you know how she is. She wants her party to be a fabulous success."

"Ah, that might be it. And you're being childish because she has focused on the party rather than rallying around you now that you've returned from travel. You are both such spoiled children, clamoring for center stage."

"You're stupid if that's what you think."

"Pardon my benightedness." The wind buffeted us once more, and at the sound of clanging I looked at the swaying array of chimes. I saw the new addition. But exactly what it was I could not ascertain. At first I thought it some freakish papier-mâché head, but as I drew nearer it looked more like a metal object encrusted with blue dusting of granulated steel. It had a kind of face. Where the mouth would have been it wore an oval aperture the size of a small egg. Two lesser holes suggested nostrils. Where a face would have had eyes there were two shallow indentions; but these were smoothly solid, sans orifices. High above these, just above what might have been a forehead, were a grouping of tiny pea-sized holes that numbered seven.

"Mmm, something new," I casually remarked.

"Oh. Yes." I sensed a change in his decorum, a sudden frigidity. Turning, I gazed at him, seeing a visage filled with wonder, and in the eyes a tinge of fear. He moved his eyes from the thing of metal and noticed my expression. Hurriedly, a torrent of words poured from him. "I found it in Bangkok, in a curious little shop. There was a main room filled with the most god-awful American junk. Then there was this little back room, dimly lit and cluttered. Just the kind of place where I find those wonderful old books that so delights you. And there it was, sitting among a disarray of jumble, covered with dust and cobwebs. I thought it was some kind of weird wind chime, so of course I bought it."

"It looks rather unearthly."

How nervously he cackled. "Indeed."

I raised a hand to its rough surface. How frightfully cold it was. With what an unnatural—nay—a *disquieting* texture it was composed. Frowning, I took my hand away. My fingers almost burned with chilliness, and with something else, some kind of nasty residue that clung to my numbing flesh. Disgusted, I roughly rubbed my hand on my trousers. A noise caught my attention. I leaned my face close to—the thing—and fancied that I could hear wind moving through it. Stepping around so to examine the back of it, I was startled to see a solid surface with no opening of any kind. But surely that was the wind that moaned through it, its noise somehow distorted as it sallied through the thing's apertures.

I looked at the length of chain from which it hanged, from a small but sturdy hook that had been soldered to its top. Stepping around, I again faced its front. Had the night grown nippier, or was it creepiness that tickled my flesh? I sensed the night wind fade away. The chimes above me stopped their incessant movement. All was dead quiet, except for the faint suggestion of sound that issued from the thing before me and Jonathan's soft chanting. I looked at him, with his wide eyes oddly glazed and his moving mouth strangely askew. What was it he muttered, some kind of name? Ithacaw, or Itsakwa, some aboriginal-sounding cognomen. And how strange that the name seemed oddly echoed on the wind that whispered from the metal sphere. It was an almost musical sound, and so beguiling that I leaned closer to the egg-shaped opening so as to hear the better. Yes, I yearned to listen, to press against that coarse uncanny surface and listen to the air that moved within, that cool air that smell of age that oozed from the opening and delightfully licked my face.

A hand tightened at my shoulder and pulled me away. I shouted in protest, and then saw Jonathan's troubled eyes peering into my own. Shuddering, I suddenly found myself consumed with fear. Together, we hurried from that haunted place.

## II.

I fidgeted in a chair before a fire. He had taken me to the mammoth library room, and after having prepared coffee for myself had fixed himself a large martini. I held the cup of scalding liquid tightly in hands that trembled. I brought the rim of the cup to my face, so to bathe in its steaming warmth. Now and then I glanced into the fireplace; but I quickly looked away, not liking the things that I saw—or thought I saw—within its flames. "Now. Please Jonathan. Explain to me that which has just occurred."

"What?"

"No, do not suddenly play ignorant. You will explain to me this—thing—in your pagoda and the unnatural effect it has had upon me. What is it?"

He paced the room but would not sit, nor did he look at me. "It's what I told you it is." He saw that I was growing agitated and angry. But I held my tongue, allowing him time to be more honest. "It's obviously some kind of weird wind device," he said at last.

"It's 'obviously' like nothing we've either of us ever seen before."

Sighing in frustration, he finally sat. "Okay. Yes, it's unusual, and has an eerie effect." I snorted. "I can't explain it. But, Henry, we are susceptible to such effects because of our senses. Sounds, music, can either soothe or disturb us. Look at what happened when Stravinsky premiered *Le Sacre du Printemps*. People went mad, the performance ended in riot. Or take thunderstorms, of which you are so partial. Some people run to hide, while you rush to the nearest window with eyes wide and delighted. We are creatures of senses, rational or not."

I pouted. "You are trying to placate me with calm and soothing language. Yet not twenty minutes ago you hurled me from that place with terror flashing in your troubled eyes."

"I thought you were going to kiss the damn thing! You had the oddest expression on your face. Of course I dragged you away. I haven't cleaned it yet. God knows where it's been or by whom it has been pawed."

"I am not placated."

"Then fuck you." Jonathan rose and fixed himself another drink. My pouting deepened when I saw that he would not offer me a refill of coffee. Tutting, I placed the cup on a small table nearby. "Look," he continued, standing before the hearth and trying to look sincere and friendly. "I agree that the thing is kind of creepy. Stop snorting. The thing is, I like it, whatever the hell it is, and that's the beginning and end of it. I found it, I liked it, I bought it." He glared at me with defiant eyes.

"Very well. I wish to speak to Alisha."

"She's retired to bed." He could not possibly have known this, having been entirely with me since we entered the house. However, the word "bed" had its effect, and I yawned. "You're tired. Come on, I'll drive you home. Just let me change into trousers, it's grown chilly."

"I'll meet you out by the car," I said, and he nodded and left the room. I went out of doors, into wind and darkness. I felt distraught, emotionally drained. I did not understand the events that had just passed, but was suddenly too weary to care.

The wind was blowing full force. I could not resist turning my eyes toward the pagoda. The lantern inside it swayed wildly in the gale, and in its dim, wavering illumination I saw a dark small figure standing before the thing of blue metal, standing very close. I was momentarily distracted when Jonathan came out of the house. The front door slammed shut behind him, pushed by violent wind. When again I looked into the pagoda, it was vacant of human occupant.

## III.

Days passed. I had received a wee note from Alisha, apologizing for the "nonsense" of the previous evening and formally inviting me to her ball. I decided to go as the Red Death. An obvious choice, perhaps. My other idea was Little Red Riding Hood, but there are limits to even my perversity; plus I had grown too plump to look decent in a dress. A flowing crimson robe would conceal my girth and look superb.

The days slowly passed, and I oft reflected upon that strange evening. I dwelt on that face of encrusted blue metal; I saw it in deepest dream. Betimes I caught myself listening attentively to the evening wind, fancying that it sang a variation of the weird tune I had heard whistling inside the—thing. I knew not what else to call it, and so it was—the thing. Yet the more I pondered on it, the more mysterious a thing it seemed, something alien, something from a bad dream. It was grotesque, and bizarre; it absolutely would not let go of my imagination. Oh, how it haunted. I burned to look at it once more, to touch it; perhaps to kiss it.

At last the festive night arrived. I taxied to the mansion and was let through the gate by an awaiting knight. I wandered below high swaying trees, moved through oscillating shadow and roaming wind. My eyes followed the line of Japanese lanterns to the pagoda. Hesitantly, I paced toward the dark structure. Its strings of chimes danced in moving air. The sphere of blue metal was nowhere to be seen.

"Henry." Jonathan stood a few yards away, holding to me his long pale hand. I walked to him, took his hand, allowed myself to be led into the house.

"Your strange new thing …"

"Missing," he said, and shrugged. That was all; he offered no explanation or conjecture. I felt a strange sadness, and a kind of panic that I did my best to conceal. We stood in the hallway, examining each other in candlelight. He looked resplendent in black tux and cloak. The only red was in the contact lens place onto his eyes. He grinned at my ghoulish makeup, shewing his two fangs. Together, we entered the ballroom.

And entered an alternative world. A diabolic one. The crowd was much as I had expected, beautiful boys in scarlet gowns, masculine women in coat and tails. Somber music was piped into the room from unseen speakers. Bowls of incense filled the room with fragrance. From a darkened corner I espied Alisha, who smiled and slightly bowed. She was magnificent and original as the Lamanite king, Amalickiah. My eyes feasted on her indigenous beauty as I stepped to her. With masculine courtesy she offered me her hand to kiss.

The room was like some fantastic phantasm. The walls had been elegantly covered with drapery of ebony and maroon velvet. Cushions of similar shade littered the floor, upon which groups of youngsters sexually explored one another. I watched as from one of these groupings a young figure arose. Despite the wild orange wig I recognized him as a lad who had oft frequented my bookshop, and who had a fascination for the yellow decadence of the late Victorian age. I was charmed to see him dressed after Beardsley's splendid work of ink and color wash, "The Slippers of Cinderella." He took from his apron one of the disintegrating roses that had been pinned thereon, and this he offered me with benedictional bow. "To the Great Lord Thanatos, the only god before whom I grovel." I took his flower, cupped my hand below his chin and pulled him to me. His breath reeked of champagne. Bending to him, I kissed him hard.

"Well," Jonathan muttered, tossing back his long dark hair, "how swiftly you get into the swing of things. Come, I've a special concoction just for you." He led me to a serving station at which a manservant poured dark liquid from a sparkling silver coffee pot. I took the delicate cup proffered me and brought it to my nostrils, breathing in the brandy with which my coffee had been laced. Normally I had no stomach for liqueurs, but on this night I refused to be a prude. I sipped, and smooth delicious nectar spilled into my mouth, warming my face.

Time passed. After a number of coffees I fell upon a cushion and smiled idiotically at the surrounding sexual frolic. Finally, Alisha clapped her hands and the music ceased.

"Mesdames et Messieurs, the Dance of the Seven Veils."

True decadence crept into the room. What they were, I could not fathom. I had read somewhere of a race of cannibalistic semi-human dwarfs who dwelled in some plateau somewhere in Central Asia. These creatures could have hailed from such a tribe. The twisted features of their hateful faces had a sobering effect. They profoundly repulsed. I watched as the ones who carried flute instruments sat in semi-circle and placed their pipes to misshapen mouths. The room was filled with discordant piping. A diminutive figure wound in flowing veils danced into the room. Its gyrations moved in rhythm to the esoteric music, and one by one the veils gradually fell from its stunted torso. I saw the small dry breasts and the twin genitalia both male and female.

People began to hoot and applaud as Alisha slowly danced toward the

nude monstrosity, holding a silver platter on her upturned palms. A
sheet of black silk covered the object that tilted on the platter. Ally knelt
before the bestial thing, and I watched as the creature removed with
knobby fingers the covering of silk. I had, of course, read Wilde's play,
and thus expected to see a grisly replica of the head of Iokanaan. Instead,
I beheld a sphere of blue metal.

Shrieking pierced the room. Rushing wildly to his sister, Jonathan
took up the sphere, clutched it to his heaving breast, and dashed madly
from the room, into night. Trembling, I arose from my cushion. Figures
surged around me, shouting cries of drunken confusion. Blindly, I ran
from the scene, seeking silence and solitude. Somehow I found myself in
the lonesome library, with its soothing and familiar world of books. Ah,
the wonderful scent of ancient paper bound in leather. And there was
the large soft leather sofa, where on more than one occasion I had
delightedly slept when allowed to spend late, late evenings pouring over
Jonathan's volumes of disremembered lore. Moaning with aching
pleasure, I staggered to the sofa and fell upon it. Happily, I succumbed
to dreamless slumber.

A delicate hand smoothed my hair and pulled me out of sleep. Alisha
sat beside me. "What time is it?" I asked.

"Almost dawn. Everyone's gone."

Swiftly, I sat up. "Jonathan!" She shrugged. "What on earth do you
mean by that absurd motion?"

"He's vanished." Her face was very pale, but her eyes were dry.

"Then we must find him. He has that—thing."

"It can wait. You need to rest." Her voice was soothing, calming,
hypnotic. I tried to meekly protest, but her hand—so smooth and
white—pressed against my lips. "Hush." Groaning in suitable protest, I
allowed myself to sink again into the depths of comfortable leather. My
heavy lids began to shut as Alisha hummed a haunting melody, one that
was disturbingly familiar.

When again I awakened, I was alone. I felt rested, yet worried.
Something, some unwelcome sensation, had shaken me from slumber.
And then I heard it, from outside, the sound of whistling. And my blood
froze, for the dissonant din was identical to the horrid music played by
that gang of goblins on their evil flutes, played to a gargoyle wrapped in
seven veils. I pushed out of the sofa, stumbled over my long scarlet robe
and hurried to the library door. All was still, and the dull light of early
dawn was skulking through the surrounding trees. Fearfully, I found my
way outside. The air was cold and very still. I saw the figure that knelt
within the pagoda. I went to her. How strangely she smiled as I
approached her. I wanted to speak, but some unspeakable fear kept me
numb and silent. I bent my knees and knelt beside her. Leaning toward

me, she pressed her cool mouth to mine. She puckered and exhaled. Both she and Jonathan were skilled at whistling, with a tone that was clear and forceful.

"Please," I begged her. "Stop."

She did not heed me, but rather gazed into the early light, her eyes suddenly rapt with wonder. The chimes above us began to sway. I turned. The thing stood just outside the pagoda. I took in the dark torn garments. It had lost its splendid cloak. The long dark hair was too caked with blood to stream in the growing wind, and some of it was crudely wound around the metal hook that pushed out of the top of the human head. One crimson contact lens still covered a wide dead eyeball. The open mouth was imbued with gore, and from that orifice there came a low unearthly sound of moaning air. Here and there the flesh of the face was torn, and thus I could vaguely make out the blue metal beneath the skin, the damnable blue metal that had somehow conjoined with once-living tissue.

Alisha's lips pressed against my ear. "It hungers for our hot mortal breath." Like a thing possessed she rose. I was too deadened with terror to try and stop her as she walked to that which had once been her brother. My blood was icy sludge, my limbs heavy with immeasurable horror. I watched as the gale increased in potency as the young woman pressed her mouth to the outrageous countenance. How oddly her frail body jerked, what ghastly noise rattled from her pretty mouth. At last she fell before me. I wept to see that she was a lifeless shell, her once-lovely mouth bruised and blue.

The thing that towered above me did not move, yet somehow I felt it beckon me. I heard from beneath the dead face a noise of ravenous air, air not borne of this terrestrial realm. Sobbing, I shut my eyes, trying to exorcise the nightmare before me. Upon my eyelids I could see the tendril shadows of swaying chimes, and my ears took in the sound of wood on wood, metal on metal, glass on glass. But most horrible of all, I could feel the hunger of the dead thing that summoned.

I opened mine eyes. I stretched my sensitive limbs and rose. I lurched to that shell of dilapidated humanity that had once been my friend, but was nigh my awful, my inescapable doom.

*6?*

# AFTERWORD

My buddy John, who worked with me at Cyclops Café, was the inspiration for this yarn. He whistles a lot, and has a clear, strong whistle, like one hears in a Disney film, with perfect pitch. He had just returned from Thailand, and that got my imagination rolling. He's into horror, wears custom-fitted fangs, and—like me—adores Barbra Streisand.

Did anyone catch my little tip to Lovecraft in this tale? "The Host of Haunted Air" is original to this collection.

My brother Alaxander and I were not native-born of Sesqua Valley, but we had dwelt within her haunted shadow since infancy; we knew her well. Her supernatural ways were as normal to us as if we had been her congenital offspring. We had but a vague memory of our Sesquan father, who vanished when we were children. I remembered sitting on his lap and listening to his whispered song, a melody that was echoed in the wind that moved between the dancing trees. There are times, now, when the wind blows above me, that I hear my father's voice. I know that he is not far. He watches from within the secret realm of the valley.

My brother had always been a wild, unruly beast. Defiantly, he would wander the poisoned patches of land near the twin-peaked mountain, those places that felt too deeply the shadow of Mount Selta. The darkness of those places crept into his pulsing heart and altered my brother's sanity. I loved him dearly, but ours was a relationship built on pain.

We watched out native-born friends leave the valley when they came of age, so as to journey to other places, near or far. I had no desire to do so. Mother's health had grown fragile, and I felt it my duty to manage the household, to secure employment. I could not depend on my irresponsible brother for any kind of assistance. And yet I felt an odd panic when, in his twenty-second year, he announced that he would be leaving us so as to spend time in the city.

Alexander was gone for months, during which time we had no word from him. Although a young man, he was still very much a child. I was not surprised when he suddenly returned home. What did startle me was that he was not alone. His companion was a very young lad named Thomas, who despite his youth had about him an air of profound world-weariness. An aspect of pain haunted this boy's beautiful face, and I knew the origin of the needle marks on his arms. To see those same marks on my brother's arms caused me to tremble with a sort of subtle hysteria. I knew that I could say nothing. When Alexander begged for money, I gave in silence. He and Thomas would leave the valley for a day or two, then return with new supplies of the poison that dulled their pretentious woes.

Thomas *had* been a victim of the world's cruelty, but my brother's "suffering" was not authentic. His madness gave him no pain; he was merely playing a part for his beautiful young lover. But Thomas was not fooled. He had lived too long among the genuine victims of society. The young man loved my brother, I suppose, or at least was amused by him; but his real passion was for heroin. He would sometimes shew me a lump of the dirty substance, trying to tempt me to join their ecstasy of habit. I was never enticed. The sight of that dry dirty substance turned my stomach.

I found Thomas, one evening, sitting alone on one of the stone benches in our back garden. His shockingly stunning grey eyes were glazed, and I knew that he was, as he honestly called it, "smacked out". He sat gazing unblinkingly at the silver moon. The long sleeves of his black shirt hid the scars on his arms. I sat next to him.

"I love how the moon looks over this valley, Alma." His low voice spoke in whispered words. "Over the city the moon looks so dead, yellow, kind of mocking. I hate it, hate how it seems to sneer at me. But here, damn, it's awesome; so silver, so—majestic. Look at how those soft beams drift to the mountain, at how Selta's white rock seems to drink in their splendor. It's so cool."

Without thinking, I ran my fingers through his soft dark hair. He took my hand and brought it to his mouth. I trembled at his tender kiss. "Your brother's crazy, Alma."

I sadly smiled. "I know."

He shrugged. "It's cool. I like crazy. I like Alex. He's added an element of interest to a nothing life. Funny, though, how I can't shake off this sense of— doom."

I took his hand and brought it to my mouth, kissed the stains on his fingertips. "Not to worry, Thomas. I'll look over the both of you." Yet even as I spoke the words I felt a chill of dread, of uncertainty. I, too, had felt a sense of foreboding. A few weeks later the disaster struck. I heard from my bedroom window someone weeping in the garden. Looking out, I saw Alexander bending over the body of his friend. I fled my room and rushed to my brother's aid; but he pushed me violently away. I sank to my knees and stared at the pool of brown vomit in which the dead boy's face rested. My bones began to shake. I opened my mouth and joined Alexander in his woe.

We buried Thomas in the cemetery where outsiders to the valley are interred. Alexander seemed lost and more unhinged than ever, and I realized for the first time how much his love for the young city boy had meant to him. Alex began to spend much time in the old brick tower in which natives of Sesqua Valley keep an amazing library of arcane lore. Against better judgment, I stepped into the tower one moonless night. I could hear my brother's uttered chanting. I found him sitting in a circle of candlelight, a book of magick in his lap. I watched as he sliced with a ritual knife the flesh of his palm, forming into the ripped flesh an alchemical symbol that he copied from a chart in the book before him. He seemed not to notice my presence. Quietly, I knelt beside him, understanding the heavy glaze of his eyes. His thin lips were twisted in lunatic mirth. Sliding yellow eyes so as to glance at me, he stupidly giggled and waved his wounded palm before my face.

"What are you doing, brother?"

He brought his bloodstained hand to his mouth, kissed it, and smiled at me with crimson lips. "Thomas," he croaked in a low dry voice. "Thomas, Thomas, Thomas." I slowly rose on shaky limbs and vacated the tower. Leaning against a heavy tree, I wept in darkness. From somewhere in the shadowed valley I heard my father's whispered song. Upon reaching home, I found mother on the living room sofa, fast asleep with an open book at her side. I took the book and closed it, found a blanket and covered her frail form.

Alexander began to sit in the garden at evenings, knitting needles in his hand, a ball of yellow yarn in his lap. I could hear his whispered mantra carried to me on the evening wind. Occasionally, he would stop and dig with one of the needle's points into the symbol carved into his palm. He would hold the palm to moonlight, bring to it a strand of dark hair. I watched as he drenched the hair with his gore. I listened as he spoke his lover's name.

I went to him the next evening, curious yet cautious, so as to observe his work. I was surprised at his almost kindly smile. The ball of yarn lay next to him on the bench, and in his hand he held a thick strand of human hair. Seeing me stare at that hair, he brought it to my nostrils. "It smells of him, doesn't it, Alma?"

I took in its potent fragrance. "Yes."

"Yes." He took it from me and picked up his doll of yarn. I saw the strands of bloodstained hair that were twined into the tiny figure. "I'm weaving a conjuration of memory, sister dear. I'll share it with you once it's completed. You loved him too, I know."

I gazed into his moonlit eyes and did not recognize the creature before me. He seemed to sense my distress, for his eyes grew wide and wild. Suddenly, he held one of the knitting needles threateningly before my eye. A low growl issued from some deep place in his throat. And then his body convulsed and contorted. Madly, he stabbed a needle into his bloody palm. Gasping, moaning, he held that stained hand to the moon, chanting again and again his dead one's name.

I ran into the woods and screamed my father's name. I tried to summon forth the mauve shadow that was the unseen realm wherein those borne of the valley eventually returned. I did not know if I was Sesquan enough to enter into that sacred secret realm; I knew only that life in my mortal world had become too unbearable. Finding myself within a clearing, I entered a ring of ancient stones, knelt and wept. A Sesquan breeze came to me, brought to me the scents and sounds of the valley, and beneath the usual sounds I heard my father's voice, forbidding me escape from mortal destiny. I clawed into the sod and screamed, and blended with my frenzied grief was another scream, in a voice I knew.

Trembling, I rose. Slowly, I returned homeward. Entering the back garden, I saw the still body that was sprawled on the ground. I knelt in wind and moonlight beside my brother's corpse. Oh, how chilly was that wind, how morbidly frigid that moonlight. Gently, I removed the needle that he had insanely thrust into his throat. Beside him lay small yellow doll. It writhed in silver moonbeams. Within one woven paw it weakly held the other knitting needle, which it clumsily tried to thrust into its arm. Bending to it, I gently took it up. Bringing it to my face, I tenderly kissed it. I took in its smell of blood, of Thomas, of magick.

Yes, my brother. I, too, had loved the city lad. And so I took up the knitting needle that I had pulled out of your neck, that implement with your blood upon its tip. I held that needle to her majesty the moon, uttered the words of wonder that I had learned from listening to you. I thrust that needle into my palm and etched thereon the arcane symbol. I held my dripping hand over the doll of yarn, pressed into my liquid essence the needle's tip. I touched the bloodstained needle into the thing of woven yarn and dead man's hair, that thing of occult sentience that I would nourish lovingly for the remainder of my sorrowful life.

*¿?*

# AFTERWORD

This is one of my most autobiographical stories, containing as it does many memories of my relationship with a street punk named Todd, whom I seduced and who lived with me for four years. Our traumatic eleven-year relationship (a non-sexual love affair) ended with his death by heroin overdose, dying as I held him in my arms. He had slumped over, and I thought he had merely passed out. But something alerted me that all was not well, and when I moved his head, I saw the pool of vomit spreading on my bedroom carpet. This death has haunted my fiction for many years, but found its most eloquent expression herein. The strange thing is that I began to write about Todd's death long before it actually happened. My first pro sale, to the anthology CUTTING EDGE, was about Todd's death. Eventually I based a Sesqua Valley character on Todd, naming the character "Nelson," Todd's last name. This way I could write "about" my lovely boy and not always kill him off. Much of my writing, you see, is a form of dealing with my dark reality. It is not, as some would claim, a form of escape. When it comes to reality, my darlings, there is no escape.

"The Woven Offspring" was first published in LORE #9, and featured an amazing illustration by my great friend, Jeffrey Thomas.

*"I'm a little girl."*

—H. P. Lovecraft

## I.

Sinuously, she twined around the tall stone pillar, licked famished lips and watched the young man run away. She laughed at the memory of his scolding words.

"It won't do, Martha," he had yelled, emotional blood pumping patches of red into his usually pale face, the blotched face that was so close to her own.

"Sod you, little man, it *will* do. *I* will do. You cannot control me."

"Someone needs to try, damn it. You obviously can't control yourself. That's what scares me. Lordy, you think you're so damn clever, calling forth storm and shadow. That's plain common in this place. But when you start hanging out with bad types and dancing on tainted ground ..."

"Enough. I haven't time for adolescent jealousy."

"Pah!" he shouted, spitting at the ground. She spat also, and watched as her saliva joined his, mingled slime.

Martha licked her smirking lips. "I have no interest in your boring sense of caution. Look." She fingered one of the symbols carved on the old stone pillar. "Don't these arcane etchings call to your soul and boil in your blood?"

The young man grabbed her hand and moved so as to block the pillar from her view. "You're new to the valley. You're intoxicated. I've lived here since childhood. I know to avoid the places of tainted air and lunacy."

Her eyes grew fierce. Savagely, she grabbed his spiky hair and pushed her body against his. Peter cried as she dug the nails of one thin hand into the flesh just beneath his chin. She forced his cheek against one of the symbols carved onto ancient stone. "Looney, am I? Is that what you're saying? But, little man, I was with you and Catherine last night, when together we conjured flowing darkness and kissed the pulsing air. I saw your occult passion."

"You're hurting me."

"Poor lamb," she cooed, then let go her hold. What was it that she saw in his eyes? Fear, certainly, and panic; and excitement. He had secretly enjoyed the pain and panic. Grinning, she bent to kiss the little bloodstained rips on his neck. Then, raising her mouth to his soft ear, she began to laugh, with laughter that soon grew in depravity. Peter suddenly pushed her from him and fled. She watched him, barking lunatic laughter; then she turned and sexually wrapped her limbs around the pillar. She kissed an arcane symbol, and listened to the distant sound that spilled from some dark place in the woodland. Turning, Martha raised her face to sunlight and playfully moaned. She knew that sound, knew from whom it filtered. Her legs moved, stepping to a steep incline that led down to Dark Swamp. The young woman scurried down the slope, clinging to the slender trunks of pale narrow trees for support.

He stood in pitch of darkness, in the place where edacious sunlight could not filter. She could just make out his conservative dress, the dark grey suit, the clean white shirt. His Panama hat was rakishly tipped over his wide brow. Her eyesight accustomed itself to the lack of light, and slowly she walked to him. Yes, now she could see the sallow face, the intelligent eyes. She discerned the flute pressed to the bestial mouth. Martha went to him, this creature so absolutely a spawn of the valley, its first-borne. Her hand reached out to stroke the pronounced cheekbones, the aquiline nose. Trembling, her hand stroked the weird instrument. Martha shuddered at the thick and chilly air that issued as notes from the mouths of strange wooden faces.

The creature took the flute from his mouth and smiled. She gazed up at him, this tall man who, the enormous width of his shoulders notwithstanding, was prodigiously lean. Ah, his silver eyes, how mischievously they gleamed and tempted. Martha turned to the reeking swamp and felt her companion move behind her. He placed the flute against her lips, then pushed it into her mouth. She tingled as the cold wooden stem subtly shaped itself to the contours of her mouth. Something in the substance of which it was made seemed to filter through her mouth and sink through her lungs, churning her gasps of breathing. It pulled her hot living air from her and pushed it through its openings. The still swamp air was filled with low weird music.

"Yes," said the lips pressed sweetly to her ear. "Assist the moan of music. Succor the gases that brood beneath the viscous slime. Let it rise in coils that shape themselves outlandishly. Evoke, Martha, evoke." Things began to filter through the ooze and rise above the water. They shaped themselves in imitation to the faces that had been carved onto the flute, and when they opened wide their mouths the noise that issued forth froze her blood and chilled her brain. "Call them to you, darling. Taste their diaphanous kisses." Oh, yes, how she longed to do so. How they called to her, these things that stank of slime and magick. They breathed their poisonous song and called to the lunacy that hungered deep within the drooling woman.

With savage force the flute was torn from Martha's mouth. Catherine

Leigh stood beside them, quivering with rage. "This is inexcusable, Simon. Take this *thing* and go." She slapped the flute into his wide white hand. Saying nothing, but secretly smiling, he departed.

The fog of faces spiralled still above the swamp water, and Martha reached out to them with longing. Catherine took her lover's hand and brought it gently to her lips. "Let me be your link to sanity," she whispered, bending to Martha's temple and brushing it with a kiss. A wonderful warmth dissolved the mordant chill that had enveloped Martha's brain; and as she slowly closed her eyes, the filmy faces dissolved into wisps that sank into the swamp.

Martha shivered. "It's so cold here."

"Come." They turned from the dark water and hiked up the slope, into sunshine. Hand in hand, they walked toward town. "Why do you associate with that beast?"

"He's fun."

"He's dangerous."

"Same thing. Don't be such a mother, Catherine."

"Darling, you're being reckless. I don't like seeing you so out of control."

"I don't desire control. I supposed little Peter blabbed."

"I made him, when I saw the cuts on his neck. Why must you be so savage with him?"

"He likes it. Anyway, he was treating me as if I were some infant. Hah, the gall." She stopped their walk and sat upon a patch of thick green grass. Catherine knelt next to her and stroked her auburn hair.

"Peter is young, and so are you. You've lots of time. You needn't be in such a hurry to experience things. There's no need for rash behavior."

"You both think I'm crazy."

"Nonsense."

"Oh, but I am. Yet wasn't it my wildness that attracted you when we met in the city? Isn't that why you seduced me and brought me here? And when I came to this valley and sensed—its power, felt it in my heart and soul, didn't you say that, yes, I was one of the adopted ones? I'm a creature of this wild and wanton place, passionately so. You are, too."

Softly, Catherine laughed, and Martha kissed the mirthful mouth. "My darling Martha, how I love you. And so let me be precise. I've hinted before of the places one must avoid. Now I shall be blunt. There are places here, not many, that are not safe for outsiders such as you. They are places where earth and air are poisoned. To breathe that air, to walk that ground, is to be seduced by lunacy. Most inhabitants can easily ignore the calling of such dark realms, but there are those—those sensitive few—for whom these are seductive territories."

"Why do you always call me an outsider? I feel like I belong here."

"You do belong, with me. The valley enjoys your human warmth, your passion, your evocative dreaming. But there's a part of you, an emotional element that lacks caution. It often controls you. And then, yes, you act a little mad. I'm asking you to let me teach you how to avoid that little patch of madness in your psyche. May I?"

Martha bent back her head and gazed at the white mountain that towered above the valley. She blew into the shimmering air and stroked her blouse, undoing its buttons. Her delicious breasts were exposed. "I'm the putty in you hands. Knead me to your desire."

Catherine licked her lips and bent low. Their limbs entwined.

## II.

But madness is a thing that cannot be contained, cannot be controlled. It broods, and waits; it smiles and lays its plots. Sesqua Valley, wondrous though it is, wears its taint of insanity, as Catherine had mentioned. Yet even she did not fully understand this potent lunacy.

Madness called to madness. It was not by chance that, hand in hand, Martha and young Peter had found themselves approaching the tainted loam of Sesqua's poisoned place, that place where diseased hunger broods beneath moist soil. Ah, how that hunger yearned for the wild free woman; how it called to her in dreaming.

The day had been extremely hot, and Peter had been obsessed with watching sunlight shimmer on Mount Selta. "Look at how the white stone glistens, at how the waves of heat bend and flow just above the surface. And, man, that surface, like something composed of pure crystal. Come on, I want to touch it."

"No, Peter. It's too hot for mountain climbing." She was nude from the waist up, and wiped her belly and breasts with a discarded blouse. She had appareled the boy in one of her summer frocks, through which his nude silhouette could easily be viewed. She held out her hand. He returned and took it, then placed his other hand beneath one heavy breast. They kissed, and playfully she bit his tongue. A chase ensued, and in his hot frolic Peter paid no heed to the direction of their running. But fervor suddenly subdued as the grass beneath his naked feet grew stiff and dead and queerly cold. And then there was no grass, but only moist dark earth. And just to his left was a stunted distorted tree from which a wretched stench fouled the thickening air.

"Martha, no! Stop."

"Why?" She slowly sauntered to him. "What ails thee, timid youth?" He could not reply, could only look nervously about. "Peter, must you be such a milksop? We're here together. Safety in numbers." He watched as she walked to the tree and tore a sliver of bark from it. The sap that spilled onto her hand was thick and red. She held to him her scarlet hand, then pressed it to her face. His fear blossomed into anger.

"Come on, we're going. Look at you, you stupid freak." Ripping the blouse from her hand, Peter prepared to wipe the mess from her lovely face. But when he went to touch the cloth to flesh, he saw in horror that the thick ruddy substance was sinking through pores, into her skin. Martha opened her mouth and deeply sighed. He shivered at the touch of her frozen breath. "Martha, please."

Deeply, with altered voice, she laughed, then sank onto her knees. Greedily, she clawed into thick dank mud, then held the stained hand to Peter. Clumsily, she moved forward, dragging legs, her knees growing thick with filth. He gazed in terror at the glistening black grue that darkly coated her hand, that awful stuff that she was going to smear on him. Like a frightened child he turned and fled. Martha stretched her mouth with maniacal laughter.

A low note of music floated to her. She looked and saw his slow approach, the one who understood her. He offered her a hand and happily she took it. Simon watched in wonder as the viscous slime with which she was coated crawled into the texture of her flesh, that flesh that subtly darkened with unnatural hue.

"Your friends will worry, and they won't enjoy seeing me with you. This place is very cold, don't you find it so?" At the suggestion of his words, Martha began to tremble, to shiver. He placed an arm around her waist and gasped at the chilliness of her altered substance.

"Hungry, it's oh so hungry," she muttered, digging a foot into the earth. Then she reached for the flute that peeked from the inside pocket of his jacket. She slid it out and held it to sunlight, then forced it into his mouth. "It wants your noise."

Simon pushed breath into the instrument. Music filled the heavy air. Martha laughed, a low guttural sound. She pointed at a place in the mud before them, a place that subtly moved with whirling motion. The black mud spread with opening. Fiercely, the woman ripped the flute from Simon's mouth and, falling again to her knees, thrust the instrument into the grime. Her arms wrapped sinuously around Simon's leg.

"See, it sinks. It's covered up. Hungry, the ground is so hungry. It wants your face. It likes your silver eyes, your soft jelly."

He looked at where the flute had sunken from sight. Something touched him, yea, even he, with a velvet kiss of fear. "Time to go," he whispered, lifting her in his sturdy arms and carrying her away.

## III.

Catherine looked deeply into the tall man's eyes. Simon's slight expression of unease, much as he tried to mask it, perplexed her. Still, she could sense his cunning, his refusal to tell her complete and naked truth. He always had to play his little games, this one. "Thank you," she said at last, "for bringing her home. Martha hasn't been herself of late."

"She is unhinged. Did little Peter tell you where she was wandering? Really, why you must go to city dwellings and seduce these innocent outsiders and bring them ..."

"Once!" she shouted, then looked at the ceiling and hoped that her anger had not been heard in the room above. "Only once. And although I'm not as ancient as you, I know when a soul belongs in the valley."

"Pah!" He twisted his oddly-formed mouth with scorn and blew out air.

"So do you, else you wouldn't be taking such an especial interest in her. But that will cease."

He raised an eyebrow and smiled a cryptic smile. "Indeed?"

"Indeed. Really, you're so queer, Simon," she continued, going to a window and gazing at the benighted woodland. "I suppose it comes from being the first-borne of Sesqua's shadow and lingering here for, how many centuries? Why is that? Have you become so debauched by daemonic magick that the valley no longer wants your return?"

"Oh, it's called—often. I do not care to return, not yet. I'm having far too much fun."

"Ah. Well, then, I'll let you go so that you may resume your games." She turned to stare at him one last time. "You will not taint Martha with you sport. She is mine."

He donned his hat and smiled beneath the shadow of its rim. "I think, you know, that the valley has claimed her as its own." And uttering low laughter, he departed.

She stood in silence, listening to her heartbeat. The awful creature had expressed her secret fear. At the sound of footfalls on carpeted stairs, she wiped tears from eyes and commanded equanimity. Peter came to her, stood behind her and wrapped his thick arms around her waist.

"So the fiend has gone. I heard you yelling at each other." He leaned to kiss her face and saw a single teardrop that had escaped her fingers. "He's upset you. Shall I kick his ass?"

She forced laughter. "No, darling, he's of no concern. How is Martha?"

"I don't know. She's ... different. That stuff she was covered with, she reeks of it. I've bathed her twice, to no effect. She smells of that devil ground, totally tainted. It's sickening. And her breath," he went on wildly. "It's so cold, like death. And she won't let me hold her. Sometimes, the way she looks at me ..." He shuddered, moaning.

Catherine turned to face him and gently took him into her arms.

Above them, Martha woke from dreaming. Oh, those dark visions, and the thing that had called to her. It was a thing that she had buried in the moist hungry mud. Its many faces had partaken of the slime that had oozed into mouths. In vision she had seen the slender wooden thing supernaturally expand, stretch as the filth of that place had mingled with its structure. Those small chiseled faces, deep beneath the denigrated dirt, expanded in transformation. They clumsily opened their expanding mouths and called. They sang to her in dreaming, and dreamily she answered, with low moaning that issued as a cloud of glacial exhalation.

Quietly, Martha got out of bed. Dressed only in a nightgown of amber silk, she stealthily walked to the back stairway that led down into the pantry. Gently, she opened the pantry door that led to the back of the house. Quickly, softly laughing at silver moonlight, she rushed into the waiting woodland, in answer to the thing that called and called. The cool earth became chilly as she stepped on tainted loam. She sighed in twisted pleasure at its touch upon her naked feet. A nearby twisted tree leaned toward her, as if to drink the contaminated cloud of breath that issued from her mouth.

She found the place wherein the flute had descended, and there she knelt and clawed with one small hand into the filth. The fragrance of her warm humanity spilled to the thick distorted thing that had called her, that large ravenous object that slowly rose to meet her hand. Martha lowly moaned at its touch, then scooted back and watched the creature lift itself out of dark moist earth. It rose, like a mutated trunk of some diseased tree. One by one it revealed its many faces, those chiseled visages that now were twice the size of her own. It rose, this massive beast of converted wood. The mouths opened with howls of foghorn potency, a sound that shook awake the sleeping denizens of Sesqua Valley.

Oh, the cold cold air that issued in fetid clouds of poisoned air from those mouths, an aether that enveloped her, that became a part of her. She crawled to one of the wailing mouths and reached into it, deeply. It tightly shut.

Martha turned to the sound of human tumult that grew in force behind her. With a free hand she crazily waved at the terrorized faces of those whom she knew. She laughed as Peter screamed her name and tried to reach her but was repelled by the swirling mist of baneful air that protected the nameless thing. "Do something!" the boy frantically cried to Catherine, as the mud beneath Martha began to spread, to open, to devour. The madwoman turned to the monstrous face that had her arm clamped inside its mouth and bent to kiss it as slowly they descended into hungry earth.

Simon Gregory Williams smiled excitedly at the scene before him, at the crowing crowd that grew in number, a crowd that seemed paralyzed by fear. A few brave souls feebly attempted to brave the noxious mist and save the laughing woman, but were utterly repelled. Simon marveled at the bestial thing that had once been his favorite flute. Yuggoth, how it had blossomed with heinous permutation. Yet it was still the instrument that he had found decades ago, that he had nourished with dark magick. He understood it, and thus he opened wide his mouth and called unto it. His voice issued as low howling not unlike the sound that wailed from the churning mouths of the blasphemous entity. Those horrid faces shifted so as to gaze at the valley's first-borne. He approached, still bellowing, and from atop the twin peaked mountain other beasts raised their snouts and joined in the vociferation. He raised a sallow hand and pushed it into the rancid brume, that mist that seemed to melt away at his touch.

Catherine watched, and despite her rage and horror, she could not help but be impressed. Yes, Simon was a creature of arcane knowledge, a wizard *par excellence*. And although this secret learning had affected his powerful mind and twisted it toward the darkest of evil things, still one could not watch his performance without secretly longing to taste the things he knew, to wield such potency.

Simon wailed, touching the tree-like entity. It opened the jaws that held Martha's arm. Peter scurried to join them and helped Simon pull her, screaming as she fought them, from the hungry sod. Oh, she fought; she bit and clawed, and with a fury of strength, she escaped them.

"You dare to deny me my heritage?" she screamed in frenzy. "The valley *calls* for me, for body and soul. We will not be denied!" She fled the scene with a fury of speed that those who followed could not match. She screamed and laughed at their calls; she howled an ancient name. She stumbled over root and bush, yet still they could not catch her, those would-be rescuers. Martha found at last the slope that led to Dark Swamp, and with unholy glee she rolled down that hill, coming at last to thick dank water.

## IV.

*From ye journal of Simon Gregory Williams, Esq.*

I thought it best to vacate the valley for a time. Perhaps my absence would help to soothe emotional seething. I did not, of course, blame myself for what most others saw as tragic consequences. Catherine was unusually quiet, compared to her immature and emotional boyfriend. I think that she understands how the valley will not be denied its longings, its appetites. I felt no need to follow the others in their wild pursuit, far too exhausting. And, really, I had no need—I followed with my *mind.* I alone knew exactly where the wretched soul had fled. We have some kind of link, poor Martha and myself. Deep beneath the gloop of swamp water she may dwell, dead yet dreaming; yet in her sodden bed of semi-death she calls to me. She has, indeed, become a thing of Sesqua Valley, combined as she is with the rotten swamp substance that mingles with her rotting carcass.

It was deliciously hideous, this situation; and yet I knew a way to salve the dilemma and shew unto all and sundry that—beast though I undoubtedly am—I was one who cared for one's own. I have long existed on this terrestrial plane. I have been a searcher after horrors; have haunted the strange far places. I have learned much, in dark secret corners of the hideous world outside the valley. I have poured over the black lore of antient tomes that lie in a plethora of hidden libraries. I recalled something that I had read in one crumbling worm-infested work. I remembered reading of an object, remembered too the rumor of where it might be located. I had been there before, decades gone: the quaint, mist-enshrouded town of Kingsport. I had visited an old man who lived in a centuried cottage, a terrible old fellow. I had also ascended the northern crag, that high, high place where the cliff extends into strange clouds, just beyond an even stranger house high in the eternal mist. I lingered in thought of that fascinating place, and enthrallment beset my hungry heart. I desired to see Kingsport in the glare of modernity.

Thus I journeyed, by tram and train, to the dream-soaked town of Kingsport. Although a place still quaint, I was abhorred to witness how the old town had been ravaged by modernity. Fah, how loud and fast and uncouth, this contemporary world. Still, still the antient settlement wore remnants of its beautiful heritage. I took in the chunks of solid past in the cobbled streets, the tottering houses from whose planks of wood I could smell the psychic residue of anterior aeons.

I sauntered through a public square and slowly passed a small crowd. They listened to a bearded man of middle years who was clad in quasi-religious vestment. He was an awful sight, standing on his plastic milk crate and stabbing fingers into the late afternoon air. Yet even more absurd were the wide-eyed idiots to whom he advocated. There was the frantic twitching woman, whose hair was a matted mess, who gazed at all and sundry with tremulous affection as she muttered the name of Christian deity. And, Yuggoth, there—the two gentlemen (sic) who reeked of the whiskey they surreptitiously passed one to the other. Ah, how they nodded their dull-witted approval.

"No pestilence of alcohol has stained these lips," proclaimed the bearded one, as the two gents looked at each other with secret guilt. "No courtesan perspiration has soaked these godly limbs. This mouth has paid no homage to the other gods." Ah—now *this* caught my attention. I moved into the crowd of on-lookers. The fanatic man seemed to sense my keen interest. We locked eyes. "There are no other gods before me. The filthy cults have whispered their secrets into the ears of dreaming, but we have paid no regard. Heed not the dead-yet-dreaming devils, or the promise they portend. Utter not their foul names, nor make to them their loathsome signals."

This bloody hypocrite. He spoke as do the television evangelists who decry depravity, all the while burning for the touch of whoredom. I held him, this prince of fools, within my steady gaze. I raised my hand and made unto him the Elder Sign. Ah! How he did twitch and shriek and totter from his crate, foaming at the mouth with fear. Whistling "Onward, Christian Soldiers", I walked away from the confused people who bent helplessly to their prostrate preacher.

I walked beneath the leaning roofs of timeworn houses, breathing in the time of twilight. I walked over wooden bridges, down old lanes, coming at last to the iron gate that was black with age. Behind it, gathered in peculiar groupings in the overgrown yard, were oddly shaped stones on which had been painted curious designs. I looked and saw in assembling nightfall the venerable cottage. How it sagged with age as it huddled beneath weird dark trees. How black were the small paned windows that still contained their delicate antique glass. From out the low-hanging gutters there spread an outcropping of grey weed and yellow grass, thick and pale as the beard of some East India sea captain.

I looked, and saw the faint glow that dimly illumed the small front porch. He sat there, in the gloom, a man who read by lantern light. I pushed open the gate, and its groan alerted the bloke of my being.

"May I help you?" the reader asked, closing his book.

"I don't mean to disturb you, sir. It's only that I visited this place many years ago. I was wondering if the elderly gentleman still resided here. But I sense from the unkempt atmosphere that he is gone."

"Yep, died some years ago."

"Ah, how sad. I was hoping to listen to more of his peculiar stories."

"He had his store of those," said the other, laughing and extending his hand. "Winfield Scot."

I bent forward and took his hand. "Simon Williams."

His eyes grew large as his lantern's glow fell upon my Sesquan visage. "Jesus, what happened to your face?"

I smiled at his earthy lack of manners. "Genetics," I replied.

"Huh, too bad. So, you spoke to the old codger, eh?"

"You knew him?"

"Only to wave at. But I've always loved this place. It feeds my dreams. Sometimes I'd come and sleep beneath that tree over there. He'd never bother me. After he passed, I just kept coming. Found this lantern out in back. Looked so old I didn't think it'd work, but it works just fine."

I inspected the lantern. It was, indeed, an apparatus of antiquity. I could easily imagine it being used one century ago so as to light the procession of some nameless festal rite. "You've never been inside then?"

"Oh, a couple of times, with some artist buddies who were here for a season. It's a weird old place."

"I'd like to see it again."

"Yeah? Well, it ain't too late just yet." I faintly smiled at this cryptic remark. He took from his coat pocket a bottle of spirits. "Just need a little fortification. Want a nip?"

"No, thank you."

He shrugged. "Suit yourself." After an uncertain pause he rose and walked to the door. Stupidly, he merely stood and stared at the brass doorknob.

"Allow me," I said, walking past him and pushing open the heavy door. It made no sound, but we did, as the smell of antient secrets pushed into our enquiring faces.

"Maybe we'd better not," he mumbled, but I was already inside. The amber glow of his lantern flowed behind me. I saw the curios that crowded every corner. There was a huge rusted ship's anchor, and there a shelf of queer clay figurines. On a long low table I saw a row of dusty old bottles, inside which, from a length of string or wire, hung unusually shaped pendulums. I moved so as to investigate them, but felt a restraining hand upon my arm. "You don't want to go near those. Something inside them's gone bad, they stink of death."

I backed away. Somewhere in this cluttered area was the potent thing I sought. I shut my eyes and called to it. Something tickled my brain in response. I opened my eyes and turned to one murky corner. The ceiling there sagged low with warping. I detected the shape before slowly discerning it— dim, pale, *outré*. Slowly, I approached the bestial thing that stood like some mould-shade in the gloom. I reached out and touched its rough white fur. The lantern's glow found me and fell upon the creature of dark continent.

"Great Christ, I forgot about her," Mr. Scot exclaimed as I pressed my hand upon the wide dead face. "Almost something familiar about her, isn't there, like some link to the forgotten past. Check out her tits."

I'll do no such thing, I thought. Rather, I reached for the thing that nestled between those ample mammiferous organs, the object that I sought. I had seen its likeness in diagram, on a mouldering fragment of *Al Azif*, whereon its occult properties had been vaguely explained. This was exactly what I needed.

I felt a shadowed form behind me, very close. I sensed that he too was studying the object that I held. "It's like a Janus head, but of opposite genders. Notice the clasp? We couldn't figure how to open it. Not that we cared to, really. Didn't like the way it felt in our hand. Don't you sense it, a kind of nasty foreboding that creeps into your skin? Ugh!"

I let go of it. "Put it on me."

"*What!*"

I turned, took the lantern from him and held it high. "Remove it from her and place it around my neck." I gazed steadily into his troubled eyes and felt my own eyes darken with daemonic vim.

"Whatever," he mumbled. Stepping to the beast he softly cursed, then reached for the chain and pulled. I enjoyed the way he shuddered at its touch. I loved his quizzical, worried expression as he raised the work of antient sorcery above my hat. I leaned close to him as he slipped it on me. Oh! The memories that sailed into my mind. Dank wet darkness, distant esoteric drumming. Ah, the epicene faces that praised me with glistening eyes. And below each face swung an amulet identical to my own. Heavily, I sighed. "Jesus, mister, you look like you're gonna kiss me."

Queerly, I smiled. Leaning to him, I kissed his eye, and felt the fearful vision spread from my mind into his own. He lacked the Sesquan nerves, and screaming fearfully he turned, fell over an object in the dark, and crawled from the terrible old cottage.

## V.

Peter Wentworth knelt before Dark Swamp and wept. Martha was there, restlessly beneath. This he knew, for she had called to him in woeful dream. Her once lovely essence, distorted by the ingredients in which she had been submerged, longed for the touch of his hot human flesh. Go, little man, and she will kiss you with her spreading, splitting lips. She will lick you with the sponge that once had been a tongue. He dipped a tremulous hand into the filthy water.

"Peter." The woman's voice mingled love with caution. Her hand pressed gently into his blond crew cut. "Come away, darling."

He turned his glistening eyes to Catherine. "She calls. She hungers for my kiss. Come on, we'll twine our three bodies just like we used to and scream and soak and pump and bite ..."

Catherine fell to her knees beside him. "Martha is gone. What you hear is a trick of this cursed place. You must fight the lure of lunacy."

A noise snapped in the deep shade of another portion of the swamp. The tall figure was vaguely discernable in the copious gloom. Shaking with rage, Peter rose to his feet. "You stay away from her! Infernal devil, be gone!"

The sallow face beneath the wide-brimmed hat sardonically smiled and stifled a yawn. "A pox on you, ignoble youth. It is I and I alone who can bring you and your beloved together again."

Catherine dipped a hand into swamp water, raised it high, watched the liquid return in droplets to the swamp. "How?"

"Don't listen to him!" Peter shrieked, spittle foaming at his mouth.

Simon slowly approached. "You know that I've been away, to a strange mist-enshrouded town. There have I found a most marvelous thing and a wonder. A thing of potency." He gazed steadfastly at Catherine. "You know I do not speak idle chatter. You realize my abilities."

"And although I want to fight it, I know that I can trust you, diabolic though you be. Depraved or not, you are my brother of the valley."

Simon's silver eyes flashed with emotion. "I am indeed. And you, young sirrah, who has lived in this region since childhood, who had been adopted by the valley's song and shadow—do you trust me?"

Catherine rose and tenderly linked her arm with Peter's. "Yes," the young man whispered.

"Excellent." Simon drew close to them. "You will place this amulet around your masculine throat. But first, I will place my finger here and—lo!—see how it opens. You, my sister, will intone this potent chant. You read Arabic, of course."

"Of course." She took the piece of yellow parchment.

Simon reached for Peter. "No!" the youth yelled, moving away and shuddering with repulsion. "I don't want you touching me. Let her put it on me."

Tutting, Simon handed Catherine the amulet. "Will you oblige the child?"

"Of course," she answered, trying not to smile. Taking the object from Simon's hand, she studied it. It was tremendously old, and she could feel its potent promise of magick in its heavy weight. Both sides wore an oval face, one male visage, one female. Each countenance had been formed with androgynous beauty. It was fastened to a chain that was composed of material she could not name.

"*May* we commence?" Catherine laughed at Simon's impatience. Yes, he is such a child of the valley, this first-borne son. He is so hot to work dark wonder. Magick was a mighty drug to him, an addiction that insisted on submission. She obeyed. Leaning to her lover, Catherine deeply kissed Peter's mouth, then raised the amulet over his head. Nature died in the woodland around them as the valley seemed to hold its breath in anticipation. The lovers joined hands above his head, and together they placed the amulet around his throat. Peter gasped and sighed. He closed his eyes and cautiously listened. From some other place and time he could hear a distant drumming, and slowly he began to sway to the sound that only he could apprehend.

Catherine brought the piece of parchment that had been folded into the amulet before her silver eyes, those eyes that saw easily in the darkness of the haunted habitation. She spoke the spell and felt its force on her vibrating lips. Nearby, the tall sallow man, who had memorized the spell, softly echoed the words. Catherine turned to Simon and saw that his hand was held toward the swamp water. She raised her hand, a hand that trembled with excitement. Mauve mist began to form above the water, and something slowly surfaced, breaking through stagnation. It was a soggy husk of flesh that had once been mortal woman.

Peter moaned and swayed as the deteriorated thing moved with aching sentience, dragging itself through the liquid sewage, toward him. The creature raised a sagging face, opened what had once been a mouth, and gagged his name. Screaming Martha's name, the young man clumsily moved into the water so as to meet her. He pulled, his voice a strangled cry, until both he and his burden were free from the swamp. Utterly exhausted, he crashed to the ground, clasping the thing of sodden flesh in tight embrace.

Suddenly overwhelmed, Catherine rushed and fell beside them. Gently, she touched the seaweed hair, the remnant of a remembered face. That ruined countenance turned to gaze at her with half-dead eyes and raised its shapeless mouth to Catherine's hand. The porous sponge that had once been tongue slid forth and nestled in her palm.

Simon watched with eyes that danced excitement. He chanted still the mighty spell, the words that had awakened death and would conjoin it with vital life. He chanted, and that which had once been Martha dropped its heavy wet head to Peter's neck. It moved as if in copulation, trying to squeeze its dome under the chain around the young man's throat. Catherine lifted the amulet and watched the soggy face spread beneath the chain. The amulet began to alter, and Catherine dropped it, shocked. She watched as its metal became soft and liquid like unto the rotted flesh of the woman she once had loved. She watched the weird metal melt and coalesce its fundamental nature with the flesh of the embracing couple. And they, the living and the dead, also began to liquefy and fuse, becoming mingled flesh. The valley's mauve mist, that supernatural entity of which the children of Sesqua Valley were a part, billowed toward them from the woodland and enveloped the congealing flesh.

The combinative forms shuddered. It raised a double head composed of faces that blended and solidified into one beautiful mixture of he and she. The healthy masculine flesh womanly softened, and Catherine wept with joyous wonder as that flesh became solid and healthy and sensual. He who was she raised itself to its knees and took Catherine into its embrace, their heaving breasts meeting in ecstasy as faces passionately pressed together.

Simon took a flute from out his jacket pocket and, playing with manic motion, began to move in rich redemptive danse.

*¿?*

# AFTERWORD

This new story is a combination of two old stories. Ever since John
Pelan forced me to write my story for THE CHILDREN OF
CTHULHU three times, so as to lengthen it, I've suddenly found it
easier to write stories of length. I simply needed to try harder and
discipline myself, and thanks to John I found my way to longer wordage
and real story telling. With this story, I continue to investigate the life of
my favorite new character, Simon Gregory Williams, the first-borne
spawn of Sesqua Valley. I hope to write many more tales of this dark
and twisted wizard. This story is published here for the first time.

"From childhood's hour I have not been
as others were—"

—Edgar Allan Poe

## I.

It was music that brought me into a twilit world of wonder and mystery. I had lived in my new quarters for a few days, delighting in my escape from my wretched former existence. I had savings enough so that I could live in frugal comfort for six months. Gladly, I left my dreary job, my boring friends, and my unsympathetic family and found a lonely apartment in a forgotten and nigh desolate section of the city. My escape was complete. I had kept only my books, my typewriter, and my cat. No one had a clue as to my departure or destination. I had deliciously disappeared. For one half year I would live a fantasy life of reading and writing in complete solitude. Discovering a wonderful Asian restaurant, it became my habitual mid-day haunt. Other than that and infrequent shopping, I stayed inside my spacious and inexpensive rooms.

Before moving in, I had told my landlord—Mr. Bullon—that I was an author working on a new book and thus needed a room that was very quiet, not one with windows facing the street. True, there was not much traffic noise, the building existing in such a deserted and unpopulated part of town; but the slightest screech of modernity was to me an abhorrent torment, and thus I procured rooms facing the back courtyard. All was very silent indeed. Until, one late evening, as I sat in my comfy armchair with pen in hand and cat on lap, that there came from directly across the hall a faint sound of someone at their pianoforte.

I was at first annoyed at this intrusion of sound, subdued as it was; yet the longer I listened the more beguiling I found the music. It contained a quality of sorrow such as I had never experienced from song. As I continued to strain with listening, tears welled within mine eyes. And when, abruptly, the music ceased, I found myself longing for its continuation.

The next morning I encountered the ancient landlord in the laundry room. "Things are going well, Mr. Stone? Your writing?"

"Yes, very well, thank you."

"Your rooms are very quiet, yes?"

"They are perfect. I do hear, occasionally, the piano playing from across the hall, but that is all."

"Ah, I shall tell Miss Greive to keep it down, as they say."

"Oh, it's not at all a nuisance, my dear fellow. It's so late at night when she plays, I'm usually finished with my work at that hour."

"Late at night! No, no, it cannot be allowed. I shall inform her." And he rushed off before I could protest any further, leaving me feeling frustrated and annoyed. I spent the afternoon feeling agitated, so much so that I could not concentrate on reading and writing. When early evening came, I made bold enough to step into the hallway and knock upon my neighbor's door. After a brief wait, it opened. My nostrils were delighted with a lovely fragrance. The woman who stood before me was very beautiful, so much so that for a moment I could not speak. She raised her brows in query.

"Do forgive me. I'm from across the hallway …"

"Ah, Mr. Stone. I had meant to speak to you later this evening. Mr. Bullon …"

"Has misunderstood me," I interrupted. She spoke with a slight European accent that I could not place. Her green eyes were kind but guarded. "I was in no way complaining. Your playing is very faint, not at all disturbing."

Disarmingly, she smiled. "You are very kind." Then she stepped back and opened the door more widely. "I was just preparing my evening coffee. Will you join me?"

"I'd be enchanted." I crossed the threshold and entered another world, an older one. I could not believe that this apartment was identical to my own, and yet I knew that it was. I sensed that Miss Greive had lived here for a long time, as the room looked so utterly dwelt in. Soft lamplight illuminated many pieces of fine furniture, obviously antique. One entire wall was taken up with sturdy oak bookcases, crammed with hardcover editions. There was a simple elegance, a delightful feminine grace, to the place that I found delightful and cozy.

"Please be seated, Mr. Stone."

"Albert."

She lightly smiled and bowed her head. "And I am Lucretia. Pardon me one moment."

Rather than sitting, I crossed to the bookcases and examined titles. She soon returned, holding a tray of coffee cups and scones. "You are an author, I am told."

"Yes, of short stories," I replied, wanting so to take up the volume of Henry James' unfinished novel, *The Sense of the Past*, in its original New York Edition. My rule was never to handle books belonging to another's library unless invited to do so. Setting down her tray, and perhaps sensing my bibliophilic hunger, Miss Greive reached for the volume and placed it in my anxious hand. "Oh, thank you. I am, actually, thinking of beginning work on a first novel, although I tremble at the required discipline."

"Discipline is a lesson one learns with years. You are very young."

"I'm twenty-eight."

"As old as that?" Her smile was slightly sardonic. "And what is your genre, Albert?"

"Human relationships, with a touch of the uncanny. James has been a gigantic influence, so much so that my editors sometimes object to my 'Victorian' prose style. But of late I have found an editor who is sympathetic, and with him I am preparing a hardcover edition of my finest work."

"Excellent. I, too, adore James. There is much poetry in his prose. Much digging into strange human psyche. His tales of innocent Americans lured to the debaucheries of European lifestyle so amuse me."

"You are from Europe?" I hesitantly queried.

A slight nod and blink of beautiful eyes. "I was raised in a very small village; but I have lived in this country for many years."

I tried to deduce her age. Although she looked in her early thirties, there was an air about her of someone much older; but perhaps that was merely the European manner, to which I was unaccustomed. Returning the book to its shelf, I joined Lucretia at a small sofa. The coffee was perfection.

We sipped, and munched, and spoke of literature. Often, I glanced into one corner of the room where sat a small pianoforte. She seemed at last to notice. "Do you play, Albert?"

"Alas, no. I am not at all musical. But I love listening."

She hesitated, sucking at her lips. "Pardon me if I do not play for you. It is a very personal expression for me, perhaps as your writing is for yourself. I simply cannot play before others." And, apologetically, she shrugged.

"Of course I understand," I said, hiding my disappointment with a smile.

"Perhaps you can write a story about such a one, the person who can perform only in solitude. That would have a touch of the—what was your word?—uncanny. A potent word, that one."

"Indeed. I adore reading biographies of authors and artists. The lives our race have lived! It is often incomprehensible."

"And intimidating. I fear I am not a brave soul. I live in this secluded world of books."

"So do I. It's the best of worlds. I mean, I am a student, of sorts, of human nature, of the human mind, of the events in human history. But from a distance. Friends have accused me of being a coward, but that's a mistake. I'm an artist. I observe the world from a distance, so to express what I behold in poetic prose. In doing so, I do not escape 'the world' and my place in it. I feel my emotions as deeply as anyone."

She thought in silence for a moment. Then: "No, we can never escape our destiny, our fate." How sad and weary she suddenly looked. I sensed that she was perhaps tiring. Faking a yawn, I made my excuses. She walked me to my door. "You will visit me again, Albert?"

"I shall be delighted to do so." Feeling a bit foolish, I took her hand and kissed it. She rewarded me with one of the loveliest smiles I had ever seen. Returning her warm smile, I closed my door. Falling into my armchair, I took up my current book but did not open it. Rather, I sat with eyes closed, thinking about my new acquaintance.

## II.

For the next fortnight I was consumed with creativity. Ideas and imagery buzzed inside my brain to the point where sleep was nigh impossible. I burned to write. For days at a time I would neither dress nor bath, but simply sit upon my hard bed mat, with pen and pad. If I had the energy or interest, I would brew coffee. My two interludes from this frenzy of productivity were evenings spent with Miss Greive, at one of which I read the rough draft of a story inspired by her idea of the solitary artist. I based my main character on aspects of Lucretia's personality, and this delighted her.

After the second meeting, as I was at her door, she stopped me. "I know that you are busy with your book, and not a social person; but I wonder if you would go with me next Tuesday afternoon to visit … an old relation. He is a lonely old man who loves literature as we do." She hesitated, as though thinking over what she had just spoken, as if to judge the wisdom of a rash decision.

"I should be delighted, of course. A grandfather?"

"No. An … uncle; a great, great uncle, recently come to America from our small village. I've told him of your writing. He's never met an actual author, and is keen to meet you. Really? You will come?"

"It will be my pleasure." She widely smiled, and bent to kiss my cheek. Blushing, I crossed into my rooms.

Now, I have always been an introverted soul, a person self-contained. The only possible society, as Wilde once wrote, is oneself. Thus is life simplified. But as I looked over my wardrobe that evening, I regretted the lack thereof. My clothes were deplorably unsocial. Then I remembered seeing, in a second hand shop where I had gone in search of kitchen items, an inexpensive summer suit of beige cotton that has slightly attracted me. It would do superbly. Happily, I prepared for bed, where I sat up for a long time, pen and pad ready, thinking perhaps I would write. Instead, I merely daydreamed about my new life, at how it had unexpectedly worked out, at how delighted I was to have found a new friend who was such a congenial companion. For once in my life I seemed to have really made the right, the wise, decision. Things were working out.

Finally drowsy, I set aside my writing utensils and extinguished the bedside lamp. As I was nearing the tide of dreams, I could vaguely hear, from across the hallway, the faint playing of the pianoforte. The sad music, like some lonely mother's lullaby sung for a child irretrievably lost, cradled me to sleep.

### III.

Tuesday arrived. How delightful it felt to stride beside a person who so enchanted me, this beautiful woman. I glanced at her as we strolled, trying once more to guess her age. Her complexion was so smooth, sans wrinkles or spots. Her eyes were clear and gleaming as they took in the surrounding beauty of Nature. She drank in the gorgeous day; and yet beneath her cheery disposition one detected a profound sadness. It was a feeling that confused and depressed me. It filled within me a longing to protect her from whatever secret woe brought that lonely, faraway look in her eyes.

The distance was not lengthy, she said, and the day so lovely; and so she suggested that we walk the entire way. She could thus point out interesting portions of the city, which I had not yet thoroughly explored. At one point we passed along a high granite wall. The swirling air was heady with blossom fragrance, and as we stopped at an open gate I beheld a small, quaint cemetery. It was crowded with trees and shrubbery, and its tilting stones looked very old indeed.

"I often stop here," Miss Greive said as she guided me onto graveyard ground. "It is the oldest cemetery in the city. The lilac smells wonderful, does it not?"

The air seemed to have grown a few degrees chillier, and the wind rose in strength. I watched the swaying laburnum, with their poisonous yellow flowers. I watched the plumes of white and pale pink lilac move in wind. At one corner of the old stone wall stood a gigantic willow tree, its long pale vines writhing as they dropped to the ground. Atop one aged tomb a cat washed itself in sunlight. How strange that a place of death should seem so alive.

"You have such an odd expression on your face, Albert," Lucretia said, lightly laughing. "Does the place unnerve you?"

"On the contrary. I feel almost audaciously at peace. As a child I often spent many happy afternoons investigating an overgrown and abandoned graveyard high on a hill, Graham Hill, as I recall its name. The place was overrun with sticker bushes and shrubbery and bending trees. Neighborhood hoodlums had violated the markers. But I loved it there. Among the happy dead."

She oddly laughed. "The dead are happy?"

"Of course they are. They're dead, you see." We laughed together.

"And what of the spirit?"

"I never think of that. I abhor the notion of eternity. You and I are material things, chemical components. We end as dust and ash. That, at least, is my fervent wish. To go on as spirit, or as anything ... God, what could be more damnable than eternal life?"

I saw her momentarily stiffen. The sun was suddenly sheathed by clouds, and then shone brightly once again. It illuminated her pale face, and the pearls of teardrops that glistened in her eyes. "Let us go," she abruptly said. "It grows late."

We vacated the place of mortal repose. Eventually we arrived at our destination, a neighborhood that seemed utterly abandoned. Most of the large houses were boarded and in stages of appalling decrepitude. A smell of decay tainted the air. I was led to a house that was tall, tilted, and black with age. When I looked at Lucretia, as she escorted me up porch steps, I saw again her nervous expression, as though she was uncertain that she was right in bringing me with her. I smiled as pleasantly as possible and squeezed her hand.

Before we reached the front door an elderly gentleman, lean and haggard, opened it to us. They exchanged words in a language I could not place, and we entered the house. "My uncle is in his courtyard," my companion informed me, leading me through a dimly lit corridor that took us to a back door. We walked out of the house, into an expanse of yard that was surrounded with a sturdy growth of tall shrubbery that served as fence. Beneath a fig tree, fanning himself as he lounged upon a large divan, was a creature so grotesque it made me gasp. If the caterpillar in Alice in Wonderland had risen from its grave a bloated, lichenous thing, it might look something like the creature upon which I gawked.

As we neared him, I sensed that he was fantastically ancient, the oldest person I had ever encountered. Not an uncle, but a great, great, great uncle! Lucretia motioned for me to wait, then went to her relation, and spoke to him in the same strange tongue with which she had addressed the servant. Then, turning to me and raising a hand, she spoke in English. "Mr. Albert Stone. This is my uncle, Sebastian Greive."

Screwing my courage to its sticking place, I stalked toward the figure on the divan. I took in greeting his outstretched hand and felt the heavy press of his moist and flabby fingers. He held tightly, and too long. I could not help but stare at his face, with its bumps and rolls and growths. The face was a mask of pretended mirth, from which a pair of sapient eyes closely examined my own visage.

He would not let go of my hand. His touch, the fabric of his flesh wrapped around my own, contained a kind of force, an energy, such as I have never experienced. I thought that I could detect something, some essence, enter into the texture of my skin and claim my body, my soul. The dewy lips stretched, and a voice that dripped with pleasure spoke. "You are very welcome to my home. Lucretia has spoken of you, and read to me one of your remarkable stories. I am delighted to make your acquaintance." His accent was far more pronounced than that of his niece.

"Thank you. You are very kind." At last he freed me from his grasp.

"Please to sit," he begged, motioning to a nearby lawn chair. "Lucretia ..." He hesitated and gazed at the younger woman, as if to query whether it was proper for him to so address her. His formal habits seemed quaintly European. "Lucretia is not one to form so fast friendship. Where we come from, we keep mostly to our own selves."

"You've never really told me where you're from," I said to Lucretia, who sat in the chair next to the one I had taken. She looked about to speak, but was interrupted by the ancient one.

"A very small village, that no one is heard of." He shrugged.

His cordiality seemed slightly overdone. I sensed secret meanings and implications under intonation and furtive glances to his niece. At the same time, I intuited his anxious need for conversation. He looked a lonely figure, with his fan held limply in one hand, with his grotesque form encased in what looked like pajamas of yellow silk. His pale green eyes seemed to implore compassion and friendship.

"I've never been abroad," I ventured. "Lack of time and money. Too, I am very stupid when it comes to learning languages. Now and then I have borrowed recordings from library in attempts to learn French or Latin, but my lazy brain revolts at such education. Alas."

"It is not so difficult when there is little else for passing time. I learned your language from an Englishman who was my friend in prison." A pregnant pause. "I spent many years incarcerated. (Is that the word?)" This last to his niece, who said something scolding in their native idiom. He shortly answered in like. "With little to do except read from inadequate libraries, I passed time learning your so peculiar tongue."

"You speak it very well."

He bowed his head in thanks. "I had long time for learning. Many decades behind unfriendly bars. I am only recently released and come to your so amusing country."

It was obviously not a subject his niece wanted discussed. "An unpleasant experience, prison life," I mumbled.

Sebastian shrugged. "One finds companions, but misses the little freedoms. I do not live so differently now, old thing as I am. Except, of course, in my way of dressing. The great tragedy of prison life is prison clothes." I good-naturedly laughed, he sounded so like a passage from Wilde. "It is not easy life, incarceration in a small ignorant village. I was so long locked up that in time I think they forgot my great offense, or lost record of it. But their fear and hatred for my kind, that does not become forgotten. They never fail to remember that I am imprisoned for necromancy."

"Enough," came Lucretia's stern voice.

"Basta! Our guest is an author, a student of the life. I give him a glimpse of life he cannot imagine."

I felt distinctly uncomfortable. Miss Greive smiled apologetically. "This is my eccentric uncle," her smile seemed to say. Her face told me, also, that he was someone she loved very much.

"I'm not much versed in the black arts," I lamely offered.

"Black? No, no. The old arts, Mr. Stone. The very old religion. Not like what one sees on the television, the what do you call it, psychic hotline. When I see that, I laugh."

"You mentioned necromancy, which is conversing with the dead."

"In part, yes. And the brewing of potions to sell to those not of our race."

"You were Gypsies then?"

"Gypsy?" He frowned in confusion to his niece, who mumbled a strange word. "Oh, no! Not as respectable as that. We were much beneath, like the women in Macbeth—you know the play?"

"Ah, witches."

"Yes, we witched. And in our little village, especially when I was young—one-hundred years ago—that is so great a crime." These words alerted something within my mind. Yes, I could imagine that he had been young one-hundred years ago. How long had he existed, this bizarre creature? I found myself believing every word he had uttered. Then he coughed and rubbed his throat with thick round fingers. "But we are parched. My dear, could you assist Franz with refreshments?" Rising, Miss Greive looked heavily at the ancient one, then nodded and was gone.

Sebastian Greive and I watched the rising moon, an orange medallion that glowed in the demi-jour of dusk. "Were you very young when they placed you in prison?"

He sighed. "Oh, I had been there, you know, now and again as a child;

for stealing and begging, you know, the things a child must do to not go hungry. They knew, of course, my heritage. Once I was imprisoned for raising a storm that frightened the governor's horses." He chuckled at this memory. "But my great crime, for which I spent many decades in tiny cell, was necromancy. Some of my people had been falsely accused—and executed. It was injustice, and so I raised them up, returned to them their innocent mortality. An unthinkable crime, in that place, at that time." He paused, deeply frowning. When again he spoke, it was more to himself than to me. "That was when I learned my arts were flawed. I watched from my tiny window in my cell as they tried once more to execute my convicted innocents. They could not. I do not understand what I did that was incorrect. I was very emotional when I threw the rune stones. Those I raised, you see, they could not again return to death. Ever." He gazed at me with weird green eyes. "Is that not unspeakable, Mr. Stone?"

"Yes," I whispered, as my flesh prickled with unnatural chilliness.

From out the house came Miss Greive and the servant Franz. The elderly man carried a large tray filled with an assortment of refreshments, the woman three long-stemmed glasses and a very tall and tapered wine bottle. I smiled, as Brazilian banana wine was a favorite vintage. Franz, wobbling just slightly, placed the cumbersome tray upon a low table. Handing to him his fan and yellow book, Mr. Greive said something to the servant in their native tongue, motioning to the great expanse of lawn before us. The servant took from Miss Greive the bottle and glasses, filling the latter with golden liqueur. Then he went out into the yard and set alight a number of braziers fastened onto tripods. In the flickering light I saw that which had hitherto escaped my notice, a small yellow tent some distance from us.

Sebastian spoke to his beautiful young relation, and she beautifully laughed. I had emptied my glass of wine like the greedy thing I am, and seeing this the elder one bent and took up the bottle of wine, replenishing my glass. Then, swiftly, he tossed the bottle high into the air, then caught it on the circular tips of his gigantic fingers, where he balanced it with dexterity. I laughed and applauded.

"You are a shocking show-off," his niece scolded.

He gazed at me with wide, innocent eyes. "Am I, Mr. Stone? Am I a shocking show-off?"

"Appallingly so," I assured him. He beamed, delighted. It came to me, with sudden enlightenment, that I had lost all trace of my former repugnance for this horribly old and ill-formed creature. Surreptitiously, he had charmed me with his manner and delighted me with his talk, outré as the latter had been. Much of this had to do, I knew, with the great affection my beautiful young friend had for her old, old uncle.

"And now," Sebastian spoke in a low, hushed voice, "entertainment." With odd emotion gleaming in his green-hued eyes, he raised a hand to the moon and made with it a curious movement. I heard the soft tinkling of bells. The noise seemed to emanate from the small tent at the far end of the yard. I watched, and saw the bent-over figure that emerged from the flaps of egress. Slowly, it unwound and rose. I trembled when I saw how tall it stood, how lean its frame appeared. It was dressed in motley, and the thin long arms it held to the moon seemed composed of smooth white wood. With a jerk of its head it jangled the bells of its cap to an unusual rhythm, and from its face there came a high weird wailing.

I felt myself shrink into my chair. The wailing sound was song, a tune that I had first heard weeks before, one that had ushered Lucretia Greive into my life. Originally I had heard it just barely, in quiet playing beyond two closed doors. Here I heard it clearly, and the sound of it chilled my blood.

The figure jostled through the darkness, then entered the lambent radiance of one of the burning braziers. I looked upon its face and moaned in fear. The too-thin visage was a pallid mask of woe. In size it seemed no larger than a skull, although in shape it resembled nothing remotely humanesque.

Stopping, it stomped a slippered foot upon the grass. From within the tiny tent there came a profusion of jangling. Slowly, inexorably, they filtered through the flaps: the tall, the lean, the pale companions of the first being. They raised horrific hands to the moon, moving bony figures as if in signal. In time to eldritch wailing song, those bony hands bent forward, until fingertips touched elbows; then, awfully, they bent the other way, until colorless nails pressed impossibly against wrists.

They danced toward us, with heads like canine skulls that jerked spasmodically, with unnaturally lean limbs bending in peculiar manner. The sight would have been clownish if not so grotesque. As they neared us, I looked imploringly at my hostess. How pale was the face that watched in ecstasy the awful jesters. She seemed to have forgotten my presence. I watched as she slowly rose and moved in rhythmic danse into the inhuman herd. Her lovely hands lifted to moonlight and made strange signals to that globe of lifeless dust.

The wailing beast was very nigh. My blood was heavy ice that weighted me to my chair. I could not move, but merely watch as Sebastian Greive heavily moved from his divan and with arduous effort stepped into the danse. He clapped his hands and stomped his feet, he punched his ponderous belly in time to enchanted noise. And his face, his large fleshy face, with eyes of jade that so eerily reflected the sallow glow of moonlight, wore an expression of profound woe that was identical to the expressions of that skeletonic crew of his conjuration.

They danced in hungry moonglow. They encircled the young woman and took her lovely hair. I saw pearls of sorrow that gathered in her awesome eyes, and felt my heart grow cold with anguish at the meaninglessness of existence. I saw the impossibly old man make signals to the moon, saw him leap on prancing feet as if he were a child trying to fetch a piece of darksome sky. Suddenly he jerked and placed a hand upon his breast. Horribly, the canine creatures did the same. With a strangled cry Sebastian fell to the ground, with a thud that seemed to shake the floor of earth. And they, the nameless buffoons who had danced in jest of all existence, they also fell, and melted into pools of shadow.

And she, oh great heaven, the beautiful she, finally floated to the ground, where she lay twitching spasmodically until, with great effort, she commanded her composure. Slowly, achingly, she crawled to the prostrate form of her rasping relation.

I quavered in the dull silence, then somehow found the strength to creep out of my chair and pull my shivering body to my friends. She had placed his head into her lap and was murmuring alien words while holding a smooth hand to the moon. I watched that hand move in esoteric fashion. The old man's arm heavily raised, and his awful hand made exactly the same movement to the lunar sphere. Then his hand fell upon her tear-dewed face. He whispered words in a language I did not know.

His hand fell to the grass. With eyesight blurred by stinging tears, I reached for it, that hand that had once so revolted me. I felt a dim memory of the former power that I had experienced when I had first touched that hand. Sebastian glanced at me and managed a feeble smile; then looking to his kinswoman he whispered, "Forgive me."

The fading force of alchemical sustenance crept from the fingers that I held, those fingers that grew still and cold.

"In pace requiescat," I wept, as Lucretia blessed me with a gracious smile. I gazed hard into her magnificent face. "Why did he beg your forgiveness?" I boldly asked. "What was your uncle's awful woe?"

"He was not my uncle," she sobbed. "He was my son."

*6?*

# AFTERWORD

This is my definitive tribute to Oscar Wilde, and contains numerous elements from his life. While reading anew Wilde's letter from prison that has become known as *De Profundis*, I came upon this: "Our very dress makes us grotesques. We are the zanies of sorrow. We are clowns whose hearts are broken." I instantly knew that I had found a germ, what Henry James lovingly called, in his notebooks, "a little donne". The same thing occurred when I was reading Julius Caesar and came upon Antony's wonderful "... whilst your purpled hands do reek and smoke," and knew that I had a title looking for a story.

It was the life of Oscar Wilde that initially made me really want to write, and to write beautifully, poetically. I had just come out as queer and was reading homosexual authors. Wilde was at the top of my list. As happened with Lovecraft, it was reading the story of Wilde's life and his correspondence that made me link emotionally to him, and want to emulate him aesthetically. These outsiders are my artistic mentors, my brothers in the art of fiction. It is to them that all of my heartfelt writing is ultimately dedicated.

"The Zanies of Sorrow" was first published in *Tales of Love and Death*.

# Beneath An Autumn Moon

*Dedicated to Antonie Francis LaChappelle III*

## I.

It was dreary midnight, and the beasts of Sesqua Valley sat in silence, listening. The sobbing from above had ceased, replaced with clumsy fumbling.

"It's a curious thing about dreams, Edith," Simon Gregory Williams languidly replied. "They are so apt in peeling away the mask and shewing the naked visage one tried so desperately to deny. Thus is bestial reality revealed."

"Bestial booze is my nephew's affliction. He staggered in at dawn and promptly fell upon the floor. I helped him crawl to his bed, and there he's been all day."

"I dare say, Edith, that the locals have given him a taste of Sesqua brew. He's proved quite popular, has your young man, in the fortnight that he's been with us. I've never known anyone so social."

"He's been socializing with those bohemian blokes at the local, Cyrus and his gang. No telling the mischief they've been leading him toward."

"Yes, they are a delightful pack of rogues."

"And that is why you'll accompany Antony when he leaves to join them tonight."

The tall, lean man was about to protest when the object of their conversation staggered into the room. He looked, this lank outsider, like animated chaos. The red-rimmed eyes lacked focus, and the idiotic mouth hung open. Stubble darkened a remarkably handsome face. His hair was very dark, and it was amazing that hair so short could look so unkempt. A stale alcoholic stench hung about him, tainting the fragrance of the small room.

"Oh, good, a fire. It's cold up in my room," Antony said as he crossed the carpet and knelt before the hearth. He studied the flames as if seeking something within them.

"Will you have some tea, dear?" Edith asked, lifting a pot of liquid from a nearby stand.

"Of course he will," Simon said, rising from his easy chair and pouring tea into a delicate cup. "Drink up, young man."

"Thanks," the lad replied, taking the cup and setting it on the floor as he continued to gaze into flame. Then he started as wind rattled a window. "Did you hear that?"

"Yes, it was the wind," Simon replied.

"No, beneath the wind—my father's voice."

There was an uncomfortable silence. Edith vacated her chair and sat next to the young man. "Antony ..."

"I didn't really think he'd come here. He hated this place. Over and over again, as his mental condition worsened, he would mutter more and more about Sesqua Valley. 'The valley of the beast,' he'd call it. There's no way he'd come here. Except that he got really crazy near the end, just before he vanished." His low voice was laced with quivering emotion. "I hate to think of him out there, lost in the woods and raving mad. Or dead in some ditch." His tears returned.

"My dear boy," Simon coolly replied, "you're far too handsome to speak in so frantic a fashion."

"Yeah, I sound crazy. Lunacy must run in the family. Tell me, Aunt Edith, are there any familial skeletons rotting away in the local wackhouse?"

"None that need concern you," the elderly woman replied, then slyly smiled as she combed her fingers through his hair.

"It isn't easy, you know, taking care of a father who is growing mad. It messes with your mind. You begin to question your own sanity. You find yourself mumbling mindlessly."

"Personally, I adore conversation with myself. It's so intelligent."

"You wouldn't, Simon, if you were drunk."

"You do, Antony, drink to excess," Simon quietly replied.

"Of course I do. I'm alcoholic." At this he got to his feet, and yet he was still so wobbly that his boot lightly kicked the ignored teacup, spilling its contents. "Oh, wow, I'm sorry, Auntie."

"Not to worry, darling. Not your cup of brew, so it wasn't."

Sweetly, the lad smiled. "Nope. Actually, the gang turned me on to some local moonshine last night, and I've a hankering for more."

Edith looked significantly at Simon, who deeply frowned, irritably sighed and said, "I'll go with you."

"Holy cow, will you? Coolness! The guys all speak of you in hushed tones of awe."

"As well they should," Simon muttered.

"I'll meet you outside. Let me get my jacket."

Simon nodded and waved the youth away. Slanting his eyes at Edith's playful smile and winking eye, he stormed from the room and stomped onto the front porch. The moon was a dim outline behind a covering of clouds.

"Ah, the gibbous moon," said Antony as he joined Simon. "That always sounded such a foreboding phrase. It's rather strange, though, how sinister the moon looks in these dark bucolic surroundings."

"There's nothing sinister about a sphere of dead dust, dear boy."

"Yeah? Well, for something so deceased it sure has an effect on this sphere of dust, and we insects that crawl all over it. Maybe I've just been too overly influenced by dad's constant raving about this 'wretched place,' as he constantly called it. Dang, he was obsessed. 'Those silver-eyed devils with their wolf-frog faces!' I used to have, as a kid, a necklace with this huge amulet on it, a face made out of stone. That thing fascinated me. I wore it always, secretly. I sensed that dad wouldn't want to know that I had found it in the attic among Mom's old stuff. I used to go into the bathroom and try to imitate the thing's facial features in the big mirror. Dad finally caught me at it and, holy hell, he freaked. He *tore* that thing from my neck with such force that I fell and split my lip. Dad hurled the necklace at the mirror, and both shattered at the force of his fury. When he saw that I was bleeding and crying, he took me in his arms, and I saw such naked fear in his eyes. 'They'll never get you,' he whimpered."

"Your father was a coward, afraid of his destiny. Although not borne of the valley, he was born of woman on this shadowed sod. This is where he belongs—as do you."

"I don't know what the hell you mean by that, Simon, but I ain't staying. I'm a city boy."

Simon slowly stepped down from the porch, onto valley ground. Hesitantly, Antony followed him, not liking the way that the older gentleman snuffled at the evening air. The beast of the valley scanned the tops of trees, his silver eyes twinkling. He took in the titanic mountain of white stone as the moon emerged from out its blanket of clouds. He stopped and turned to gaze at the young outsider, as streams of leprous light fell upon his bestial face. "You know that you will never leave us."

Antony stared at that moonlit countenance and was suddenly filled with terror. Yelping, he rushed away, toward the center of town and its well-lit confines. Simon's snout curled with mirth. His cunning eyes watched a pale cloud that hovered near the moon. Gazing intently, he whistled to the sky, watched as the cloud began to coalesce with cosmic shadow, to shape itself into a semblance of Simon's face. Simon hissed, and the cloud began to bubble, to separate and dissolve. He raised a hand to feel the texture of his fantastic face, glorifying in his nameless origin. From atop the mountain unseen snouts rose toward the moon and bayed. Moaning softly, Simon looked to the direction where the young outsider had fled in panic. Smiling, the beast of the valley continued his casual stroll toward town.

## II.

It was a festive scene at the Valley Pub. Horton was playing at the

saloon piano, pounding queerly discordant honky-tonk. Cyrus, extremely inebriated, was dancing atop a large table around which stood the gang, happily banging bottles and glasses in time to the music. Antony, already crapulous with drink, tried to lose himself in the surrounding merriment; yet his soul was heavy with foreboding, and he could not help but continually glance at the door with a sense of dreadful expectancy.

"Come hither, Antony," Cyrus playfully coaxed, reaching for the outsider. Antony protested by placing his hand on his stomach; but the crowd would have none of it and boosted him up onto the table, helped by Cyrus's happy hand. The eudaemonic crowd cheered and clapped as Antony tried to join Cyrus in his caper. This he found difficult, however, for the rhythm of the danse did not make sense to his clumsy feet. The more he tried to find his way into the crazy tempo, the more audacious it became, until at last he lost his footing and began to fall. His flailing hand caught onto Cyrus, and together they crashed into the crowd, then sprawled upon the floor, soaked in sweat and brew.

The pandemonium suddenly stilled, the music silenced. Antony looked to the entrance and met with Simon's cynical gaze. His stomach began to ripple, and he pushed himself to a standing position and hobbled to the men's room. He knelt before the toilet for quite a while, shuddering; then he washed his face with cool water and returned to the bar.

Simon motioned to the beautiful woman behind the bar. "Amber, two of my special potions."

"No more alcohol for me, Simon," Antony pleaded.

"Don't be absurd, child. Alcohol has never touched these lips. This is something quite different. It will calm your digestial storm."

"No, really," Antony insisted, as the barmaid playfully smiled and handed him a cup composed of queer metal. He looked at the designs embossed upon the cup, and then at the dark liquid within. He brought it to his nose and smelled sweet herbs. "What is it, tea?"

"To your health, reckless youth," Simon said as he tapped his metal cup to Antony's. Breathing with deep resignation, the young man drank. The liquid was thick. It crept slowly down his throat, spreading soothingly through him. He felt instantly more relaxed. The drink had been but half consumed, and yet it was enough. Handing the cup to Amber, he watched as she devoured the remaining brew, closing her eyes in ecstasy.

Simon turned to face the silent crowd. "So, Cyrus, you've come of age and will soon be leaving us."

"For a wee while, just. I have the hankering to roam."

"I'll look after your place, if I may. I'd enjoy doing some work there.

Are you finished with your new piece?"

"Only just."

"I didn't know you painted," said Antony.

"No, dear fellow—I sculpt. Your aunt has been good enough to teach me some techniques."

"Cool. I'd love to see your work," the outsider enthused.

"Yes," Simon replied. "To see it in early autumn moonlight, that might be quite splendid. Shall we?"

"Well, if you insist." Clumsily, Cyrus looked for his jacket, then led the way out of the bar, into night. "Here, Antony," he said as they walked beneath the silent trees. "Let's be of support to one another." And he tenderly wrapped his arm around the other's waist. Drunkenly, they walked, and when once Antony looked behind him he saw that many persons from the bar were following.

"Feeling better?" Amber asked, catching up with them and linking her arm with Antony's. He smiled and nodded. How amazingly better he felt, absolutely relaxed. And his senses seemed somehow heightened. He could smell the valley as never before, all of its myriad scents. The sight of shadowed trees was cool upon his eyes. He was especially aware of Simon's musky odor, and was amazed at how very ancient that aroma seemed. It was an earthly smell, but unlike anything on earth he had ever experienced.

Moonlight filtered in streams through the canopy of spreading trees, and in that soft light Antony studied the facial features of the young man who stumbled beside him. He took up the young man's hand and kissed it, breathing in its Sesquan fragrance. Cyrus smiled idiotically and bent to lick Antony's throat. When he raised his drunken face before Antony's own, the outsider recalled his father's scornful mutterings about "those silver-eyed bastards with their wolf-frog faces". Yes, there was an oddity of features; yet as much as it repulsed, it beguiled. He remembered his mother's amulet. She was a presence he but faintly recalled, for she had left them when he was very young, and his father refused to speak of her. Antony associated the strange stone amulet with her, keenly so. It was his secret link to her memory, one that he knew instinctively to keep from his crazy father. He could but dimly recall her face. Was it the influence of his new surroundings that made him think that she, too, had slightly wolfish features?

They came to a bungalow in the woods, and Cyrus unwound himself from Antony and stumbled to the building's crooked door. There was a small stone table with benches, and Antony, suddenly weary, sat down. Amber sat down close to him, and he nestled his head upon her bosom. She did not smell of the valley. He studied her lovely face, the smooth and human features. She looked down at him and beautifully smiled.

Simon leaned against a tree and produced from an inner jacket pocket a lean black flute. Shutting his shining eyes, he brought the instrument to his mouth and dreamily played. As he played, he slowly swayed, and as Antony watched it seemed to him that the surrounding trees swayed likewise, moving to weird music. He watched as a thin branch bent so as to touch Simon's fantastic face.

At last Cyrus emerged from his bungalow, holding in his hands a large and heavy bust. This he placed on the stone table, inches from Antony's face. Beams of moonlight fell upon the sculpted face, a face that seemed familiar. Antony took in the tired, fretful eyes of the stony face, the thickness of eyebrows superbly etched. He knew those eyes, that face, and yet it had been altered. The nose was longer than a human nose should be. One ear poking from the covering of thick hair had been slightly tapered at its tip. Antony suddenly laughed.

"Cyrus, you've given Poe the Sesqua look!"

Surrounding figures slowly moved toward the table. Antony could see their shadowed faces, their eyes as pale as silver moonglow. A hand smoothed its fingers through his hair, and he looked at Amber. "You're not one of them," he whispered.

"Not of the valley borne, but I'm a part of it now, inexorably. The valley knows its own, Antony."

"I don't understand."

She kissed his questioning eyes. "You will." Raising her head, she smiled at Simon, who began once more to play his flute. Cyrus jumped onto the table, nearly capsizing his creation, and began to sway. Antony watched as the young man began to undress. Others, too, near and far, were removing their clothing. He lifted his head as Amber reached for her blouse and pulled it off. Her ample tits fell heavily before him, and he kissed one dusky nipple.

Completely nude, Cyrus leapt from the table and hunkered before the young outsider. Digging into dirt, he scooped up a handful of soil, into which he spat. Dipping fingers into the stuff, he brought his soiled hand to Antony's face and began to push particles of earth onto the young outsider's flesh. Then he bent to kiss the mucky face.

Amber bent low and dug a dainty hand into the earth. Humming Simon's haunting tune, she raised her hand above Antony's head and let the soil sift through her fingers. Others approached, with hands full of sod, and the young man shut his eyes at their touch. He felt Amber move from him, and opening his eyes he watched as she danced beneath trees upon black earth. Others joined her, and finally Cyrus pulled Antony off the bench and led him to the danse.

There came from beneath the ground a solid pulse, a weird rhythm similar to the one that Antony had tried to dance to at the pub. He tried once more to find his way into the measure, and once more he could not. Giving up, he fell to his knees and watched the ones who moved about him. He watched them hunker obscenely, watched them dig into the ground and bring up handfuls of soil, which they sprinkled onto each other. Antony clawed into the floor of earth and smeared his face with Sesqua's aromatic muck.

They danced around him, beneath tree and moonlight, and the rising wind accompanied the tones that issued from Simon's flute. And underneath that wind Antony could hear, mutely, the call of his father's voice.

"I'm here, father. I'm here." He wanted to rise, to flee into the woodland and find his pa. But the earth of Sesqua Valley held him down, and all around him moved the dancing beasts. He tore off his shirt, clawed at soil and smeared dirt onto his body. Cyrus knelt before him, grinning wildly. His face was the face of the amulet, the face that Antony had tried to impersonate before a bathroom mirror. Antony flexed his facial muscles, trying to imitate the features on the face before him. Cyrus laughed and flashed his silver eyes, then raised those eyes to moonlight and loudly bayed.

Oh, what ecstasy was in that sound. Simon's music grew in intensity. It utterly beguiled. Ripping off the remainder of his clothing, Antony arose and tried once more to join in the lunacy of ritual.

### III.

He awoke in speckled sunlight, to the call of birdsong. Amber's head lay on his naked chest, and Cyrus's nestled at his groin. He unwound himself from their nude forms, rose and found his clothing. Somewhere in this woodland, he knew for a certainty, was his father. Antony stumbled through overgrown pathways, calling. There were dark forms that scurried about, leaping through the trees. Perhaps they were squirrels. Coming to a clearing, he espied the titanic white mountain, Selta, towering over the valley, like some silent sentinel. There were curious stone idols and other aesthetic oddities placed in various locations, and as he bent to touch one anomalous statuette he thought that its shape held some arcane significance that he could not comprehend. Everything in this godforsaken valley held some secret meaning, even the sound of the wind as it soughed through treetops seemed esoteric. He listened carefully to the wind, but heard no sound of calling underneath its murmur. How lonely he suddenly felt, how lost. His low sobbing haunted the air, and when a figure knelt next to him, Antony took the young Sesquan in his arms.

"I couldn't find him, Cyrus."

"No."

"But he's here …"

"A portion of him, yes. Look, there are things you can't yet understand."

"Then stay and teach me. Why are you going? What's all this weird talk about children of the valley coming of age?"

"When a child of the valley reaches a certain age he goes out into the world and explores its corners of legendary wonder. It's what we do, it's how we grow. My time has come. You don't need me to teach you anything, the valley will do that."

"Dang, it creeps me out the way you talk about the valley as if it were some kind of entity. This whole thing is getting too freaky. I admit I've fallen under some kind of spell of enchantment. Everything here affects me oddly, and as much as it tweaks my little brain, I kind of get off on it. But I'm not staying. As you and everyone else keeps reminding me, I'm an outsider. I need to return to the city. I know you all want me to stay, especially Simon. That cat creeps me out big time."

"Simon is cool. He's very powerful."

"You see, there you go. Saying things that have some kind of deeper meaning that somehow I'm supposed to comprehend. I can't take anymore of this brainfuck bullshit. I'm returning to the city. Come and stay with me at my dad's house. I know some degenerate punk clubs that you'll really grove on. I can show you some 'legendary wonders' the likes of which you'll not find elsewhere. Come and stay with me."

Cyrus looked thoughtfully away. "Perhaps. You make it sound intriguing. I do like hanging out with you, pretty boy." Coyly, they smiled to each other, and Cyrus ran a hand along Antony's waist. "But for now we need to get you home and into a tub. You're covered with debris. A good hot soak will do you good."

They helped each other to a standing position. Antony looked once more at the curious sculpture, at the dark surrounding trees. "Why do I feel so weird? What's going on inside my brain? What is this place doing to me?"

"The valley has claimed you. Don't look like that, Antony, it's an awesome honor."

"It sounds a little threatening, dude. Becoming a part of this place was never in my plans for the future."

"How did it feel, Antony, dancing with us last night? Didn't it feel wonderful and right?"

"Once I got into it, yeah. But I was intoxicated—by everything. What was in that drink that Simon so cunningly got me to ingest? Was I drugged?"

"Ha, you make yourself sound like a victim in a conspiracy plot. It's all so simple. You know that you were born here, that your mother was one of us."

"Yes, yes. So that seals my fate? Have I no choice in the matter? I don't like feeling doomed."

"Is that how you felt last night? Rather, didn't you feel wantonly free?" The young outsider frowned and blew out air. They walked to where Cyrus's clothes lay in a pile. Antony watched him dress, then followed him to his aunt's house.

They found Edith in her spacious kitchen, and the delicious smells helped Antony to realize that he was ravenous. Edith clucked her tongue at her nephew's grimy appearance, but smiled as she noticed that it was only his flesh that was dirtied; the clothing, though stained with alcohol, seemed clean enough. "I don't know what you've been up to, but your breakfast will wait until you've bathed. Cyrus, will you partake of morning meal?"

"Absolutely," the lad replied as he ushered Antony from the kitchen to the upstairs bathroom. When they entered Antony's bedroom, they found fresh clean clothing laid out on the bed. And there, on the pillow, was something that took the city boy's breath away. Antony felt a chill run through him as he reached for and lifted the amulet. It was almost identical to the one that he had worn in youth, except that the facial features were of a more masculine cast. Looking at the bestial face was almost like locating a lost friend, and bringing it close to his face, he traced the wolfish features with a finger. He moved his facial muscles and flexed his nose.

"Like this," Cyrus whispered, then moved his facial muscles so that his wolf-frog visage took on a monstrous form.

"You're not human."

Cyrus smiled and tilted his head. "I am borne of Sesqua Valley."

"I was born here," Antony said, looking very serious.

"Of woman thou art born; I am borne of the valley, bred in distant shadow. Unto that shadow I will return."

Antony laughed bewilderedly. "It just gets weirder and weirder. Where is my father?"

"Can't say. Only Simon knows for certain."

"Did Simon kidnap him? My father would never have come here on his own, he *hated* this place."

"He feared the lure of haunted homeland. He fought the song heard deep in dreaming. He knew the allure of legend, yet thought he wanted to escape, when all along he truly desired destiny and heritage."

"You sound insane when you talk like that," he said, undressing.

Cyrus sniggered. "Your father lost his sanity, that's what city life did for him?"

"Oh, but all this crap you're telling me is the stuff of sanity," Antony mocked.

Cyrus shook his head. "You're just like him. Fight and fight, and flee."

"Yes, I'm my father's son. And I'm returning to his home in the city. You'll come with me?"

Cyrus closed his eyes and deeply listened. Outside, the rising wind remorsefully moaned. Some creature of woodland sadly cried. Opening his silver eyes, Cyrus bent and took the amulet from Antony's hand. Pressing against the boy's naked flesh, Cyrus raised the leather cord over his friend's head. Softly, as he lowered the cord so that it rested around Antony's throat, Cyrus hummed a tune that was weirdly echoed on the wind. The face of stone fell heavily against Antony's left breast, just above his heart.

## IV.

Late afternoon sunlight shone upon the huge round tower, playing on its old, old stone. Cyrus stopped to look at the tall edifice, and smiled as the notes of music sailed into the air as they issued from the tower's topmost room. He watched the tower for a little while, watched it against the background of a darkening sky. Then he stepped into the slim entrance and climbed the small stone steps that, circling, led upward. Small square openings served as diminutive windows, yet even on the brightest of days the modicum of light they allowed inward was quite restricted. As he neared the topmost level he took in the ever-increasing scent of ancient books, of moldering manuscripts. He heard distinctly the playing of the woodwind instrument.

Reaching the room, he stepped onto its stone floor and leaned nonchalantly against a wall. Simon sat at a long oak table that was littered with books, manuscripts, pads and fountain pens. A single candle feebly glimmered on the table before him. Cyrus took in the array of flutes, apparatus of varied design and size. The device at Simon's mouth was an antique thing of brass stained green with age. Finally, Cyrus pushed away from the wall and stepped to the table. He stood akimbo before the old one, waiting.

The beast took the flute from his lips and set it down beside the others. "What is this I hear, Cyrus, that you'll be accompanying the outsider on his return to city life?"

"What of it?"

Angrily, Simon smashed the candle with his large dark hand, extinguishing the flame. "Have we worked our influence upon the child for naught? The valley has claimed him, as it claimed his father before him."

"And the valley is not to be denied. I know all that. You think that because you're the first-borne that everything has to be exactly as you desire and go unequivocally to your plans. You're not a god, Simon."

"I am lord of this realm."

"Oh, I think the mountain would disagree."

"Do not dare to lecture me about my place, thou newly-formed. The valley keenly longs for that young human."

"As do you, and that's really why you've summoned me, isn't it? What, jealous because I've tasted him and your tongue has yet to lick so succulent a fare?"

"Be gone, insolent youth. And take heed to work your influence while with him in the city."

"I doubt that I'll need to."

"Away, away."

Cyrus made a sign of religious mockery. "Deus vult," he intoned, bowing low. Then he turned and, whistling, exited the chamber. Simon listened to the departing footfalls, his eyes smoldering in thick darkness. Then he took up another flute and brought it to his wide wet lips. He played to gloom until a faint calling came from a distant place. Sighing, he rose and vacated the tower.

Gazing into darkling woodland, he raised a hand and made with it a curious signal. He waited and watched, and soon, like some emanation leaked from dreaming, it billowed toward him, the oozing mauve shadow that was especial to the region. It surrounded him, boiled around him, lapped at his heels like some fawning creature. Simon moved deeply into it, and all about him transformed fantastically. He wisely smiled and almost danced as he entered the dream-soaked heartland of Sesqua Valley.

Gossamer trees, pale and spectral, trembled with genuflection as Simon pranced past them; at a crimson tarn frogs with children's faces sang a chorus of praise unto the ancient one. Simon waltzed onward, until he came upon a stump of white wood. Touching his hand to the bleached bark, he waited as dark cracks appeared and formed a woeful countenance.

"I want to kiss my son," the entity begged.

"And so you shall, in time. He has decided to return to that squalid city to which you stupidly dragged him when he was but an infant. You thought to escape us, to deny how deeply enmeshed you are with supernal shadow."

The pale thing moaned. "I felt the dancing last night, felt the stomping in my roots. He's been anointed?"

"To a degree. But you will have to writhe those roots deep into his dreaming when he departs. You will have to call and call."

"I long to taste him."

"And so you shall," Simon assured him, bending to the brow of the quasi-face and examining the mark etched upon the forehead.

"It is dry, and I so thirsty."

Simon traced the insignia with a fingernail, slowly digging that pointed talon deeper into the substance of which the thing before him was composed. Liquid, thick and dark, bubbled from the opening and trickled to the moaning mouth. Simon listened for a while to the sound of feeding, then turned away and began to walk again toward the crimson tarn. Dancing, he undressed, then leapt into the rich red depths. When he emerged, he dripped gore. The ancient beast snarled at the delirium of sound that vibrated all around. He gazed at the reflection of his face, then flexed facial muscles until that visage resembled the face of stone worn on a length of leather cord. Raising his snout, he laughed and laughed.

## V.

They moved, these beasts of dubious gender, to the pulsing beat of modernity. Myriad lights of various hues zoomed and swirled above the smoky room. Antony leaned against a pockmarked wall, his sober eyes hidden by thick dark glasses. A fantastic creature, like something from a deranged Charles Addams illustration, sauntered to him.

"*Where* have you been? Haven't seen you for an age."

"Hello, Jackie. I've been visiting relatives in the country."

The hellish creature blinked and took a sip from its drink. With its free hand it reached for and removed Antony's glasses. "Great Jesu, Antony, are you sober? This *won't* do. It'd too disconcerting. Are you broke?"

"Nah. Don't worry about me, babe. I'm okay."

"None of us are that, stud boy. Well, time for my duet." Tenderly, the creature bent and kissed the lad on the throat, replaced the sunglasses over his eyes and skipped to the steps that led up to a small and beer-stained stage.

"Jackie, I want your ass," someone in the crowd yelled.

"You couldn't afford it," Jackie replied into a microphone with sultry voice. "I'm ... expensive. Ursula?"

Another creature of dementia staggered through the crowd and climbed the steps. Tall and *outré*, like something from a perverse science fiction film, it drunkenly reeled near the edge of the stage, and the crowd raised hands in preparation to catch it should it fall into their midst.

"Hey, Ursula, suck my chopper," someone cackled.

"I doubt that it would reach this far," the creature sneered. Then rock music filtered through the speakers, and the two drag queens broke into unruly song. Antony smiled. For all of their *bizarrerie*, the two performers were hugely talented and obviously popular with the surging audience. And yet, as Antony watched, as he looked at the crowd who sloppily moved to loud and obnoxious music, he could not help but compare it to a different bar scene, to a different dancing that he had but recently beheld. Suddenly bored, he turned and found his way to the exit.

The chill of late autumn greeted him. He scanned the skies for the moon, but that empyreal sphere was hidden behind an ugly skyscraper. Walking slowly past a wall that had been decorated with broken pieces of mirror, he looked at his bits of reflection. The streetlight above cast dim illumination, but it was enough to shew the amulet that hung behind the open shirt. Antony gazed at the reflected image, deeply frowning.

"Hey, pretty boy." Cyrus drunkenly ambled to him, smiling stupidly. "That city grog is lame. One has to drink so much of it before there is any kind of effect. What's wrong, why the long face?"

Turning, Antony held the amulet up to his friend for inspection. "Does it look different to you? When Edith first gave it to me I thought it kind of looked like Simon. But now … it rather resembles myself."

"Not half as hot as you, dear boy."

"Dang it, be serious. Is this more Sesqua Valley weirdism?"

"Lordy, what a word! Just go with it, child. Come on, Jackie wants to buy you a drink."

"I'm bored with that scene. You stay if you like, I'm going home."

"As you wish." Hurriedly, Antony led them from that place, toward the waterfront, followed by his friend.

A truck sped by them, belching exhaust. "Hell, this city stinks, doesn't it? Fumes and garbage and alleys reeking of piss. It's gross. And look, you can't see the stars. The sky above the valley was brilliant with starlight. And the moon, on the rare occasion you can see it, looks so dead and weak here. The moon above the valley is awesome, isn't it? It feels so close there, so—intimate. Doesn't it?"

They approached at last the waterfront, and suddenly Antony rushed from his friend and ran to a pier. Cyrus slowly followed, smiling a secret smile. He found his friend kneeling on the moist old wood of the ancient peer, gulping mouthfuls of air.

"Here at least I can smell some nature, rotting as its stench may be. And there—ah!—the rising wind." Then he froze, as beneath the moan of windsong he heard another sound. "Did you hear it?"

"Yes."

"My father's voice …" And he began to shake with stifled sobbing.

"Why on earth did I come back here?"

The beast of Sesqua Valley knelt next to his friend, shoulder to shoulder. "So to realize where in fact your heart and soul belong."

Antony wrapped his arms around his friend's waist. "I'm frightened and confused."

"For naught, Antony. You were born in the valley, by a woman bred of shadow. You have tasted Sesqua's magick, and it has tasted you. Stop shuddering. It's not just your father calling you back; it's awesome destiny."

"I still don't understand so much, and yet I know you're right. Will you return with me?"

"No. I'll come home in time, and then we can resume our wild delicious ways.

"I'm driving back tonight. I can't breathe in this skanky city air. I'll miss you." Cyrus bent to him and they kissed. "I can taste the valley on your mouth, smell it in your skin. It smells like home. Isn't that strange?"

Cyrus softly laughed, and they kissed once more.

## VI.

He parked the car before Edith's house, but the house was vacant of beings. Going up to his bedroom, he sighed with joy at the comfortable bed, the familiar surroundings. He removed all clothing, then went to the window, knelt before it, took in the light of the harvest moon. Before him spread the valley, and he gasped at the enthralling sight of it. Never had anything seemed to him so beautifully alive. Gazing intently at the titanic mountain, Antony marveled at how it seemed almost to stretch its twin peaks toward the majestic moon, as if to drink the lunar light.

Someone entered the room and knelt beside him. She was nude except for the amulet that nestled between her young breasts. He took her in his arms. His face swam into the thickness of her dark hair, hair that was richly scented with valley fragrance. Amber joined him in kissing, her amulet clanking against his own. Rising, she took his hand and led him down the stairs, out the door, into night. They walked into the moving woodland, toward the sound of woodwind.

Simon leaned against a tree, dressed in his usual antiquated style. His hat was rakishly tilted to one silver eye, and his favorite flute was at his lips. In the clearing to which Antony was led Edith danced upon dank soil. She, too, was nude, and in her bestial nature the young man saw something so unspeakably beautiful that it made him moan. From beneath his naked foot he felt the pulse of Sesqua's heartbeat, that strange and uncanny rhythm to which he had tried unsuccessfully to move on numerous occasions. Now it found his heart, and he felt that organ slow in beating until it matched the valley's cadence. He stepped into that measure, smoothly, easily, joyfully.

Antony joined in the danse.

Amber raised her lovely arms and swung dark hair to the sound of Simon's playing. Her pretty hands made secret signals to the moon. From somewhere on Mount Selta, beings bayed in ecstasy. Edith spat onto the ground and etched a symbol into the earth with her foot. She hunkered and dug into the turf. When she raised her panting face to starlight, Antony gasped to see how absolutely nonhuman she appeared. His aunt was truly and completely a creature of this supernatural valley. He studied her look, the image that for so long had beguiled his senses, his dreams. He moved his facial muscles in imitation of her monstrous face.

Edith watched him and roughly cackled. She brought up hands that were filled with sod and danced toward him. She pressed to him her ancient breasts, those breasts that reeked of Sesqua's heady fragrance. She covered her sculptress hands over his moving face, pushing earth into a phizog that began to alter.

Simon danced to them, his pale eyes feverish with wanton magick. Mindlessly, he played his pipe. Amber wildly danced as valley shadows caressed her face. She howled as Edith took her hands from Antony, thus revealing the young man's altered visage. Antony raised his nigh-bestial face unto the moon, that silver sphere that kissed with beams that were reflected on his eyes, eyes that grew pale and altered in shape.

Simon raised a hand to the woodland, welcoming the misty shadow that began to billow toward them. Antony gazed into that mauve mist, then fell to his knees as he saw the stunted thing that crept closer and closer. It stopped at last before him, the bleached entity that wore his father's face. Weeping, Antony placed his hand upon that hideous visage and felt its mouth hungrily kiss his fingers. Then he bent his face, his face that now was the twin of the stony image of the amulet he wore, and touched his lips to his father's liquid eyes.

*6?*

# AFTERWORD

Lovecraft once complained to one of his correspondents that he had his Poe pieces, his Dunsany pieces, but where were his Lovecraft pieces? As is obvious with the publication of this book, I am writing works that express my fanatical identification with Lovecraft. Once in a while, however, I compose a story that seems very much a Pugmire piece. "The Zanies of Sorrow" is one such tale; "Beneath an Autumn Moon" is another. When I now write a story of Sesqua Valley, I try to evolve the series and expand the mythos. It is no longer enough to simply set a story within the valley and have cool creepy stuff occur. A new tale *must* contribute information to the lore, to the growth of legend. That's what makes it fun for me, and hopefully for you as well.

"Beneath an Autumn Moon" is original to this publication.

# The Balm of Nepenthe

*To ye memory of Samuel Loveman*

I had been feeling execrable that day, plagued by an appalling apathy toward everything in life. Oppressed by an ocular tugging that made reading an impossibility, I sat for hours in my armchair, dwelling on the sweetness of oblivion. How I longed to escape the tedious trifles of life, to sink into the secluded refuge of a slumber from which one never need awaken. My gloom deepened as the day grew dark, and as I watched the waning moon rise over the valley's rim I did not care for the way it peered at me through vast, vaporous heaven. Churlishly, I shut the shutters.

I sighed, and the gathering wind outside the house seemed to echo my melancholy. Closing my orbs, I listened to the wind as it shook the window pains. How envious I was of that daemon wind, of its wild unfettered freedom. Perhaps if I went to walk in that majestic current of air it might teach me the secret of its sovereignty.

I dressed warmly and walked outside. Oh, the treetops that swayed in night's exhaling pant. Ah, the pale clouds that navigated above Mount Selta's vaulted peaks. I gazed for many moments at that slumbering titan of white stone, jealous of its antediluvian repose. Then the wind pushed at me, and I wandered into the center of town. Most of the buildings were dark as death, but I noticed a pale light that illumed the ticket booth of Sesqua's dilapidated cinema house. Approaching it, I smiled at the studious young man who sat within the cubicle, lost within the reading of some slim volume of literature. "Hello, Howard," I softly spoke.

He started at the sound of my voice, squinted through his spectacles, then smiled in recognition. "Mr. Randolph, good evening, sir."

"What is it that has you so captivated, young sir?"

"A most curious volume that two young men that were knocking on doors in the valley gave to me, all about a Great Old One who filtered from the stars and dwelt among the mongrel hordes of ancient America. Very odd indeed, but not as queer as this film we're shewing."

"And what is the queer film about, pray?"

Howard oddly frowned. "Strangely, I cannot quite recall. I remember the faintest of images, and this memory so disturbs me that I find I do not wish to clearly ponder upon it. There was something about a moon—I think it was a moon—and ..." He closed his eyes in contemplation, went a deeper shade of pale and shuddered. His worried eyes opened, and shaking his head in rueful fashion, he took my dollar bill and pushed to me my entrance ticket. I watched as he returned to his thin blue book, then took my ticket and entered the building.

I climbed the steps that ushered me into the diminutive auditorium, of which I was the lone occupant. I sat, and the house lights dimmed. On the screen before me was thrown an image of some African jungle. The camera slowly pushed through unwholesome growth, until at last was revealed a Cyclopean ruins whose megaliths seemed unwholesomely ancient. Their design was so utterly alien that I thought it impossible that they had been the creation of human civilization. Above one weird turret the gibbous moon queerly shone, and I watched that yellow orb sink into the veldt of elder secret. I did not like the ghastly hue of that moon, nor the dark winged things that accompanied it in descent. I gazed at the surface of that sphere of dead dust, at its face of supernal mockery.

I closed my eyes so to dispel the sense of fright that had overcome me. Reopening them, I beheld the figure of a man. I gasped at the beauty of his regal face, that black visage that smiled as he raised his hand before me. I saw that he held a curious key fashioned of obsidian glass. Hesitantly, I took the proffered relic. How strange that glass can feel so cold. How the touch of it in my hand began to soothe my silly fears. I pressed it to my forehead, felt its wintriness sink into my flesh and find my brain, which became preoccupied with the delicious image of my death, my sweet death.

I was suddenly alone. Rising from my padded chair, I slowly stepped down the wooden stairs and into nocturnal air. The ticket booth had been vacated. I smiled at the memory of young Howard's queer nerves. Upon the window of the booth I saw the reflected moon, and smiled at its dead refracted light. I turned to face that pale distant disc, and laughing I did a little jig. I danced homeward, then entered my quiet dwelling, where I undressed and slipped between bedclothes. I placed the key of semiprecious stone above my heart, then listened to that organ's steady pulse, that rhythm one sometimes heard in drumming from unseen inhabitants atop Mount Selta. It was a stress that was echoed deep beneath the valley's sod; down in a place of unfathomable obscurity. I found myself drifting like sand to that lightless realm. There I floated, waiting for the one wrapped in textiles as red as sunset flame. Then he was there, the regal shape that held before me a chalice of white gold. The liquid that swirled within the goblet seemed to have caught particles of celestial inferno. The black man reached with his free hand for the key clutched to my chest; sycophantically I gave it to him, in trade for the chalice, which I brought to my lips. The elixir was as sweet as exotic sickness.

Smiling, the black one took back the goblet, then motioned to something that simpered at his feet. I gazed in disbelief at the impossible creature that hunkered there, watched as it brought a flute to its nebulous mouth, marveled at the whistled tune that issued from its instrument. It was a music of the spheres that contained within its notes a potent alchemy. Closing my eyes, I whistled the abstruse notes, whistled it for aeons. And then I seemed to awaken from mysterious slumber, with limbs that ached from wading through dark dreaming; and I was in bed, alone as always, contemplating a remembered song that echoed in memory.

I spent the day in bed, recalling vision, evoking song. At dusk I rose and dressed, then wandered to the old cemetery where, for decades, those who are outsiders to Sesqua Valley are buried. I found my favorite place, an ancient mausoleum wherein, one century ago, a wealthy gentleman interred his beloved son. The unhappy young man had taken his life. Oft times, when especially lonely or sad, I would visit this cold dark place, sit upon the young man's tomb and sing to his memory. On this haunted night I did not sing; rather, I whistled the tune that I had heard in dream. The airy notes vibrated in the lifeless air, the air that began to quiver. From the rotting stone on which I sat there rose a cloud of dust, dust that shaped itself into a human form.

"Why have you awakened me?" the gloomy figure asked.

I smiled. "You've slept for one hundred years. And, god, look at you, so young and beautiful. This is not a place for one such as you. Look at these weary eyes set deep within an old man's face. Who better deserves this eternal repose?"

Nigh it was the specter that smiled. "Fifty is not old. I did not like this shadowed valley when I lived. I abhorred the way its shadow crept into my dreams. But now that I have slept within that shadow for many decades, I do not fear it so."

I rose and went to him. "You are so lovely. Beauty such as you possess should caress the material of flesh. Come into my arms."

He drifted to me. I pressed my lips against his phantom mouth, whistled into it the remembered daemon tune. My hot living breath filled his unearthly frame. The dead thing drank my life. And now I rest within this depth of balmy shadow. At times I remember the hideous thing called life, but I push its madness from me. I snuggle here in this blessed realm of darkness. Sometimes, from somewhere far away, I hear the sweet singing of a young man, whose voice is as sad as the existence of flesh and blood.

*¿?*

©WIEDEMANN 2000

# AFTERWORD

This is another of the stories I wrote in memory of a member of the Lovecraft circle, my queer brother Samuel, who was a brilliant poet. He was one of a few of Lovecraft's great friends who were gay, although it is extremely doubtful that HPL was homosexual, or knew that such deviants were numbered among his pals. Strangely, Lovecraft experienced two amazing dreams concerning Loveman, which he transformed into minor stories, "The Statement of Randolph Carter" and the brilliant prose poem "Nyarlathotep". "The Balm of Nepenthe" was first published in *Tales of Sesqua Valley.*

# The Phantom of Beguilement

*"Light seeking light doth light of light beguile;
so, ere you find where light in darkness lies,
your light grows dark by losing of your eyes."*

—Shakespeare

## I.

Katherine Winters halted for one moment on the small wooden bridge and watched the trickling water of Blake's Creek as it flowed beneath her. Dim October sunlight shimmered on the water, and the scent of autumn perfumed Kingsport's misty air. She was happy that she had stayed beyond the tourist season. The old town enchanted her, as did its strange, old-fashioned inhabitants. Continuing along Orne Street, she arrived at last at the quaint shop of curios that was her destination.

She hesitated for one moment, then entered the dark and chilly place. Closing the door behind her, Katherine stood in silence, waiting for some sound of life. It was, this place, like a tomb of the forgotten past. Slowly, she walked by dust-enshrouded items, coming at last to the thing she sought. Reaching, she took up the small framed painting, lightly wiping a thin coat of dust from the glass. A scent of lilacs wafted from behind, from a shadowed presence that soon stood beside her.

"Hello, Miss Winters," the liquid voice gurgled. "I see that the wee painting continues to captivate."

"Indeed. Luckily, my mother has sent a rather generous check, so I can at last be extravagant and do some reckless spending."

The older woman smiled with thick mauve lips and lightly swept fingers through her scented hair. "Mothers are such a wonderful invention. With some exceptions." She took from Katherine the painting and studied it with a faraway look. "His didn't understand him at all."

"You told me that his name was Jeremy Blond."

"Aye, that it was. Poor sod. A nervous young artist, with dark wounded eyes and pale lifeless hair. We get the type often in Kingsport, but I've never known one to look so hunted. Poor strange lad …"

"And this is the only work of his that you have?"

"It is, love. His mum collected the rest after his vanishment. Aye, she had a lonesome look about her as well. She hated that her only child had chosen to be a painter and poet, but when his body was never found, well, his art was all she had with which to remember him. But this piece she never saw. I found the wee photo frame and popped it in there, nice as you please. 'Tis an old, old frame, you see, and somehow compliments the mood of the piece. So you'll be taking it off my hands?"

"Yes, please," Katherine answered, reluctantly surrendering the painting. "It's almost like an experimental photograph, so indistinct and surreal. Is it a woman on a raft, surrounded by shadow and eerie mists of light? And those things that float above, like a flock of primeval psychopomps—are they gulls, and if so, why so disfigured? He had a wonderfully unique style. How old was he?"

"Oh, very young, little more than a child. Very preoccupied, so he was, with his strange books."

"Occult books?"

"Aye, so they were. When he first arrived he would come in seeking old editions of classic poetry, biographies of poets and such. But then he became seduced by local legends. Used to listen to the stories of that drunken lout who hangs about the vacant cottage where the terrible old man used to live." Katherine smiled to herself, secretly. The older woman began to wrap the painting in thick paper.

"And Jeremy was a poet as well, Mrs. Keats?"

'A very peculiar poet, miss, as we get betimes in this old town. Ah, wait a tic." She reached behind her for a large old book upon a shelf. Opening it at the middle, she took from it a folded piece if paper, which she handed to Katherine. Tenderly, the young woman opened it. "I'll toss that in as well. He called it one of his 'Shakespearean sonnets,' and surely it's as daft as anything Shakespeare wrote, if I may be allowed to say so."

"You may," Katherine allowed. "How ancient the paper looks, and smells."

"Yes, he found a box filled with centuried foolscap. Utterly delighted, so he was. How did he phrase it? 'Antique paper on which to pen my antiquated poesy,' something like that. Ever read Oscar Wilde, Miss Winters? Well, when Jeremy spoke, he rather reminded me of Wilde. He was of another time. Too young to be so old, that was his paradox. And then one day he was taken from us, but how or where or why we shall never know. The world is queer, Miss Winters, a very queer place all told."

The proprietor handed Katherine the wrapped object, in exchange for proffered money. Dreamily, Katherine departed with her prizes, holding both painting and poem to her breast, skipping down the cobbled streets in time to happy heartbeat, and followed by vague shadows in the sky.

## II.

She danced upon dark water, enshrouded in shadow and eerie mists of almost-light. Above her loomed the craggy silhouette of Kingsport's prehistoric cliffs. Salted sea spray swirled about her, a light and fanciful haze in which she could almost distinguish the forms of fantastic things. She cried out, and was answered by the muted ululation that issued from the mouths that flocked above her. Again she cried, wanting so to see the pallid faces of the strange winged beasts. And then the mist thickened, became a brumous wall that encircled her, that spilled its essence into her gasping mouth. It found, this stuff, her aching soul. She transformed into a thing of spreading aether.

She awakened to the sound of a north wind shaking her bedroom window. In accompaniment she moaned, not wanting to shake off slumber. But the wind was insistent, and finally she crawled out of bed and staggered to the window, before which she knelt. The bedroom curtain was never closed, as she loved to view the nighted sky from the cozy confines of her bed. Katherine gazed at the panorama spread before her. Legend-haunted Kingsport. She had come with money left to her from an aunt who also loved the arts, and who continuously encouraged Katherine's talent as a poet. Having heard of this charming New England town where thrived a vigorous artistic community, she came to seek solace from an absurd emotional breakdown. She came in search of creative flow, and slowly her poetry began once more to issue forth. Within a two-month period she had completed her cycle of sonnets. But Kingsport had given her more than creativity; it had provided a rich artistic fellowship of which she had become increasingly fond.

One of its rich characters was the "lout" spoken of by Mrs. Keats, one Winfield Scot, a fellow poet. She had met him in Kingsport's public library, where he spent his days reading, keeping warm, and pretending to write. (He had not produced new work for many years.) His nights were spent at a vacant centuried cottage, famous among townsfolk as the home of a curious creature always referred to as "the terrible old man." This gentleman was said to have been a former sea captain, and was at the time of his death of an incredible age. It was whispered that he had learned strange rites and secret ceremonies during his sea journeys, and people did not like the large oddly-painted stones that leaned in the tall unkempt grass of his yard, stones that were positioned in esoteric groups, like prehistoric idols.

Winfield Scot was not liked by the respectable Kingsport inhabitants because he slept in a place that was shunned by all reasonable people. His monthly check kept him in good supply of the alcohol with which he fought off personal daemons. Katherine had taken a part-time job in a small café, more to kill tedium than for financial relief, and it became her habit to pack a small evening meal after her shift, which she would take to the lonely poet. She found his conversation pleasant, and noted an aesthetic intellect belied by a disheveled appearance.

So Winfield had known the young artist who had so mysteriously vanished. Katherine rose and walked to the bed, above which she had hanged Jeremy's painting. She touched a finger to the indistinct figure on the raft, studying the strands of hair that issued from a ghostly dome. But was it hair, or a garland of fluid vines; or rags; or, perhaps, shredded seaweed? She studied the small flock of spectral things that hovered in the foggy air. How strange that they never seemed to take on solid form. They were gulls, or perhaps large mutated bats. Did bats have such pale faces? She could never satisfactorily count their number, at times finding seven, or ten. How superbly Jeremy Blond had captured their ethereal grace. To look at them brought a fever to her brain, a longing to be numbered among them.

She studied the curious raft. Was it composed of rotted wood bound by rope; or was it a network of large splintered bones wound with bloodless veins? The phantom figure stood at the very edge of the craft, wrapped in a robe of sparkling mist and inky shadow.

Katherine suddenly needed coffee, and as it brewed she read once more the sonnet that had been scrawled upon a sheet of olden paper. Having worked so ruthlessly upon her own sonnet cycle, she had grown weary of the form. But this piece queerly captivated her. She spoke the words aloud.

"Oh, drift to me in coils of rotten smoke
And kiss my dome with mouth of ancient breadth.
Oh, kiss my dome with mouth as cool as death,
From which a mortal tongue hath never spoke.
A mortal voice hath never stretched thy throat,
And mortal passion never pumped thy breast,
And mortal sanity thou never quote,
And mortal moan is naught to you but jest.
I hear your utterance croak in the mist,
Above the whisper of their singing wings,
Those wings that stretch from out those shadow-things.
I hear the spell with which my soul is kissed.
I hear the spell that mutates flesh and bone.
I spread these new-formed wings that now I own."

Interesting, she thought, if a bit clumsy. Obviously it was a companion piece to the painting. Surely, it was a captivating image, both as poem and painting. It stirred strange passion within her heart. She wanted so to understand the soul who created it. At last she dressed and left for a quiet day of work. When her shift came to an end, she found herself carrying a small paper bag and hurrying to the vacated cottage on Water Street.

The day had been sunny, but blessed with cool autumn chill. She waltzed to her destination, slowing only once as she came upon a group of small children who were playing at tableau. Each held a thin wooden wand to which had been attached a pale papier-mâché mask. Katherine lightly laughed as the young ones danced and frolicked, then froze into living picture. The childfolk heard her laughter, held out to her their tiny arms. Beguiled by innocence, Katherine joined momentarily in their pantomimic play. Daintily, she danced, then fell to her knees. Pale paper faces formed above her. She raised her arms as if they were wings, and as she did so the late afternoon wind gushed about her, as if it would release her from a prison of gravity. A lovely child bent to kiss her neck; then they fled *en masse*, laughing lightly at the sunset.

She walked, and the huddled cottage came into view, enshrouded by bending trees and gathering shadow. Her hands pressed against the cold metal of a gate, and she paused momentarily so to gaze at the curiously-painted stones that were grouped in the tall yellow grass. The sight of these stones always disconcerted her. The manner in which they were grouped seemed slightly sinister, as if they were so assembled as to function in a weird and wicked way. It was the stones, and the way that shadow and light played upon their painted surfaces, that had kept people from bothering the sea captain when he lived; and it was they that kept folk away after the terrible old man's demise. Indeed, a subtle yet increasing sense of alarm had seized the innocent seafolk of Kingsport after the old gent's death, for now there was no one to control the possible cosmic influence of the disquieting stones.

Katherine walked past the high iron gate, into the yard. Smiling at her from the darkness of the front porch, a bottle of whiskey in hand, was Winfield Scot.

"Ah, sweet Kate. Come to keep an old man company."

She settled next to him in the cool shade and handed him the bag of food. "It's not much, just cheese sandwiches and grapes."

"Delightful. Here, have a swig." It was his playful habit to offer her his booze. Frowning momentarily, she took the proffered bottle and pressed it to her lips. When she began to choke and cough, her companion happily patted her and took back the bottle.

"Ugh, how can you drink that wretched stuff?"

"This nectar is my dearest friend, sweet Kate. It warms the dread chill of mortality."

"It wouldn't do anything for me, except give me bad dreams …"

"Ah, no—it's the stones that give me dreams. Wonderful, terrible dreams."

"Actually, I've had a rather wonderfully terrible dream of my own, inspired by a work of art, a painting by Jeremy Blond."

The fellow at her side smiled into the night, reflecting on past acquaintances. "Yes, his work would do that, poor haunted fellow that he was. A true Kingsport artist was Jeremy Blond."

"Meaning what?"

"Well, we get our tourists, and we get many student artists who are little more than tourists. They are charmed by this lovely old town, but they never penetrate its magick, never see its soul. They see the surface only, suffused with misty light. They never see the darkness where lies its haunted heart."

She bent to him and lightly kissed his mouth. "I love it when you talk like a poet."

"Yes, I'm like Wilde now, a poet who merely talks, but beautifully. I live in a world of whispered words and remembered glory, just as Jeremy Blond dwelt within a world of haunted imagery."

"With what was he haunted?"

Scot obliquely smiled. "If you've one of his paintings, you know. An image of Death upon a raft, sailing the river Styx, surrounded by harpies. I implied once that he had been inspired by Joachim Patnir's famous work, but this he utterly denied. A queer, morbid boy, was Jeremy Blond. Near the end he became very odd. And then he vanished."

"Fascinating. But you've misunderstood his art, dear Win. It wasn't Death that he envisioned, but something far more beguiling."

"More captivating than oblivion? You jest." Then he closely studied her. "And you've been dreaming of this thing?"

"Yes, last night. A wonderful vision. I didn't want to leave it."

Scot was silent for some moments, a troubled frown on his face. Opening the bag, he took out a cheese sandwich and thoughtfully began to feast. He was troubled at what he sensed was his friend's preoccupation with Blond's eerie obsession. When Katherine suddenly arose, Scot's eyes filled with panic for one moment, then seemed to dim with a kind of resignation. "Leaving so soon, sweet Kate?"

"I'm restless. Need to walk, I think."

"Then come and kiss me sweet and twenty."

"Once, and quickly. You've such a curious expression on your handsome face." She bent to kiss his cheek, then quickly rushed to the gate and departed.

Rather than going straight home, Katherine took a late bus to Central

Hill. A vigorous north wind blew from the harbor, and she pulled her heavy shawl about her as she passed through the high iron gates of Central Hill Cemetery. Most of the tottering, crumbling tombstones dated to the mid-1600s. She leaned against a tall ivy-covered marker and gazed down the sloping field of death, beyond the hill's crest, to the sleepy town. Kingsport was illumed with lamplight. A faint fog crept over the sea's dark water, while a heavier cloud enshrouded the fantastic form of Kingsport Head, which rose one thousand feet above the water. How ancient everything was, and how poetic was this age-old beauty. Little wonder that the town had become so widely populated with poets and painters. Her own cycle of sonnets had benefited greatly from her surroundings, as had her psyche.

"A pox on modernity," she sighed to night. "My soul is as ancient as this sod I stand upon. See, my shadow, illumed by antediluvian moonlight, blends so easily with the shadows of these centuried stones, a sibling shade." She danced among the stones, beyond them to one of the willow trees that stood near the high iron fence. Dancing, she lifted her arms into the streaming vines, the vines that twined around her wrists and wove into her hair. She danced until exhausted, then fell upon the ground. The moonlight was cool upon her brow. She gazed at its ageless beauty, then noticed the creature that hovered in dark sky. Rising from bended knee, she grasped the tasseled ends of her shawl and raised her hands to heaven. She could almost distinguish the pale face that floated far above her. Suddenly, from behind, a wild rush of tempestuous wind pushed her, upsetting her balance. Heavily, Katherine fell to graveyard ground. When again she looked into the empyrean of night, she saw naught but thickening fog.

### III.

She waded through the opaque air, relishing the residue of moisture that kissed her face. Some uncanny instinct led her along the winding streets and pavements, over worn and weathered bridges. She could feel the heavy pulse of Kingsport's psyche, its remnant of dream and darkness. She could almost smell the ghostly past, the haunted future. Ah, the muted creaking of spectral ships that had slipped beneath the harbor. Oh, the moaning souls that sighed beneath the sea.

She walked the narrow cobblestone streets of Harborside. Like one lost in fanciful nightmare, she stumbled past the silent buildings that leaned improbably over the streets. Katherine knew that she was on Foster Street, for there was the tall, dilapidated building that had once been Mariner's Church, but was nigh abandoned. Slowly she moved on, to Water Street, toward the piers that were sheathed in yellow fog. Oh,

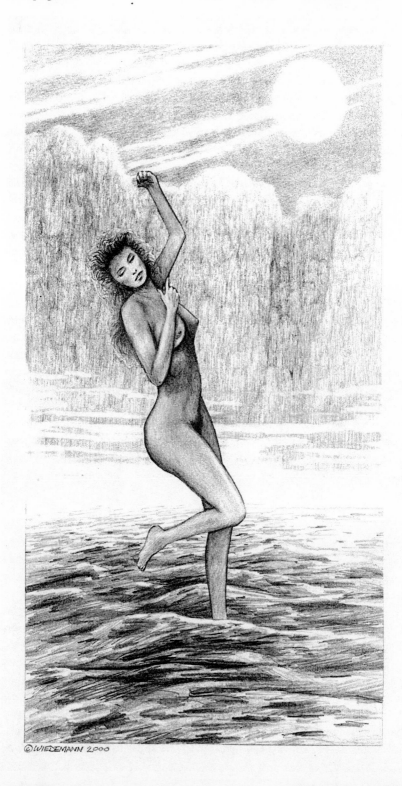

the heavy smell of the silent sea; how it filled her nostrils as she pranced upon the rotting planks of an age-old pier.

She reached its end and knelt, gazed outward, waited. Dimly, sailing toward her in the fog, came the hazy silhouettes of weird winged things. Her lips trembled, aching so to call out to the pale faces that watched her from above. The sighing wind rose from the water, brought with it the putrid stink of the sea; and of something else, something not of this world.

It glided toward her, out of the fog, over dark water. As it neared the pier, Katherine realized that Jeremy Blond's painting had not exaggerated the unearthly nature of the creature on the raft. He had caught precisely its essence.

The young woman pressed her palms against the damp wood of the aged pier. She leaned toward the apparition that stopped just inches from where she knelt. The figure bent to her. Its ropy hair writhed and reached for her, wove into her own. Its spectral claws wrapped around her shaking fingers. Stagnant shadow filled her pores and sank into her soul. It blessed the texture of her skin. Phantasmagorically, she shivered with mutation. How she stretched her tingling mouth and warbled the new words that writhed within her burning brain!

The creature of wondrous nightmare drifted from her. Katherine raised her strange pale face to those twilight things that watched her from above. Joyously, she unfolded her wings and floated above dark water, to the flock that waited for her in the foggy aether.

*6?*

# AFTERWORD

I originally wrote this story for an anthology that never saw the light of day, a book of tales set in Kingsport. My buddy Chad Hensley loaned me a copy of *Kingsport, The City in the Mists*, an extremely groovy Call of Cthulhu by Kevin A. Ross. I had for a long time been extremely skeptical about the whole gaming thing: Lovecraft was *literature, not* a game. But I became enchanted with the Kingsport gaming manual, and soon began to collect many more such books from Chaosium, Inc. The real gems from Chaosium, however, are the amazing Cycle Books of Mythos fiction edited by Robert M. Price, himself the author of some superb Lovecraftian fiction. Often, when I'm burned out and long to find that elusive muse that will get me writing again, I'll return to one of my favorite Cycle Books, and therein find excitement for our beloved genre once again.

These books, both fiction anthologies and gaming manuals, are created by devoted Lovecraft fanatics, people who have studied in depth the fiction of HPL and used that fiction to create their own—often extremely clever and fascinating—adventures. Not only do these books pay homage to Lovecraft's genius, they at times actually *evoke* a sense of Lovecraftian awe. I have been assured by gamers whom I've met at conventions that gaming brings people to Lovecraft as *readers*, and thus I have had to put my snobbery aside and realize that this whole gaming thing ain't all that bad.

"The Phantom of Beguilement" first saw print in my chapbook, *Tales of Love and Death*.

The thing before me shook with vulgar motion as it vomited hilarity. The absurd mop of tangled hair fell before wide blank eyes, and the torso jiggled so violently that I expected the dummy to slip from its chair. Backing away from the large cabinet of wooden frames and thick plates of glass, I smiled. Then all motion ceased, the thing stood dead still; my minute was up.

The round man behind the counter grinned with impious glee and softly chuckled. "My granddaddy made it 'fore I was born, when he built this store in '78. It was a modern wonder back then, pulled in huge crowds. Great for business. Course, back then it worked with pumps. My daddy rigged it so as it would work with electricity. It's something, ain't it?"

"It is indeed, Walter," I agreed, glancing at the nickel slot and fighting the temptation to watch it one more time.

The old man gazed at me with wide eyes set deep within a rubbery face. Then he pushed buttons on the antiquated cash register and totaled my bill. Opening my wallet, I gave him money. He eyed the food and drink items as I dropped them into my backpack. "Gonna take in some sights, are you?"

"Yes, I want to hike into some country. Thought I'd follow the railroad tracks along the riverside and head toward those distant hills."

"You want to watch out for rattlers, Joe. It's crawling with snakes up there. Ain't tryin' to put you off, but jest be careful."

"Will do, Walter. Thanks." Turning to the door, I moseyed outside, squinting at pale autumn sunlight. A cool breeze was blowing from the river. Pulling on my backpack, I strolled toward the water until I came upon rusty railroad tracks. In the week that I had been in this small town, I hadn't heard or seen a train go by, and thus assumed that the line was not in use. Happily, I hopped onto one of the rails, balancing as I walked with arms outstretched. I had been quite adept at this when a kid, but adulthood had dulled my talent. Slipping onto dirt and rocks, I bent to pick up a smooth round stone, which I threw so that it skimmed on the river's surface.

I walked for about an hour, following the track as it turned away from the river and headed into an area of rocky hills. Cautiously, I scanned the ground and nearest hill for snakes, but saw no living thing. The air was still, which I found odd. Surely the breeze I had experienced would sail between these hills of red rock. But nothing stirred, and I slowly sauntered through the hushed surroundings, until at last the hills were behind me and I looked out onto a great expanse of open land.

The curious object stood in the still and silent distance. At first I thought that it was a derailed freight car of odd and diminutive design; but as I approached it I saw that the metal wheels were not intended for railroad tracks. The wooden surface had once been painted yellow, but now a faint remnant of color covered the vehicle's splintered wood. Spectral letters formed a name that was too faded to make out, large though the letters had been. This was obviously some kind of carnival car, from a sideshow that had long ceased to exist.

As I neared a doorless entryway, an unpleasant meaty odor assailed my nostrils, and I wondered if an animal had somehow become trapped inside and was rotting in death. Gingerly, I leaned into the doorway and peered into a world of curious horror. Shelves had been built into the walls, and upon one long shelf I saw a series of mannequin heads covered with deteriorating rubber masks, the decaying facial features barely human as their split and rotting pieces peeled and bent like the brittle leaves of a dead plant. Upon another shelf I espied a series of fantastic bestial forms, creatures of absurd combinations, looking like the work of some magnificent artist who was superb in creating macabre fakes. How strangely realistic they looked, these concoctions; how brightly their black eyes shined, reflecting the sunlight that filtered through the great holes in the compartment's roof.

I heard no sound of movement, saw no sign of feasting vermin. Placing my hands flat on the wooden floor, I heaved myself into the car. My clumsy feet stumbled as I rose to a standing position, and my arms grabbed onto the nearest object so to prevent my falling. The object before me was an old kinetoscope, such as I had once seen in a curio shop back home. I knew that this neglected, timeworn machine before me could not possibly work, especially as there was no source of electricity; and yet I could not keep from rummaging into my pants pocket for a nickel. Feeling foolish, I dropped the coin into the slot, and softly gasped as the machine began to whir and creak. Hesitantly, I pressed my forehead against the rim of the rectangular peephole. I saw nothing but blackness, and supposed that the machine's source of inner illumination had long expired. Yet, as I continued to watch, lulled by the mechanical purring, I detected a suggestion of moving shadow in the blackness into which I peered. Something obscenely flowed, growing in size as it expanded closer to the viewing glass. It seemed, this crimson-tainted blackness, to bubble, as if hungry to leak its blasphemous essence into my eyes. Frantically, I backed away and blinked at sunbeams that spilled from above onto my trembling eyes.

The antique gizmo shuddered and died. My panic subsided. Again, I became aware of a rancid stench, and when I looked behind me its source was discovered. There, on a long low table, was a grouping of large glass jars. The pulpy objects inside them gently swirled in thick ruddy liquid. As if on cue, one of the soft spongy things paused in circulating and bumped against its glass prison. I thought at first that it was a variation of the weird rubber masks, albeit one of more lifelike rendition. I did not like its wide liquid eyes, and felt peculiarly nonplussed by its idiotic smile. As I gazed at the wretched thing, its carrion smell seemed to increase, filling my mouth with bile. Hurriedly, I rushed to the doorway and jumped onto solid ground, where I stood and gagged.

Beneath my retching I heard another sound, a curious kind of music. It brought to mind a damaged jack-in-the-box from my poverty-stricken childhood. The tune that played as I gently turned the crank was distorted, seemingly incomplete. The mindless music that fumbled from the other side of the car was of a similar nature. Beguiled, I sought the source of sound, feeling again that sense of keen expectancy I knew as a child as I turned a little crank and waited for the macabre jester to pop out of the box. What I suddenly beheld was no less clownish. I could not fathom what the figure was supposed to be. At first it suggested a sad-faced hobo clown I had once delighted in while attending a circus; and although the creature before me now was dressed in hobo fashion, it certainly was not melancholy. Rather, this darkly dressed buffoon joyfully pranced to the warped music, clapping large white hands as it shook with jocundity.

The thing that squatted near to the farceur was inexplicable. It might have been a kind of deformed monkey, or a dwarf costumed very badly as a beast. Just as peculiar was the instrument that was cradled in the creature's crotch, a kind of makeshift hurdy-gurdy from which the staccato noise issued. I did not like the way the creature obscenely turned the crank that produced the sound, nor the way its partner wagged in time to the outlandish rumpus. Foolishly, the clown waved at me, then bent to a wooden wash basket into which it dipped its pale large hands. I stared as those hands emerged, now defiled with dripping gore. Happily, the funny gentleman tossed globes of grue into the air, juggling the balls as crimson drops splashed all around.

The balls of blood were thrown into the air, and the creature watched expectantly as they floated for a moment, then fell onto his gleeful face. The music stopped, and the jester turned his eyes to me. The wet red fluid entirely covered his face, and I helplessly watched as the thick lips of that face puckered and blew. Slowly, inexorably, a bubble of blood began to expand from a mouth inhumanly wide.

I stood transfixed as the inspissating liquid ball separated from the monstrous maw and rolled toward me in the air. The vagabond jiggled with joy as his familiar jerked spasmodically as it ferociously turned its crank. A cacophony of cacodaemonical pandemonium assailed my eardrums as the bubble of blood collided with my countenance. All was instantly quiet. I blinked but could not see clearly. A ghastly scarlet fog swirled all around me. Slowly, I began to make out nebulous forms. I saw a buffoonish figure hopping toward me. Scuttling at its feet I could dimly discern a shaggy object, and I suddenly realized that it held within its paws a large and empty glass jar.

Huge discolored hands reached for my face. Instantly, I was sightless. But, oh, I could *feel.* My legs seemed to slip from me, and the heavy pack no longer pressed against my back. Hot liquid baptized my dome. Flabby fingers worked my flesh into a kind of sphere. Then the hands were gone, but not the wet red mist. I floated in a carnal pond, and pushing forward bumped into a wall of glass. Through that glass, darkly, I saw the jolly man lift his bestial companion to the shelf of rotting masks. The wee creature clasped one of the shredding heads with its claws and, its face twitching excitedly, pulled the floppy rubber over its pate. How queerly snug it fit.

Winking, the masked one pointed a talon at me. I watched as the wicked member began to circulate, and as I watched I too began to slowly gyrate. Dimly, as I turned, I beheld my squashy crony in the jar next to my own. Something in the sardonic curl of his too soft lips proved intoxicating, and foolishly I smiled.

The caravan began to rhythmically thump, and though I heard no sound, I could see the twin grotesqueries flailing playfully about the room. The dwarfish thing leaped into its master's arms, and together they approached my prison. The shattered visage of the masked one peered into my jar. Perversely, its jaws opened, and a twin-tipped tongue snaked forth and touched the glass. How it was possible that I could feel the pressure of that purple, porous appendage slip against my flesh I do not know; but the touch of it so titillated that, god help me, I laughed until I split.

*6?*

# AFTERWORD

Although not obviously Lovecraftian, this tale has as its source "The Terrible Old Man" and the spurious "The Thing in the Moonlight" (the text of which was actually taken from a 1927 epistle to Donald Wandrei). That Lovecraft never wrote an actual story based on his dream (something he was known to do) makes me wonder how many other macabre tales he neglected to pen. I've never based an entire story on a dream, and yet dreaming is a vital part of writing weird fiction. I never write a story until I have fully *imagined* it. When I get a germ for an idea, I daydream about it, seeing it in my mind. When at last I begin to pen my rough draft, I recall my story as though remembering something that actually occurred.

Lovecraft remains a major source of inspiration. He is the font that never dries. Every time a new edition of his fiction is published, I buy it, and reading his fiction anew always shews things that I have missed. Recently I purchased *Waking Up Screaming*, the new mass market paperback from Del Rey featuring an introduction by Poppy Z. Brite. As I read the opening tale, "Cool Air" (a story I've not read for some time), I was amazed at how much of it I had forgotten. I was impressed anew at how superbly Lovecraft wrote. This happens again and again with HPL, from reading his fiction, his poetry, his letters. I shall be reading Lovecraft, and celebrating his genius in poetry and prose of my own, for the remainder of my life

Printed in the United States
212442BV00001B/4/P